*Prince of Time*

## The After Cilmeri Series:

*Daughter of Time* (prequel)
*Footsteps in Time* (Book One)
*Winds of Time* (a novella)
*Prince of Time* (Book Two)
*Crossroads in Time* (Book Three)

## The Gareth and Gwen Medieval Mysteries

*The Bard's Daughter* (prequel novella)
*The Good Knight*
*The Uninvited Guest*

## The Last Pendragon Saga

*The Last Pendragon*
*The Pendragon's Quest*

## Other Books by Sarah Woodbury

*Cold My Heart: A Novel of King Arthur*

# PRINCE OF TIME

by

## SARAH WOODBURY

# Prince of Time
## Copyright © 2011 by Sarah Woodbury

This is a work of fiction.

Cover image by Christine DeMaio-Rice at Flip City Books
http://flipcitybooks.com

*To my Dad*

# A Brief Guide to Welsh Pronunciation

c      a hard 'c' sound (Cadfael)

ch    a non-English sound as in Scottish "ch" in "loch" (Fychan)

dd    a buzzy 'th' sound, as in "there" (Ddu; Gwynedd)

f      as in "of" (Cadfael)

ff     as in "off" (Gruffydd)

g      a hard 'g' sound, as in "gas" (Goronwy)

l      as in "lamp" (Llywelyn)

ll     a breathy "th" sound that does not occur in English (Llywelyn)

rh    a breathy mix between 'r' and 'rh' that does not occur in English (Rhys)

th    a softer sound than for 'dd,' as in "thick" (Arthur)

u      a short 'ih' sound (Gruffydd), or a long 'ee' sound (Cymru—pronounced "kumree")

w     as a consonant, it's an English 'w' (Llywelyn); as a vowel, an 'oo' sound (Bwlch)

y      the only letter in which Welsh is not phonetic. It can be an 'ih' sound, as in "Gwyn," is often an "uh" sound (Cymru), and at the end of the word is an "ee" sound (thus, both Cymru—the modern word for Wales—and Cymry—the word for Wales in the Dark Ages—are pronounced "kumree")

# Cast of Characters

## The Welsh

David ap Llywelyn, Prince of Wales
Ieuan ap Cynan, Welsh knight
Llywelyn ap Gruffydd, Prince of Wales, David's father
Marged, Princess of Wales, David's mother
Anna, David's half-sister
Mathonwy ap Rhys, Anna's husband; nephew to Llywelyn
Lili, Ieuan's sister
Aaron ben Simon, Physician; Jewish émigré to Wales
Bevyn, Welsh knight, Captain of David's guard

## The Americans

Bronwen Llywelyn, Archaeology graduate student
Elisa Shepherd, David's aunt (Marged's sister)
Ted Shepherd, Elisa's husband
Christopher Shepherd, Elisa's son (David's cousin)

## The English

Edward I (deceased), King of England
Sir John de Falkes, Castellan of Carlisle Castle
Thomas Hartley, Falkes' nephew
Humphrey de Bohun, Earl of Hereford
John Peckham, Archbishop of Canterbury

# City of Chester

## 28 June 1285

### *Humphrey de Bohun*
### *Third Earl of Hereford*

**I** stalked toward Edward's quarters. *Stalked.* My wife tells me I stalk when I'm angry, like a caged lion or trained bear at a village fair. I don't agree. I don't get angry. Anger is dangerous. Anger implies a loss of control that I can't allow myself, not when so much depends on measured thought and careful planning. Edward would agree. Though I despise the man for his cunning and his power over me, cold calculation is more his style and it's a style I have endeavored to emulate.

*Idiots! To bungle the siege so badly as to call my leadership of the Marcher lords into question! To have Edward call me into his presence for an accounting!*

I pushed open the door into King Edward's rooms and *stalked* the twenty feet to the dais, before bowing. "You summoned me, sire?" I asked.

Edward sat, an elbow bent on the arms of his chair, his hands steepled in front of his mouth. He was in his mid-forties, ten years my senior, but still a vibrant man, with a full head of dark hair and a straight back, showing no signs of either a slower mind or body. There was a pause as he left me hanging, waiting for his response, trying not to feel as awkward as one always felt in the royal presence.

"Tell me of Builth Castle," he said, as if discussing the disposition of a minor estate.

"Prince Llywelyn came behind us with several hundred men. We couldn't maintain the siege and had to quit Wales. We have retreated to Huntington."

"Your assumption was that if you took the castle, I would take it as a *fait accompli* and allow you to keep it," Edward said.

*Yes.* I bowed again. "I apologize, my lord. I believed I was acting in England's best interests." *Damn the man! Why couldn't he be as malleable as his father? I must remember in future that when I challenge you, I cannot think as my father or grandfather did; you are a different kind of king; you do not respect the old boundaries and honors.*

"Did you now?" Edward asked. "Had you taken it, I would have had to act in England's best interests and give it to Edmund Mortimer who has prior claim."

*And who has never fought against you as I have. I learned at Evesham that there is no such thing as honor, no such thing as right or wrong. Only victory matters. You taught me that day to think as you do: no mercy for one's enemies and hardly any loyalty to one's friends. There can be no chinks in one's armor. A sword can find a weak point, even if by chance, and thrust home. Power is fleeting, drained out as my father's blood soaked the ground around him, dead on your orders. I was only sixteen when my father died at Evesham. The bitter taste of that has stayed with me ever since.*

Edward continued speaking. "I realize that you and your forefathers have treated the Marche as a child's toy that is yours and yours alone, but you may recall a conversation we had earlier in which I explained that I expected to be notified, in advance, of any major offenses into Wales."

"I misunderstood, my lord," I said. "I intended no slight to your person."

"I can't have your activities endangering my plans for Wales. Peckham has requested a meeting between us and the upstart Welsh in Lancaster in August. I have acquiesced, and I expect you there as witness."

"You intend to acknowledge them?" I asked, surprised.

"No." Edward looked at me coldly. "But until then, you will keep to your possessions." He paused, and I studied him carefully. There was something else there, something uncharacteristic of him that I'd not seen in his face before. *Glee?* "You may hold your men in readiness," he continued. "After Lancaster . . . then we will see."

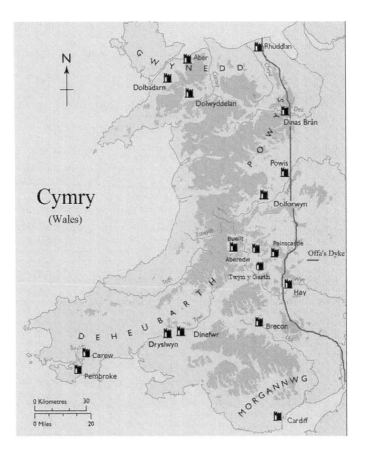

# Cymry
## (Wales)

N

GWYNEDD

POWYS

DEHEUBARTH

MORGANNWG

Rhuddlan

Aber

Dolbadarn

Dolwyddelan

Dinas Brân

Powis

Dolforwyn

Buellt
Painscastle
Aberedw
Twyn y Garth
Hay

Brecon

Dryslwyn
Dinefwr

Carew

Pembroke

Cardiff

Offa's Dyke

Dee

Dee

Ystwyth

Teifi

Tywi

Wye

Usk

0 Kilometres 30

0 Miles 20

# 1

## 2 AUGUST 1285

## *David*

Ieuan hung over the side off the boat, heaving his guts out. No doubt he'd long since stopped caring if anyone saw him, but hoped now that I would change my mind, turn this God-forsaken bucket around, and head for Wales.

I watched from the cabin doorway as Aaron, my friend and physician, stepped beside him. "Only another few hours, Ieuan. The captain says we'll reach port long before dark."

"But when is dark in this land?" Ieuan moaned, resting his head on the rail of the boat. "It stays light for hours longer than it should."

As a matter of fact, from my position I could see our destination. The Irish Sea was fickle at the best of times, but in this case, I assumed we would reach port as the captain promised.

Aaron patted him on the shoulder and continued towards my cabin. "I gave Ieuan one of my remedies," he said when he reached me, "but his stomach dispensed with it before it had time to take effect."

I debated whether to go to Ieuan, but decided he'd prefer that I didn't. He was proud, and for his lord to hold his head while he upended his innards over the side of the boat was probably not what he wanted. Quite naturally too, under the circumstances, Ieuan was exaggerating about the light. It wasn't as if southern Scotland were in the arctic and Wales in the tropics. Still, at this latitude and longitude (which admittedly hadn't been discovered yet) we could expect to see the sun for nearly sixteen hours a day, which meant that it wasn't full dark until ten in the evening, and it started to get light before five. Unless it was raining, of course, in which case it was dark all day and I had the dark moods of my men as well as the dark skies to contend with. Fortunately, at the moment the sky was free of clouds.

We docked a few hours later near the town of Annan in Scotland, northwest of the English city of Carlisle.

"Why here?" Ieuan asked Aaron, but as I'd instructed, Aaron looked blankly at him and said that when and if Prince Dafydd chose to tell him, he would know the reason. My men were used to following orders, but in recent weeks I'd entrusted Ieuan with more responsibility. Bevyn was getting older and he and I agreed that Ieuan should take his place as my first captain when the time came. Ieuan was young, in his mid-twenties, but smart—clever even—and the other men respected him.

As we docked, I emerged from my cabin in cloak and boots I'd borrowed from one of my men who shared my height. The clothes were plainer than any I'd worn since I'd become a Prince of Wales two and a half years before. In keeping with my disguise, I didn't wear my mail, but instead wore heavy leather armor under a plain, brown cloak. I could have been a third son of a minor house, which was my intent.

My men were either on shore already or crowded onto the deck of the boat when I came out, and they stared at me, surprise showing on their faces. I knew, then, that I'd made the right decision to send Sir Nicholas de Carew home ahead of me in a different boat. He would have counseled against what I was about to do.

I gazed back at my men and smiled, feeling light-hearted and free for the first time in many months. "Aaron and Ieuan, with me," I said. "The rest of you must stay here."

I strode towards the gangplank. Before I reached it, Bevyn blocked my path and tried once again to dissuade me. "My lord," he said. "You know this is unwise."

"I know it," I said. "But more unwise would be riding with a dozen men through the English countryside. Three are less noticeable, quicker, and more able to outrun any attackers."

"That was not what I meant," Bevyn growled. "This entire expedition is ill-advised. I do not like it."

I rested my right hand on Bevyn's shoulder. "I have a vision for Wales, Bevyn," I said. "What comes next is part of it."

Bevyn bowed his head and gave way, but grasped Ieuan's arm as he passed him. "You understand your charge, man? What I will do to you if anything happens to him?"

My impulse was to interfere but I didn't. Bevyn would give his life for me. He expected the same of Ieuan. Ieuan nodded and Bevyn released him.

I stepped off the boat, relieved to feel soil under my boots at last. Three horses waited for us and I mounted mine, Bedwyr. Cadwallon, acting as groom, boosted Aaron onto his mare, and then brought Ieuan his Llwyd, "Grey", named not very creatively by his little sister.

"You know that I agree with Bevyn," Aaron said. "Are you sure this journey is necessary?"

"I'm loathe to leave bits and pieces of the twenty-first century lying around unattended," I said, keeping my voice low so Ieuan couldn't overhear. "I wouldn't want them to fall into the wrong hands—or anyone's hands. They're too distinctive and remarkable. You'll see what I mean when we find them."

"Yes, my lord," Aaron acquiesced.

We rode away from the boats and left the town behind us. It was time to tell Ieuan something, and I weighed how much he could handle. "You've seen the vehicle, of course," I said.

"Yes," Ieuan said. "It came from the lands of Madoc the explorer."

Aaron breathed in through his nose and let the breath out. As it had Aaron, Ieuan's statement set me back a pace. It was an explanation for our presence in Wales that my father had latched upon a month ago which seemed to satisfy everyone. No mention of time travel was necessary if we could explain twenty-first century technology as simply being from a more advanced civilization.

"The Prince and his mother brought more from that land," Aaron said. "More possessions that they've had to hide, lest others brand them witches."

"It does take very little to arouse the passions of the people," Ieuan said carefully. "Or the priests."

Aaron's mouth twitched. "So you understand the problem," he said. "But do others see as clearly? What of Princess Marged? When others become jealous of another's talents, they can fall back on suspicion and superstition. Even had she raised our Prince in this country, she is still a most unusual woman. How much more so if she possessed . . . unusual artifacts."

"What kind of artifacts?" Ieuan asked, ever the pragmatic thinker.

I leaned forward so I could see Ieuan across Aaron's mount. "If they're where she left them, I'll tell you. If others have discovered them before us, then there's no need for me to explain just yet. Suffice to say they are of metals and quality that you've never seen, nor will ever see again, I dare say."

"Even were you to take me to Madoc's land?" Ieuan asked.

"I don't want to imagine the circumstances under which I would be forced to take you there. I hope never to see it again. I'm afraid if we went there, we'd find it difficult to return."

"You've traveled that distance once," Ieuan countered.

"And I dare not risk it a second time," I said. "Come. We have some way to ride before nightfall. Aaron thinks it's at least twenty miles to our destination. We have a few hours before full dark and I want to have ridden past Carlisle before we rest."

"Can you at least tell me where we're going?" Ieuan asked.

"To the great wall built by Hadrian," I answered, and then spurred Bedwyr forward. *These questions are so difficult.* The longer I lived in Wales, the easier to pretend that the twenty-first century was impossibly far in the future. On the outside, I was nothing more or less than a prince, the son of the Prince of Wales. I liked it that way—wanted it that way—but then the façade crashed down and I was left with a truth that only a handful of men from the thirteenth century knew. Aaron was one, and to open the circle to Ieuan was hard, even though I trusted him.

I was five strides ahead of Ieuan before he signaled Llwyd to catch up with me. I could almost hear him thinking: *The Roman Wall? What could he want with it?*

\* \* \* \* \*

We chose to rest before it was fully dark, in a copse of trees that could hide us from prying eyes.

"How much farther?" I asked Aaron.

"If we rise at first light, we should reach the place in less than two hours."

"Excellent," I said.

Ieuan grumbled. "If I knew what we were doing, and how long it would take, it would make it easier to prepare for what I might have to defend you against," he said.

"Just the English," I said, clapping him on the shoulder. "As usual."

"Oh, that's just great," he said, and turned away, but not before I caught him rolling his eyes at Aaron. Bevyn would have cuffed him but I ignored it. *Better to ignore it. I want a thinking man more than one who merely obeys.*

"I will take the first watch," Aaron said. "I don't sleep until after midnight under normal circumstances, much less on the ground with only my cloak for warmth."

"Sorry, Aaron," I said, feeling contrite. "I wanted you along for your knowledge, but didn't think how uncomfortable it might be for you, out here under the open sky without a fire."

"You're allowed a brief lapse, every now and then," Aaron said. "I'm here by my choice as well as yours. Don't think on it further."

I nodded, accepting as I often had to the sacrifices of those who surrounded me. Instead, I jerked my head at Ieuan. "Come," I said. "We'll sleep and let the old man keep his own counsel." I threw myself on the ground, wrapped my cloak around me, and used my arm for a pillow. What I hadn't admitted to anyone was my delight in being out in the open, with only Ieuan and Aaron for company. It felt great to run Bedwyr under the open sky with nothing more pressing on my mind for the next couple of days then picking up a few of my mom's things.

Ieuan lowered himself to the ground and braced his back against a tree. He rested his head against the trunk and closed his eyes. I followed suit and was trying to empty my mind for sleep when Aaron spoke.

"You Welsh remain a mystery to me," he said. His voice was so matter-of-fact, he could have been commenting on the weather.

I squinted at him, trying to make out his expression through the fading light. Then I realized he wasn't looking at me, but at Ieuan. I feigned sleep so as not to disturb their conversation.

"Excuse me?" Ieuan asked.

"You bicker among yourselves, you hate the English, you sing with fervor and you love absolutely. You have an intensity that contrasts so sharply with the English. Is that why they have defeated you time and again?"

Ieuan was insulted. "They've not defeated us this time. They will not. They wouldn't have even had King Edward survived."

"What's the difference this time?" Aaron asked, and then stopped Ieuan before he could answer. "Ah." Reflexively they both looked at me, and then away again.

Ieuan took the watch after Aaron, and I after him. This far north, dawn came quickly and I woke both of them with a shake just as the sun peeked over the horizon. We mounted and rode east, through the wide open country. After three years among the mountains and forests of Wales, the empty space disconcerted me. I glanced at Ieuan. Beneath his armor and cloak, his shoulders were tensed. "When I rode north to join Prince Llywelyn in

Gwynedd," he said, "I thought I'd come a long way from Twyn y Garth. In the last few days, I've learned how little of the world I knew."

"I'm no different from you, Ieuan," I said. "I've lived across the sea, but never traveled beyond the borders of Wales into England until this week."

We hugged the border between Scotland and England for safety's sake, but after an hour turned south and made a run for the Wall.

"Let me ride ahead to ensure it's safe," Ieuan said, once the fort came into sight.

Aaron and I slowed our horses to a walk while Ieuan spurred Llwyd forward. In order to reach the actual fort, he had to lead Llwyd across a half-filled ditch. He entered the fort through an opening in the wall. Five minutes later, he reappeared, waving. Aaron and I followed the path he'd taken.

"Let's get the bag," I said. Though I would have loved to explore the whole area, we didn't have time. We picked our way to the western side of the fort and entered a little room where Mom had found Sir John de Falkes' nephew, Thomas, a year ago almost to the day. I shifted some rocks. Her backpack lay underneath, exactly as she'd described. I turned to Aaron. "Are you ready for this?"

He nodded, his eyes bright, reminding me of Ieuan. I knelt and opened the bag. Sure enough, it was full of Mom's incredibly useful twenty-first century items, including . . . I pulled out a brown candy wrapper and sniffed. *Heaven! It's been so long!*

I tipped the bag and dumped three candies into my hand. I held one out to Aaron. "Chocolate," I said, without explaining what that meant. It would be over three hundred years before another European would taste chocolate, which without sugar would taste more bitter than coffee. I gave a second candy to Ieuan who'd appeared in the doorway of the little room and ate the third one myself.

"My God," Ieuan said. "What is this?"

"Good, huh?" I said. "Let's keep going. We've more things to collect."

"Those are your mother's possessions?" Ieuan asked.

"It's her pack," I said, handing it to him as I passed him.

He held it up. Its dark blue, artificial fibers were, quite naturally, unfamiliar. But this was Ieuan and he was intuitive and smart. Without asking, he slung it on his back, one strap hanging down unused just like a twenty-first century student.

I was glad I'd brought him.

"We've further to go," I said. "The wall passes a small lake somewhere to the east of here. My mother left a larger bag hidden near it."

Still carrying the pack, Ieuan mounted Llywd. "Why was your mother so far from Wales? I thought the land of Madoc was west of Wales, across the sea."

I was done lying to him. "She flew here in a machine we call an 'airplane.'"

Ieuan blinked. "She flew? You mean like a bird?"

"She was inside a machine much like my chariot, but with wings. The man piloting it landed here, Mom got out, and then he flew off by himself."

Ieuan picked up on the last point. "How dare he do such a thing!"

I laughed. "He obviously cared less for her than we do."

"Your mother did just fine on her own," Aaron said. "Few women could have reached Wales in one piece, as she did."

"You helped, Aaron," I said. "My father and I haven't forgotten it."

Aaron bowed his head, but seemed to shrug his shoulders simultaneously. He still had a hard time taking a compliment, however deserved. He'd lived nearly a year among people who treated him respectfully even though he was a Jew, but that wasn't enough time to overcome a lifetime of persecution in England.

We left the fort by the northern exit and again headed east. I watched the sun, trying to guess how long Mom had walked before she reached the fort. From her own description, she'd traveled for several hours, but it was hard to judge how quickly a horse might cover the same distance.

"There!" Ieuan said. I saw it too: a small lake nestled in a little valley, glimmering in the sun.

Mom had given me what I thought were clear directions, but at first we couldn't find the rock, the tree, and the specific bush she meant. I sent Aaron to the southern side of the wall to look again, and Ieuan and I walked down the hill to the beautifully clear lake. I picked up a stone and skipped it across the water. *One,*

11

*two, three, four.* Ieuan found one for himself. *One, two, three, four, five.*

"Hey!" I said. I found another stone. *One, two.* Ieuan had a handful of stones and each one he sent skipping across the water to the count of five or six.

"What did Edward say, my lord? Something about putting an 'upstart Prince' in his place?" Ieuan couldn't contain the laughter in his voice.

"Oh, now. That isn't fair," I said. I stepped back from the lake and searched until I found a large rock, more like a boulder. I picked it up, muscled it to the edge of the lake, and threw it, aiming for a spot about a foot from where Ieuan was standing. *Thunk.* It sent up a huge splash, soaking him from head to toe.

"Ha!" I said.

Ieuan, devilry in his eyes, reached into the water and threw a handful of water at me.

"Over here, my lord!" Aaron interrupted our play.

Laughing, we pawed our way to the top of the hill, racing to see who could reach it first. When we found Aaron, he had the bag out and open and was staring at Mom's laptop.

*Wow! I wonder if it still works!*

"It seems the bush was uprooted by an animal which covered over the bag," he said.

"That won't fit in the saddle bags." Ieuan said.

"It folds very small," I said. "We just need to take everything out of it and distribute the contents first." I bent forward to do just that, but before I could start, Ieuan hissed a

12

warning. I swung around: men on horseback, still dots on the horizon, rode steadily in our direction.

"Men. Coming," I said to Aaron. "Stay down. Maybe they haven't seen us yet."

"Are they from the north or south?" Aaron asked. *Scots or English?*

"The west, from Carlisle," I said, "and not riding hard, but a company of them, perhaps twenty."

"What are we going to do?" Aaron asked.

I made a instant decision. "Aaron, you take all of Mom's things and ride south, right now, away from here."

"What? I can't leave you, my lord!" he said.

"Perhaps they aren't unfriendly," Ieuan said.

"We can't risk the contents of my mother's pack," I said.

"We can't risk you," Aaron countered.

"I note your objections, Aaron, but Bevyn isn't here to overrule me. Ieuan and I are unmistakably Welshmen and in much more danger here in England that you are, even as a Jew. You may not be welcome everywhere, but we're not welcome anywhere. You, at least, can get away."

"He's right, Aaron," Ieuan said. "I can take care of him. Truth be told, we can ride more quickly without the burden of the goods you carry."

Aaron gave way. We loaded all of Mom's things into his saddlebags, folded the duffel tight, and stuffed it in with them. Then I buckled Mom's backpack to one of the bags and hung a cloak over it.

13

"Go, Aaron," I said. I glanced over my shoulder at the riders. "They're not close enough to make you out and the sun is in their eyes."

Aaron leaned down and put his hand on my shoulder. "Keep safe, my lord," he said. "I will circle around Carlisle and make for the boat. If I can't reach it safely, I'll head south for Wales by land, though I dread the thought of appearing before your father without you."

"It's my decision, Aaron."

"Yes, my lord," he said. He turned his horse away.

Ieuan had been watching the English the whole time. "They're coming this way," Ieuan said. "Do we run?"

"Can we reach Scotland before they intercept us?"

Ieuan shook his head.

"Then we mount and head back to Carlisle on the southern side of the wall. If they're so anxious to meet us, we'll let them come to us. We've done nothing wrong. We're merely two businessmen, taking in the sights."

"Except we saw their king die," Ieuan murmured, under his breath, as he threw a leg over Llywd's back.

"And we say *nothing* about that!"

Ieuan and I trotted our horses along the old Roman road that followed the wall. Before long, a man shouted. With a rueful look at Ieuan, I slowed Bedwyr. We'd reached a spot on the wall that was little more than a low barrier, some three feet high. The years had filled in the ditch on the northern side. The lead horseman came to a stop ten paces from me. He was shorter than

I, older, and dressed well, in a mail hauberk underneath a red and blue surcoat.

"How goes it, sir?" I asked, trying out my English. I'd been practicing the thirteenth century dialect.

"Who are you?" the man asked. "What is your purpose here?" He looked past me to Ieuan, who bowed but didn't speak. *Thank God! He read my mind! They might have run him through and asked questions later.*

"May I know to whom I have the pleasure of speaking?" I asked.

"Sir John de Falkes, castellan of Carlisle Castle and commander of King Edward's forces in the northwest of England."

While my mother and I had discussed the possibility that I might encounter Sir John de Falkes in Lancaster, this meeting defied incredible odds. But as my father once said, coincidences weren't something he believed in anymore.

"David of Chester, at your service," I replied, bowing slightly.

"And your companion?" de Falkes asked.

I turned to Ieuan. "Ieuan ap Cynan, of Twyn y Garth," I said. "He doesn't speak English."

Ieuan had started when I spoke his name. I gave him a reassuring smile, and turned back to Falkes, who was now staring at me, his mouth slightly open.

"Why do I keep encountering the Welsh along this wall?" he asked. "What is the attraction?"

"My lord?" I asked.

"I met a Welshwoman here this time last year. Perhaps she was one of your kinfolk? Her name was Marged ap Bran. You have heard of her?"

"Yes, of course. Marged is my mother."

"Of course she is," he said. "How could it be otherwise? How goes it with her?"

"She is well, my lord," I said. "My companion and I have traveled to Newcastle and I wished to see the wall. It is a pleasure to meet you as well, as you were so kind to her."

Falkes, however, narrowed his eyes. His astonishment in abeyance, he reverted to the custodian of the north he was. "I don't believe you," he said. He scanned our equipment and gear. "You must come with me to Carlisle."

"I was hoping to begin our return journey to Chester by this evening," I said.

"You will have to postpone it," Falkes snapped.

At a signal from him, his men surrounded us. Fortunately, Falkes didn't take our swords or search our belongings. Ieuan's bow always drew my eyes like a magnet, but as Falkes was a soldier, perhaps he thought nothing of it. At the same time, I was glad I'd borrowed Cadwallon's sword and left mine with him before we left the boat. Mine was far too fine a weapon for the man I was pretending to be. Not that a merchant should have a sword at all, and perhaps that was what made Falkes uneasy.

"This was part of your plan?" Ieuan asked me in Welsh.

"We can fit it in," I said, in the same language.

"I wish I understood the language better," Ieuan said. "I recognize words as you speak them, but then they come so fast I can't keep up."

"It doesn't necessarily help," I said. "They say words you think you know the meaning to, but then it turns out entirely differently than you'd thought. It's almost worse to know what they're saying, because you listen to the words instead of focusing on their actions."

"That is my task, then," said Ieuan.

The sun had reached its zenith and begun to descend before we approached Carlisle. We crossed the Eden River some distance from the city and then clattered through the east city gate. We wound our way through Carlisle and up to the castle which perched on the hill to the northwest of the city. I looked left and right, trying to get a sense of how the streets were laid out. Falkes noted my attention.

"You find Carlisle to your liking?" he asked.

"Yes, my lord," I said. "It's been years since I have seen such a grand city as this."

Falkes seemed pleased enough by my compliment to abandon his watch over me. He rode ahead so he could lead his men through the gate that separated the castle from the city proper. Just before he reached it, however, a rider burst from underneath the gatehouse and nearly collided with Falkes.

"My lord!" he said. His horse sidled sideways as he tried to control it.

Falkes reined in his own horse. "What is it," he said.

17

"King Edward is dead!"

Falkes asked neither when nor how, but gestured to the messenger. "Come with me," he said.

He urged his horse through the gate, his men surging to follow and shooing us along in front of them. Welsh castles were small, often merely a stone keep surrounded by a single wall. We positioned them on hilltops to augment their strength. Carlisle Castle was nothing like that. It was enormous, built of reddish stone cut in thick square blocks, and was situated in a flat area that was bigger than a football field. I couldn't begin to guess the number of soldiers it could hold. It had an inner and outer courtyard, both protected by enormous, square gatehouses.

Veering off before entering the second gate, men herded us to a rough building which squatted against the western, curtain wall, directly across from the main gate. The space encompassed by the walls had a variety of buildings in it, including a barracks, stables, and craft-houses. We stopped in front of the blacksmith's workshop. Two men worked the iron inside and the fireplace in the center of the shop shone bright in the darkness of the interior.

With swords drawn, the men urged us to dismount. The situation had an ugly feel to it.

"Why are you doing this?" I asked.

"Put your hands in the air."

Ieuan and I obeyed, and though I ran through various techniques to get free in my head, I didn't implement any of them. Falkes' soldiers outnumbered us fifty to one. They took our swords and our knives and shoved us through a door to the right of the shop.

I ducked my head under the frame and into a windowless room attached to the shop. It smelled of urine and horses. Hay lay on the floor in dirty clumps and the pumping of the bellows sounded through the thin wooden wall that separated the room from the workshop. The door closed behind us and the bar dropped. I pushed on the door. *Nothing.*

"Why didn't they just run us through?" Ieuan asked. "It would have saved time."

"Perhaps Falkes doesn't know what to do with us," I said. "We're neither dangerous enough for the dungeon, important enough for a room in the keep, nor harmless enough for him to let go."

"I don't like it," Ieuan said, sounding like Bevyn.

"The postern gate is set in the wall not far from here," I said.

"I didn't see it," Ieuan said, but the knowledge cheered him considerably. "It's almost as if Falkes wants us to try to escape. Then his men could kill us as we fled."

"Falkes has a free hand in the north," I said. "He answers only to Edward, who is dead, along with his brother and many lords of the Marche. If he were to throw half of his people into his dungeons, who in England would gainsay him? There's nobody left."

Ieuan lowered himself to the ground and leaned his back against the curtain wall which formed the rear of the room. "I would dearly love to hear that messenger's report," he said.

At that, a scratching sound came from behind me, prompting me to turn and look. A blue eye gazed at me through a knot in the wood.

"Hello," I said, in English.

"Hello," the voice answered in the same language. It was high and I couldn't tell if it belonged to a boy or a girl.

"May I be of service?" I asked.

The eye blinked, then disappeared. It reappeared in a larger knothole, two feet higher and to the right of the other one. "I'm Thomas," the voice said. "Your mother saved my life."

"So she did," I said.

The lone eye inspected me up and down. "You look like I thought you would," he said. "Will you say a few words of Welsh?"

"Of course." And then continued, "*Mae'n dda gen i gwrdd â chi.*"

"What does that mean?" Thomas asked.

"I am very pleased to meet you," I answered, in English again.

"Ask him to tell us about Edward," Ieuan said.

I stepped closer to Thomas. "Is King Edward really dead?"

"Yes," Thomas nodded vigorously. "The messenger rode into the castle just before you arrived. Uncle John spoke with him in private and then announced the news to everyone in the hall. They say it was plague but Uncle John doesn't believe it. I heard them whispering about a traitor among King Edward's men. He thinks the Welsh are involved. But you aren't are you, since your Prince is dead too?"

"What was that?" I asked.

"They found a boy wearing the red dragon surcoat among the dead. Wouldn't that be Prince Llywelyn's son?"

I turned to Ieuan and quickly translated what Thomas had said. He whistled through his teeth.

"We had no hand in the death of your King, Thomas," I said, turning back to the boy. "As a Welshman, you must understand that I don't mourn him, but don't fear for us in that regard."

Thomas surveyed me through three heartbeats. "I must go," he said and disappeared. Light shone through the hole. I put my own eye to it. Thomas ran away from us across the courtyard without looking back.

"I'd forgotten about that surcoat," I said. "Edward ripped it from me during the fight and we just left it in a corner. All that work to hide our presence and erase any trace of our camp, and I made a foolish mistake like that."

"But look how it's turned out," Ieuan said. "Falkes will never suspect who you really are now."

"It must have been Moses," I said, picturing him with his father. "He had all night to arrange the bodies as he saw fit."

Ieuan rubbed his hands together in gleeful expectation. "What mischief you could make, my lord, now that you're dead!"

I ignored that. *No more Cadwaladr! No more Robin Hood!* "I've been so focused on Edward's death, that I've given little thought to the death of all the others: Edward's brother, Edmund; Robert Burnell; the Mortimer boys"—Ieuan made a 'hooray!' sound at that—"Gilbert De Clare; John Gifford, not to mention my Uncle Dafydd," I said. "What will happen now?"

Ieuan swept a hand through his hair. It had come loose from the thong that normally held it at the nape of his neck. "Hereford," he said. "He's all that's left." *Humphrey de Bohun, the third Earl of Hereford, Lord of the Marche.*

"He's ambitious and clever," I said, "much like Edward, in fact. What will he make of these deaths?"

"Nothing good," Ieuan said. "Worse, news of your death will spread and your father may hear of it before we can reach him."

I tried to picture it: Edward had tried to kill me on the evening of July 31st. The next morning, Carew, Aaron and I had observed the Scot encounter with the camp's sole survivor, Aaron's nephew, Moses. At the news of Edward's death and the supposed plague in the camp, the Scots had turned tail and run the other way as fast as their horses could carry them. We'd departed from the fishing village of Poulton shortly thereafter.

"We docked at Annan on the evening of August 2nd, only two days after Edward's death. Tonight is August 3rd."

"It's less than eighty miles from Lancaster to Carlisle. A man can ride that distance in a day if he pushes his horse," Ieuan said.

"Hereford could have arrived in the camp with the Archbishop of Canterbury within hours of our departure. He's two days ahead of us; he's had two days to plot something we're not going to like," I said.

"First, he would have ridden as hard and as fast as he could to London," Ieuan said. "Edward II is only sixteen months old. The deaths of Edward, Edmund, and the others, leaves a huge whole in the power structure of England that Hereford will be only too glad to fill."

"He has few allies in England," I pointed out. "His loyalties have been to himself, far more than to Edward. Other men know that and won't trust him."

"He'll play that down, especially as so few men remain to gainsay him. Watch," Ieuan said, "they'll name him regent within a week."

"He holds one of those 'Great Offices of State' doesn't he? What's his—the sixth highest in England?" I asked.

"He's Lord High Constable. That makes him fifth, though at this point, he's probably moved up because at least a couple of the men in front of him are dead."

I slid down the wall until I sat on the floor, my knees bent in front of me, and placed my chin in my hands. "We'll see what develops tonight," I said. "Right now Falkes is too busy with the news of Edward to worry about us."

"So we can hope," Ieuan said.

# 2

## *Ieuan*

**I** couldn't rest. I paced around the small space, not more than four strides across, while my lord sat on the floor, his chin in his hands.

"I could break through that wall with my boot in two kicks," I said. Prince Dafydd turned to look at the wall behind him and then back at me.

"One kick if I stood beside you," he said. "But I think we shouldn't act before dark, and maybe not even then. Ideally, I'd like to see Falkes again, to better know his mind."

"Why?" I asked.

"These behind-the-scenes machinations are beyond me," he said. "The more exposure I have to men such as Falkes, the better I'll be able to treat with them when I become Prince of Wales, and better able to advise my father in the interim."

"Not if you're dead," I said. "We're Welsh. Most Englishmen think the only good Welshman is a dead Welshman."

"I've not forgotten, Ieuan," Dafydd said, his voice suddenly soft, and I felt bad for speaking as I had. He was so young and had so many responsibilities. But then, his destiny was a straight road, laid out before him that all could see. He couldn't shirk it; *nor can I.*

"You think they mean to kill us?" he asked.

"I do, my lord, and that's not just the fear talking or the hate I hold for the English. Falkes may have plans and ideas about what really happened with Edward, but it's not your job to find out what those are. It's your job to get yourself clear, back to Wales."

"You and Bevyn," Dafydd said. "You always feel the need to remind me of who I am."

"I apologize, my lord," I said, "for speaking out of turn."

"You didn't speak out of turn," Dafydd said. "You're right. That's why you're here. My father does not entirely trust my judgment and rightfully so."

"In that you aren't correct," I said. "We sons always seem to disappoint our fathers, but no father has ever thought more of his son than Prince Llywelyn thinks of you."

Dafydd looked up at me and I gritted my teeth, knowing I'd said too much. "Like you disappointed your father?" Dafydd asked, as if he'd read my thoughts. Given his other abilities, I wouldn't be surprised to learn that he *could.*

"It's not important, my lord," I said, trying to head him off. He had a disconcerting frankness that seemed to encourage a similar candidness in his men.

"Isn't it?" But Dafydd nodded. "Another time, then. I won't forget."

I groaned inwardly. He wouldn't, either. I turned to the door, pretending to inspect it while my innards roiled as I attempted to dampen my emotions. My father hadn't been a bad man, just stubborn and unbending. He'd never even beaten me unless I deserved it. *It was his silence that hurt; his cold disapproval; the knowledge that I, as his only son, was ever a disappointment. My mother had comforted me once, explaining that fathers and sons never understood each other—but I knew she was wrong; knew it even then; knew it even before she died with the son for whom my father longed, the one he hoped would grow into the man I could never be.*

\* \* \* \* \*

Darkness fell, late as always this far north. Prince Dafydd and I sat beside each other, arms crossed, waiting for the time when the castle was at its quietest. Neither of us slept.

"Falkes doesn't know you are the Prince," I repeated, more to reassure myself than him.

"It's a nice thought," Dafydd said.

"Still," I said, "he must have noticed something about you, my lord. Something that struck him as not quite right, or we wouldn't be here now."

"He didn't think my mother was quite right either," Dafydd said. "Although as a woman she'd have been of little interest. He probably forgot about her the moment she was out of his sight. That is, until he encountered me."

"You are too well dressed," I said. "Your horse is too fine, your sword to well-made to be a simple merchant from Chester."

"My original intent was to pass myself off as a younger son of a knight," he said. "I miscalculated in thinking that Falkes would view me more favorably as Marged's son, although now I'm glad I mentioned her. It will cast doubt on the notion that I was associated with the death of Edward."

"Imagine if he knew you were Prince Llywelyn's son too," Ieuan said.

Dafydd grunted, "I'd be dead by now."

I returned to my reverie. Best to not get back on the topic of fathers and sons. I leaned my head against the rough planks at my back and closed my eyes. I entertained myself by wondering what my sister Lili was up to, what kind of trouble she'd gotten into recently. I smiled, but then stilled. The door to our prison creaked open.

"My lord!" I nudged Dafydd, but he was already getting to his feet.

A small person stood silhouetted in the doorway. *Thomas.* He spoke, his voice high and excited.

27

"What's he done?" I whispered as we joined him at the door.

Thomas had our horses saddled and our swords strapped to the saddlebags. I didn't want to think about what this might cost him if he were caught—if *we* were caught. My father would have killed me.

He led us to the unguarded postern gate a few yards away and pulled it open. We slipped through the door and Thomas knelt to wedge a stone between the door and the frame to keep the door from closing completely. In single file, we walked our horses along the castle wall, keeping to its shadow. After a dozen yards, Thomas stopped. He and Dafydd conferred briefly. Dafydd nodded. We mounted while Thomas turned back to the castle. As he passed me, he patted Llywd's neck. Then a light flashed in the darkness of the wall. Thomas had slipped back through the postern gate.

Dafydd was no more than a shadow in front of me. A few men shouted on the other side of the wall, frustrating me again by my lack of English. I understood simple sentences and words, having sat with Aaron a time or two, but not enough to help Prince Dafydd. I wanted to know what Thomas had said but held my impatience in check. Now was not the time.

Carlisle Castle perched in the northwestern corner of the city, surrounded by water on three sides: the river Caldew to the south and west and the Eden to the north. We'd escaped by a western gate, which was all to the good as far as I was concerned. West was where I wanted to be, but in order to reach the sea, we had to follow the wall around to the north and cross the Eden River where it looped around the city, before heading west through Scotland to the sea.

"Thomas pointed me to a bridge to the north of the castle," Dafydd said. "When we come around the wall, we shouldn't have to ride far before we see it."

"Guarded, of course," I said.

"Of course. He apologized for not being able to encourage the guards to over-drink as he had the men at the postern gate."

"There's nothing to draw these away from their post either," I said.

"Unfortunately not," Dafydd agreed.

"We may have to kill them," I said.

"Let me try to talk our way past, first," Dafydd said. "Dead bodies will give Falkes more reason to come after us."

"Agreed," I said, albeit reluctantly. The longer we were in England, the more anxious I was to get my lord home, by whatever means necessary. Killing, at least, was efficient.

Two torches lit the wooden bridge that spanned the river, held in sconces designed for that purpose. I fell back, letting Dafydd take the lead as he'd asked. I swung my quiver onto my back, tightened the strap across my chest, and tugged my bow from its rest. I held it down at my side so as not to appear threatening.

Dafydd shot a wicked look back at me. Before I could worry about what he was up to (again), he straightened in the saddle and began to sing:

*"Ohhhh, the cow kicked Nelly in the belly in the barn,*
*Oh, the cow kicked Nelly in the belly in the barn,*
*Oh, the cow kicked Nelly in the belly in the barn*
*And the doctor said it wouldn't do any harm.*
***Second verse! Same as the first! A little bit louder***
***and a little bit worse!"***

His deep voice echoed through the trees. The song was ridiculous and dreadful. He could have been pissing his pants in fear, and instead, he *sang*. As Dafydd launched into the third verse, he reached the guards, who'd dropped their pikes and stood, one with his hand on his hip, the other pushing back his helmet to scratch his head. The guard on the left was a hefty fellow with a thick brown beard, which was all I could see of him in the darkness that the torchlight couldn't penetrate.

He interrupted Dafydd in the middle of a note. In response, Dafydd laughed and spoke. He gestured with one hand to me. I held up my hand in greeting and the guard nodded. Without questioning my lord further, the men raised their pikes and waved us through. Dafydd was whistling the song as he reached the end of the bridge and by then I'd encouraged Llywd to catch him. We trotted down the road on the other side of the Eden together.

"What did you say to them?" I asked.

"I told them I was escorting you to your wedding at the behest of Sir John de Falkes," Dafydd said.

"My wedding!"

"One of the men asked why I was drunk instead of you and I told him that I'd met the girl and you hadn't."

I shook my head. I never knew what was going to come out of his mouth next. Dafydd, however, was no longer laughing. "Do you know where to go from here?"

"North and west," I said. "As quickly as we possibly can."

"Agreed. Hopefully, when Falkes notices our absence, he'll dismiss us, realizing we're unimportant in the long run. His charge is to defend against the Scots, not Welshmen."

"That would be my hope as well," I said.

"Hey!"

I glanced over my shoulder. A man on a horse leaned down to confer with one of the guards who was looking in our direction and pointing.

"Ride!" Dafydd said.

* * * * *

To evade our pursuers, we rode hard for nearly five miles, and then trotted our horses off the main road. We then proceeded to spend the entire day and into the evening leading our horses through the trees. Now, my lord Dafydd and I crouched near a trail, our horses tethered a few feet from us. Not knowing the region at all, I'd been pleased to discover that the terrain became much more wooded a few miles from Carlisle.

I was, quite frankly, astonished that Falkes had put this much effort into finding us. With his King dead, he surely had much greater concerns than a young boy from Chester and his servant. *Unless, of course, he'd discovered that Dafydd was the Prince, after all?* I dismissed the idea. *Perhaps Falkes is simply stubborn.*

We waited, listening to the forest around us. It wasn't my forest but the feeling it gave me was similar to what I'd felt a thousand times before.

*The great Cadwaladr ap Seisyll peers through the underbrush, a massive bow on his back and a dozen arrows in his quiver. Braose's men are scouring the bushes on the other side of the valley looking for him, but of course the great Cadwaladr is invisible to evil men such as they. Cadwaladr stifles a laugh, and turns to—*

*"What are you doing, Ieuan?"*

*I twist around to look into the face of my little sister, Lili. Instead of answering, I grit my teeth at her and hiss.*

*"Are you being Cadwaladr again?" she asks.*

*"Sshh!" I yank her down beside me and we peer together through the bush to the other side of the field, where the Earl of Hereford patrols with his men. If I didn't recognize him from other visits to these woods, I would have thought him an ordinary man. He's of middle height with red-brown hair and beard.*

"Him!" Lili says, trying to whisper.

A dozen of Hereford's knights cluster around him. I can't hear his words—and wouldn't understand them could I hear them—but his men listen attentively. Watching him speak, it makes me angry to think that the man might be a good leader, that his men might fight for him for more than the gold he offers.

I shift, setting my arrow into the bow and sighting on Hereford's head. It's an easy shot, not even a hundred yards. Then, Lili bumps against me and my shoulders sag. Would Cadwaladr have achieved greatness if he'd had his little sister tagging along behind him all the time? What would the real Cadwaladr have done? Throttled her? Probably not. Nobody had been able to sneak up on him, except the last English soldiers, there at the end.

Cadwaladr has been dead for a hundred years but I still feel the weight of his sacrifices. My uncle's lands of Twyn y Garth, near Aberedw, abut those of the English usurpers, and we live with the constant reminder the English encroachment, what they've done to us, and what they still do to us daily. Braose is long dead, though the Earl of Hereford is becoming equally infamous among the Welsh. Braose or Bohun—it makes no difference to me. These English overlords are cut from the same cloth. Thieves and murderers to a man.

I look hard at my sister, still smiling at me, and then fling my arm around her shoulders. "Come with me,"

*I say. "I'll teach you to shoot a bow and that way even when I'm not here, you can defend our family from our enemies."*

*Lili skips out from under my arm and takes off running. "I'll set up the butts," she shouts at me over her shoulder. "I'll be as good as you someday! You'll see!"*

*I shake my head but she's too far away to see. She has no idea how much practice she will need. Every day I work until my arms shake but still the heavy bow is more than I can handle. And it's not even a full six feet as yet. My uncle has already cut a new stave for seasoning, and when I turn fourteen next spring, he'll string it for me one last time. I will be a man then, with a man's responsibilities.*

*Then, with my uncle's blessing, I will seek out Prince Llywelyn and join his men. And one day Hereford will pay for his family's treatment of Cymry. I will see to it. Personally.*

Hereford or Falkes; King Henry or King Edward—the names changed but the will was the same. With no Lili to interrupt me this time, I put a hand on my lord's arm. Three men approached, walking their horses past our position. They rode unspeaking and we held our breath until they were out of sight and sound.

"How long are they going to search for us?" Dafydd asked, under his breath.

"Until they find us?"

"We're in Scotland. They have no jurisdiction here. Surely this is madness."

"Only if they're caught."

"We must reach the boat," Dafydd said.

"By what means?" I asked. "Where there are three, there might be more. I don't think Falkes will be so easy on us a second time."

Then, the clip-clopping of another horse's hooves sounded. I peered through the underbrush. "It's Aaron," Dafydd said, springing to his feet.

Aaron's head and his horse's were down, draggingly tired, but they both looked up at the sight of us. I tugged at Dafydd's cloak to keep him from bursting out of the trees. "Wait," I said.

After the first brief glance, Aaron looked away from us and pulled his horse off the road. He dismounted while Dafydd and I backed into the trees, thankful for his silent warning. It was another minute before the three soldiers from before returned and stopped as they reached Aaron.

"A Jew!" one of them spat on the road. I knew enough English to understand those words, at least.

Aaron kept his eyes fixed on the ground but it didn't appease the Englishman. He leaned forward, grasped Aaron's beard in his left fist, and jerked his head, forcing him to look up. "You offend me," the man said.

A small knife appeared in his right hand. In retrospect, it's possible he only intended to trim Aaron's beard, but before I knew it Dafydd had his sword out and had charged out of the woods. I was quicker, however, and the man died with an arrow through his neck before Dafydd could reach him. Finding himself without an opponent, Dafydd swung around and met the sword of one of the other men with his blade.

Before the man could slash at Dafydd's head a second time, Dafydd whipped out his belt knife and slit the horse's throat. It crashed to the ground, trapping its owner's leg beneath it. He screamed. Meanwhile, I pressed and loosed a second arrow at the third man who'd taken flight rather than engage either of us. The arrow hit him in the back and he too fell.

All of a sudden, I could hear again. The birds in the trees sang as before, undisturbed by the violence we'd unleashed. Aaron rested his head on his horse's neck, one hand to his eyes while Dafydd dispatched the downed soldier. I handed my lord a cloth with which to wipe his sword. Dafydd took it. He shrugged. "We need to move," he said. "Now."

"A trail runs south, just there," I said, pointing towards a spot a few yards distant. "But Aaron can't ride much further."

"We don't have a choice."

We'd not gone far down the trail, Dafydd slightly behind Aaron to encourage him and not allow him to fall behind, before the scent of the sea came strongly. The hoof beats behind us sounded more loudly too. Dafydd glanced once behind us, and then slapped the rear of Aaron's horse with his hand. "Run!" he said. The horse took off.

"They've brought too many," I said.

"I know," Dafydd said.

Dafydd and I spurred our horses. Ahead, a gap in the trees revealed the end to the road, a cliff that faced the sea. Beyond, in the fading light, the gray sea blended in with the grayness of the sky. Below the cliff should be the village of Annan and the boat.

"Damn it!" Dafydd said. "Hurry!"

I glanced behind me again. The English were closer—far closer than they'd been last time I checked. Ahead of us, Aaron raced through the gap in the trees and turned left, following the edge of the cliff. In two heartbeats he was out of sight.

"My lord!" I said, "we might have to stand and figh—" But I couldn't finish my sentence. An Englishman had gotten off a lucky shot with his bow and his arrow hit me in the back, low on my right side, driving through the leather armor into my ribs.

I cried out.

Dafydd heard me and looked back. "Christ!" he said. He reined in, signaling to Bedwyr with his knees and reaching for Llwyd's reins. I struggled to stay upright but all the air had left my lungs. "Stay with me, damn you!"

He managed to catch Llwyd's reins with one hand and me with the other. He tried to hang on to me, but my weight was too much and I fell between the horses to the ground. Dafydd leaped from Bedwyr, shoving at his horse so that he blocked us from the English arrows, and bent over me. My fall had dislodged the arrow and blood poured from the wound.

I gazed into his face, trying to speak. "Hush," Dafydd said. Then a look crossed his face, one I'd seen a few times before. It was one of resolution and I wanted to shout at him, "Whatever your plan, don't do it! Your life is worth so much more than mine! Leave me and run!" But I choked on my own bile and couldn't speak.

Hooves pounded along the road. They were almost upon us. Dafydd put his head close to mine. "Can you rise?" he asked.

I managed a nod. We clasped hands and he pulled me up, but instead of requiring me to walk, he stooped, grasped my arm and my waist, and threw me over his shoulder so my head hung down his back. Without looking behind us again, he took three long strides in the direction Aaron had gone. Unlike Aaron, however, Dafydd didn't follow the path to the village. Instead, he hovered on the edge of the cliff. *Christ, what's he doing?*

He jumped.

Rocks rush passed us. I closed my eyes, waiting for the impact and the pain. But there was only darkness.

# 3

## *Bronwen*

**I** had a big bite of hamburger in my mouth, with mayonnaise and ketchup dripping onto the napkin in my lap, when word came from on high that my professor wanted to see me. I knew it was important because the departmental secretary had actually gotten up from her desk and walked down the hall to the graduate lounge to find me.

Now I faced a dilemma. Do I finish the hamburger, thus delaying my visit to Professor Tillman, or do I leave the rest of the hamburger uneaten? I'd decided that morning that I needed to augment my four major food groups (coffee, diet cola, onion rings, doughnuts) with more nutritious fare if I was going to survive a second year of graduate school. Thus, the banana I ate for breakfast, and the hamburger for lunch.

I set the hamburger on the table. It looked forlorn and I knew it would be cold by the time I got back. I left it and headed down the hall to Professor Tillman's office. I'd not seen him in some time, as I'd taken to working late to avoid him. Ever since his divorce, he'd become overly friendly. I was hardly a man-magnet (nice looking . . . sure . . . but *normal*), so it could have been all my imagination. At the same time, he wasn't helping me with my thesis as much as in past months and I feared that he could tell that my enthusiasm for graduate school was waning. It wasn't the enormous amount of work—I could handle that, including the interminable round of classes and papers—but that so much of it seemed to be work for work's sake. Ultimately, however, it was the endless self-promotion that had caught me unprepared and still left me with a sour taste in my mouth.

I knocked on the office door and poked in my head. Jim Tillman sat behind a large wooden desk at one end of the room. The office wasn't very big, but lined floor to ceiling with books. A guest chair sat on the opposite side of the desk, only two paces away. Tillman held up one hand to stop me before I spoke, finished what he was typing on his laptop, and then looked up.

"Hello, Bronwen. Come in and shut the door."

*Ugh.* I came in but only closed the door most of the way. I hoped he wouldn't notice.

"Give it another shove," he said.

I spun in the chair and kicked the door with my foot. It latched. I spun back and looked at him, trying to affect a bright and expectant face.

"Coffee?" he asked, holding out a small French press.

"Sure," I said. *It is one of the four food groups, after all.*

40

"Not that we should drink this stuff with all the latest findings," he murmured as he poured some into a cracked mug and handed it to me. "Sorry, there's only a half a cup left."

Despite myself, I smiled. "Well, I guess I don't have to worry about it damaging me, since I only have half a cup."

Tillman looked at me, and there was a pause. Then he laughed, and I remembered why I liked him so much. That was the worst part of my suspicions. Maybe I was just misinterpreting what he was doing. *Maybe it's all in my head?*

Then he dropped the bombshell.

"The selection committee reviewed your request for funding for the upcoming year. Although you've made good progress, we feel that others are more deserving of the annual stipend."

I stared at him, feeling stupid, sure he couldn't just have said what I'd heard. "They're revoking my stipend?"

Tillman smiled, in what he probably thought was a gentle manner. "Yes, Bronwen. We have forty-five graduate students. We couldn't fund all of them."

"There're forty stipends. Are you telling me I'm one of the bottom five students in the department?"

"It isn't necessary to compare yourself with the other students, Bronwen."

Not compare! Graduate school was nothing if not hierarchical. Full professors, like Tillman were at the top, followed by associate professors, assistant professors, and then graduate students. One of the secretaries had actually denied access to a

41

forty-two year old, third year student—a former tax lawyer—who
wanted to use the copy machine. Undergraduates were at the very
bottom of the heap but usually they were oblivious enough not to
know it. The whole thing would be laughable if it weren't so sad.

In the face of my silence, Tillman continued. "Your grades
are more than adequate," he said. "There were other
considerations which I am not at liberty to share with you."

*Bleh.*

"So, do I just pack up and leave?"

"You do have the option of continuing in the program, as
my assistant or through your own monies. I'm willing to continue
working with you, if you're willing to work for me in my research."

And that was it.

What to do? In truth, I loved archaeology. When I'd
applied to college as a senior in high school, the admission
programs were scrapping the 'well-rounded' motif of previous
years, in favor of students with a 'passion.' That was fine by me. I
didn't have much else to offer, what with my spotty attendance
record and worse grades. I hadn't skipped school to smoke under
the bridge. I'd been yanked time and again by my free-living
parents for another trip.

Before I was fifteen, I'd been to every great museum in the
world. I'd lived for more than three months in seven countries.
I'd crossed mountains and deserts, lived in yurts and thatch huts,
climbed Aztec, Mayan, and Egyptian pyramids. I'd attended
seventeen schools and when I wasn't in school, I'd worked with my
parents in everything from a refugee camp in Africa, to triage

medicine in Nepal, to well-digging in Guatemala. Was it any wonder that archaeology appealed to me? One, while doing it, I didn't have to talk to anyone I didn't know, always a plus; and two, I got to play with all the dead, old stuff that other archaeologists had brought back from all the ruins I'd seen. What could be better?

Sitting there in the chair, with my world blown apart around me, I accepted Tillman's offer. Despite my misgivings about him, I had no actual *proof* that he wanted anything untoward from me. *And then there's the ugly truth . . . where would you go if you were to leave here?* I told myself that Tillman's research fascinated me, which is why I'd asked him to become my major professor in the first place. His specialty was Roman Britain. Hadrian's Wall wasn't as huge as the Great Wall of China, but just as enthralling.

Right away, he took me upstairs to his lab to show me where he wanted me to start. He talked a mile a minute all the way there, as he unlocked the lab, and until we stepped inside. He stopped when he turned on the light and both of our faces fell. The lab was packed with artifacts, mostly uncatalogued. It was a mess. He knew it was a mess. And now it was my job to deal with it.

It was past nine in the evening by the time I was able to go home. The scary thing was how many people were still in the building and I waved to a couple of them as I passed their offices. I always hated walking out to my car by myself. I thought about getting someone to come with me but told myself not to be pathetic. It was bad enough that everyone was going to know by tomorrow or the next day that I was no longer a funded student, but at school on sufferance without a stipend. I was going to have to stand on my own two feet.

I pushed open the door with my shoulder, holding my keys in my left hand and my TASER firmly in my right. I was so preoccupied with my thoughts that I almost didn't see the two men, one kneeling beside the other in the shadows of the building. As I passed them, walking quickly, the one who was kneeling jerked around and startled me. He knew it, too, for he held out his hand as if to plead with me not to run.

I backed away. He wasn't as old as I'd first thought—more of a boy than a man—but he was a big guy, with a mop of unkempt, light brown hair and long legs. I couldn't see very well by the light of the street lamp, but it looked like he was wearing a cloak and a thick leather coat—*could that be armor?* What really got my attention, though, was the long sword, sticking out from his left side. It looked like a real sword, not a prop. None of the SCA folks I knew had a sword like that.

He spoke. "My name is David . . ." then paused, thinking, before continuing, "Llywelyn. Please, please help us. My friend is wounded."

*Llywelyn.*

The other man's voice spoke out of the darkness, quiet so I couldn't quite make out the words. It tickled my ear to hear him, as if I should understand what he was saying but couldn't quite catch it. David replied under his breath. I glanced from one to the other, ready to run, but not yet running. I couldn't run away from that name and there was something about the boy that wasn't really threatening, though I held up the TASER just in case. David held out his own hand again. "Please! Don't go. We really need some help."

"Why do you think I can help you?"

"You have a cell phone?"

"Of course."

"Please call 911. You can stand over there to do it, but please call. My friend's been shot in the back."

Believing him now, I fumbled in my backpack for my phone while David returned to his friend. He shushed him and began to work at his clothing, perhaps trying to get at the wound. I dialed my phone.

"911," the woman who answered said. "We have your location. What is your emergency?"

"A man has been shot. We're at the plaza at the Penn State campus, outside the archaeology building."

"Stay on the line. An ambulance will be with you shortly."

As she spoke, I moved next to David, but held the connection open. I fell to my knees beside him.

"Can I help?"

David scooped up a pile of weapons that lay beside him, consisting of, from what I could see, two swords (he no longer wore one), three knives, a bow and a quiver.

"I need you to take these and put them somewhere safe," he said.

45

"You're not serious!"

"If the authorities find me with them, we may end up in jail instead of the hospital. We've done nothing illegal as far as I know, but we're dressed strangely enough without complicating matters further."

I blinked. He talked just like a professor, but he couldn't have been more than sixteen or seventeen.

"Do you have a vehicle?" he asked.

I nodded. "In the parking lot."

"Please do as I ask. Please."

Giving in again, I took what he gave me, leaving him my phone so the ambulance's tracking device could find him. I ran to my car, though the weapons were so heavy my shoulders were aching by the time I reached it. I threw open the hatchback and dumped the weapons inside, only to find that the bow wouldn't fit. Grumbling, I scooted around to open the door to the back seat and folded down one of the seats. Slamming the doors, I ran back to the plaza. The emergency crew had arrived.

While the EMTs worked on his friend, a policeman grilled David. I ran up just as the cop said, "I need to see some ID, sir."

"I don't have any."

The policeman's mouth twisted, irritated. "Give me your name and date of birth."

David rattled them off. The policeman hesitated over his paperwork when he realized David was only sixteen—he didn't have to carry identification at all times until he was eighteen.

"How about your friend?" the policeman asked. "He's older than you, isn't he?"

"Yes, but I don't know that he has identification either. We didn't plan for him to get hurt."

"What's his name?"

"Ieuan Cynan," David said.

"Excuse me, sir," I interrupted. I'd been rummaging in my pack while they talked, and now pulled out my driver's license. "I'm Bronwen Llywelyn," I said.

David's eyes almost bulged from their sockets, but thankfully he kept his mouth shut.

"It was you who called emergency services?" the policeman asked.

"Yes, sir," I agreed. *What are you thinking, Bronwen! Are you out of your mind? Why are you getting involved?*

"He's your brother?" The man asked, gesturing to David.

"Cousin," I said, though we looked nothing alike, with David a Viking to my Celt.

"And the other guy?"

David spoke this time. "Our friend. He's visiting from Wales and doesn't speak any English."

"They don't speak English in Wales?" the policeman asked.

"Not always," I said, and gave David a speaking look. *From Wales. No wonder their voices sounded familiar.*

"Excuse me, sir, ma'am," one of the EMTs interrupted, walking over to stand next to us. "We're taking your friend into the hospital."

47

"Can I ride with him?" David asked. "He'll be lost without me."

"No, sir; I'm sorry, sir; that's against hospital policy. Anyway, we've sedated him, so he won't remember the trip."

"I'll need certification from you that this was a gunshot wound," the policeman said to the ambulance technician.

"No gunshot, sir. Looks like he fell on something sharp. It bit him between two of his lower ribs. He's lost some blood, but it missed his lungs."

The policeman glared at us while the ambulance man returned to his work. We stood and watched them load Ieuan into the ambulance, and then the policeman spoke again. "I thought you said he'd been shot."

"I thought he had!" I said, looking at David.

"I'm sorry," said David. "I must have misspoken."

"Don't make a habit of it," the policeman said. He snapped his notebook shut. "I hope your friend recovers soon."

"Thanks," David said, and the policeman walked away. David turned to me. "Will you take me to the hospital?"

I bit my lip and looked up at him, meeting his blue eyes. They were bright and sincere and fixed on mine. I shook my head to say no, but found myself saying yes to him again.

*Surely I will regret this!*

David grinned.

# 4

## *David*

**It** was an amazing feeling to sit in the car as Bronwen drove it through the nearly empty streets of State College to the hospital. The interior was dark, except for the lights of the dashboard, and when we'd pass a streetlight, the light would fill the car before dissipating again as we drove by it. I gazed out the window, watching the reflection of the tall apartment buildings, forming canyon walls on either side of the street, flash past.

I was progressing through the stages of adrenaline crash with my usual rapidity. First: *jubilation!* It was the dirty little secret of battle that afterwards it wasn't horror, or fear, or revulsion that we felt, but utter joy at having survived another day. *I'm alive! And they're not! Against all odds, I will live to see another sunrise!* The whole time we were with the police officer, I'd been in a euphoric, dreamlike state, yet so confident that things were going to go my way that I was completely unsurprised when they did.

*I can't believe it worked!* I'd spent the last two and a half years in and out of danger, but I recognized the moment with the English soldiers bearing down on us as the *end* in a very concrete sense—far worse than when Edward of England had leered at me across his pavilion. That first soldier would have run me through without hesitation if I'd not jumped off the cliff with Ieuan, who would have died from the arrow, if not the sword. I'd been thinking about possible ways to return to the twenty-first century for *years,* as had Mom and Anna. It was really Anna's idea to jump—she'd wanted to try it from the tallest tower at Castell y Bere, back in the early days. I'd dissuaded her, not wanting her to risk her life even if it left us ignorant.

This time, however, it was no kind of risk at all to jump. Now, of course, the question was how to reverse the process and go home. *Would we be able to go home?* I stopped myself before I began to dwell on those thoughts. *Put it away. Put it away. There's too much else to think about.*

The post-battle optimistic and joyful feeling was generally followed, in my case, by chills. Feeling them coming on, I rolled down the passenger side window. It was a warm night, typical for August in Pennsylvania. I set my elbow on the door frame and rested my head against my fist. I could feel Bronwen watching me, checking my profile between glances out the front windscreen. I wanted to gain some measure of control before I talked to her and tried to explain anything.

*I am so tired.* As soon as the thought passed through my head, I squashed it, told myself to *put it away* again. For the first time in years, I was safe. *Really safe—unless Bronwen was about to get us in a car accident.* I looked over at her. She looked competent. She sat, slim and dark beside me, back straight, brown hair up in a no-nonsense bun, her left hand resting on the wheel while her right worked the gear shift.

"Is Llywelyn really your last name?" I asked her, breaking the silence.

She smiled. "Yes, it is. I didn't lie. You really shouldn't lie to the authorities, David."

"I actually didn't lie either. Ieuan was shot."

"Where was the bullet? Did it just graze him?"

I didn't want to answer. "He was shot with an arrow," I said, after a moment's reflection.

"An arrow! What are you talking about?" Bronwen was looking at me instead of out the windscreen of the car.

"We were being chased by men and they shot at Ieuan," I said.

"But this is ridiculous!" Bronwen said. "They're still out there! You need to go back and tell the police."

"You heard the EMT," I said. "There's no indication now that he was even shot, much less by an arrow. What would the police say to me, dressed as I am, still with no identification?"

"What if they shoot someone else?" she asked.

"They're long gone," I said, not yet ready to explain further. "Leave it be."

Bronwen ground her teeth.

"Thank you for helping us," I said, trying to distract her.

Bronwen didn't look at me, and her fingers clenched tightly around the steering wheel. "I've had a lousy day," she said. "This feels pretty much par for the course."

"Do you live far from here? You can drop me off and I can take care of things myself."

"How are you going to deal with the hospital with no ID?" she asked.

I felt a funny twist in my stomach at her words. "I've no money either," I said. "Will the hospital treat him even if we can't pay?"

"Why would you have to pay? It's been a couple of years since you had to pay."

"Really?" I asked, and then Bronwen gave me a confused look so I didn't say anything more. *What else has changed since 2010?*

Bronwen didn't say another word for the rest of the short drive to the hospital. She was thinking *something* but maybe I didn't want to know what it was. She parked the car and got out, jerking the door handle and slamming it closed behind her. The parking lot wasn't full, and we walked across it to the emergency room entrance. The ambulance men had already unloaded Ieuan and together we peered through some glass doors into a room where he was being worked on by a doctor and two nurses. Bronwen headed for the nurses' station.

"Do I need to sign him in?" she asked.

A woman behind the desk looked up. "Yes," she said, handing Bronwen a clipboard. "I'll need his full name, birth date, ID number, and current address."

Bronwen looked over at me. I shrugged and put out my hand for the clipboard. We walked to some chairs, set against a wall in the hallway, and studied the paperwork.

"How closely are they going to check all this right now?" I asked.

"It's all in the computer," Bronwen said. "They'll know immediately if something isn't right."

This was going to be a little more difficult than I'd thought. I picked up the pen and wrote Ieuan's name and nothing else. I had no ID numbers, no address, and certainly no credible birth date, so I left it all blank and walked back to the desk.

"My friend is from Wales," I said. "I don't know his ID number."

The nurse looked irritated. "May I see your ID then?"

"I don't have any. I'm only sixteen," I said, taking a cue from Bronwen.

"Social security number?" the nurse asked.

"I don't know it."

Pursing her lips, the nurse wrote INDIGENT in big letters across Ieuan's form. I hoped he would still get decent treatment from the doctors, since that's why I had brought him here in the first place.

I went back to Bronwen. She had a cup of coffee balanced on her lap and was in the process of loading it up with cream and sugar. She ripped off the top of the packets of sugar, two at a time, and dumped them in until I lost track. She saw me watching her, and smiled.

"Like a little coffee with your sugar?" I asked.

"Coffee is one of the four basic food groups, didn't you know?" she said.

"And apparently cream and sugar are two more," I added.

"No, no, no. They're included in the coffee group." She stirred her coffee with one of those tiny straws that came with Styrofoam coffee, but were remarkably ineffective, especially given the quantity of sugar in her cup. "I don't actually *like* coffee," she confessed. "What I drink is basically hot coffee ice cream."

She took a sip and sighed. I sat beside her again.

"May I ask you a question?" I said.

"You can ask," she answered, her eyes closed now and her head resting against the wall behind us.

"Since you share his name, do you know of Llywelyn ap Gruffydd, a Prince of Wales from the Middle Ages?" I asked.

"You mean the last Prince of Wales? The one the English killed in 1282?"

"Yes, that's the one." I let out a breath, and it was like a cold rush of water had been poured over my head. I felt lightheaded, almost ready to pass out. It was as I'd feared and suspected: my Wales existed in a different dimension. We weren't time travelers, but travelers to another world, separate, and parallel to this one.

I stared off into the distance, taking in the bustle of the emergency room without really seeing it. Riding across the Scottish countryside with Ieuan and Aaron, I'd had a moment where I'd felt myself free, but Bronwen's words truly loosed the chains that held me. If I got back to Wales—*no, I wouldn't think it*—when *I got back to Wales*—I could do and be what I wanted, without fear of affecting the future into which I'd been born.

A nurse came over to us. "We're moving him upstairs now. You may follow us to his room," she said.

"Thank you," Bronwen and I said together and stood up.

Ieuan lay unmoving on his gurney. "Is he going to be all right?" I asked the nurse, before she turned away.

"We believe so. He has two broken ribs and the wound where the object entered, but we've bandaged it and are giving him IV antibiotics. We'll keep him overnight, but by tomorrow or the next day he should be well enough to go home."

"Thank you," I said again. I turned to Bronwen. "You should go home. I can come find you tomorrow, after you've slept."

"That's okay. I'll come with you," she said. "As it's tomorrow already, I might as well see this through. I would like to see for myself that your friend is okay."

She walked forward to follow the nurse and I gaped at her retreating back. My statement hadn't been a question or a suggestion at all—if I'd spoken that way in Wales, everyone would have known that it was an order. I shook my head. I'd clearly lived in the Middle Ages too long. I expected people—and especially women—to do exactly what I said, when I said it, and not ask questions. How Anna and my mother must confuse the men around them.

Bronwen signaled to me from the elevator. *"Come on!"* She mouthed.

I obeyed her. *How cool is that?*

# 5

*Ieuan*

**I** awoke on my back in a bed under white coverings with a soft pillow beneath my head, in an unfamiliar room. *And what a room!* I stared at the ceiling. It was composed of white, gridded squares, with tiny holes speckled all through them. They occupied my attention for a time, and then I started hearing sounds: one was rhythmic and high pitched, but unlike any bird call I'd ever heard; another went 'wump, WUMP; wump, WUMP, also rhythmically. The sounds were coming from some—*I don't even know what to call those things*—to my right. Little lights went on and off in the boxes and a wavy line skittered up and down on the face of the—*thing.*

A third sound penetrated. Voices talked softly beside me. *English voices.* I turned my head, and there was Prince Dafydd, smiling at me, with a beautiful girl beside him.

*Trust him to find a beautiful girl! Some men have all the luck.*

She and the Prince were seated in front of an enormous window, so clear it was almost as if it wasn't there. The window coverings had been pulled back and bright lights shone from the tops of long posts. Further along, chains of lights moved in rhythm, some white and some red. There were even lights high in the sky. They weren't stars, or at least looked like no star I'd ever seen or imagined.

The girl had dark brown hair, blue eyes, a short stubby nose, and a wide, full mouth that was made for laughter. *Or kissing.* She was laughing now at something Dafydd had said. I found myself staring at her and couldn't stop.

Dafydd noticed. "May I introduce you to Bronwen ferch Llywelyn, Ieuan," Prince Dafydd said. "She helped us find someone to treat your wound."

"I'm pleased to meet you, Ieuan ap Cynan," she said with a smile. Her Welsh was accented strangely, but had a lilt I liked.

"It is my honor, my lady," I said.

Bronwen laughed. "I'm no lady! Don't even think it. I'm glad you're awake."

Dafydd had been staring at her during our exchange, and now found his voice. "You speak Welsh! How is it that you speak Welsh!"

"As you pointed out earlier, my last name is Llywelyn. I'm Welsh, though I haven't lived in Wales for many years."

"We're . . . not in Wales, my lord?" I asked.

"What do you remember?" Dafydd asked.

"I remember being chased by English soldiers, and being hit by an arrow, and falling from my horse. You picked me up . . . and then you jumped! You jumped off the cliff!" I tried to sit up in my excitement, and pain shot through my back. I moaned, and Dafydd and Bronwen scrambled to their feet to settle me down again.

I looked up at Dafydd. "I saw the cliff rushing by, and then a blackness came over me. I remember nothing after that. How did I get here?"

"English soldiers?" Bronwen asked. "He thinks English soldiers shot at him?"

"They did," David said. "It's a long story which you aren't going to believe."

Bronwen's features stiffened. "We'll see about that," she said, and crossed her arms across her chest. I wanted to warn her that it wasn't her place to become angry with the Prince of Wales.

"You really want to know?" Dafydd said.

"Yes," she said.

"If I tell you, you can't overreact," he said. "You can't say I didn't warn you."

Bronwen opened her mouth, closed it, and then sat back in her chair and crossed her knees. "Fine. I'm all ears."

But then Dafydd hesitated, and instead of telling her anything, asked her a question. "Look at me and tell me what you see."

Bronwen shifted, uncomfortable under Dafydd's scrutiny. "I see a young man of sixteen, dressed in what appears to be medieval-authentic linen shirt, brown leather armor, tunic, trews, leather boots, and a cloak. You look like you need a bath. Your teeth are straight. You have blue eyes and light brown hair and are a couple of inches over six feet."

"How about our weapons?" he asked.

"I didn't get to examine them closely, but what I saw indicated that they were beautifully worked and . . ." she paused, her brow furrowed. "They're of a very old design. Are they antiques?"

"What if I told you that all of our clothes, including our boots, are handmade? That the weapons were handmade too and are over seven hundred years old? What would that say to you?"

"That you are very rich, obsessive members of the SCA who refuse to carry ID or money?"

"What's the SCA?" I asked.

"Society for Creative Anachronism," Bronwen said, "but from your ignorance maybe that isn't the case either."

*Society for Creative Anachronism.* I had no idea what any of those words meant, separately or together.

"Do you know about old weapons?" Dafydd asked, following his own train of thought.

"I'm a graduate student in archaeology," Bronwen said.

Another word I didn't know. "What's 'archaeology'?" I asked.

Bronwen gave me a look, and then returned her attention to Dafydd. "Why doesn't he know?"

"Because where he comes from, there's no such thing," Dafydd said. He sat beside her then and put his head in his hands.

"Would you mind leaving us for a time?" Dafydd asked. "You've been up all night. Perhaps now you could go home to sleep?"

"You haven't answered any of my questions," she protested.

"I can't answer them," Dafydd said. "Not right now."

Bronwen grimaced. "I don't get this, but that's fine. You don't have to tell me. I don't know you at all. Goodbye."

She headed for the door.

Dafydd stood and held out a hand to stop her. "I'm sorry," he said. "I want to explain, just not here, with Ieuan ill. Where can I find you again, to give you the explanation you deserve, and to get our weapons back?"

Bronwen jerked the door to the room open. "At the archaeology department," she said. "Right where I found you." The door slammed shut behind her. Dafydd contemplated the space where she'd been, his hands on his hips.

"That's hardly the way to win a girl, my lord," I said.

"Win a girl?" Dafydd laughed. "She's at least five years older than I am. She would never be interested in me."

*Really?* "You're the Prince of Wales, my lord. Every girl is interested in you."

"Trust me, Ieuan. Not this one," Dafydd said. He grabbed the back of a chair and pulled it close to my bed.

"Why did you send her away?" I asked.

61

"Because I had to tell you where we are, before I could tell her where we came from," he said.

"I don't understand, my lord. Where are we?"

"We're in the land of Madoc."

I grinned and pumped my fist. "I knew it! I knew it!" I stopped. "How is that possible?"

"Because the land of Madoc is not only far away across the sea from where you were born, but hundreds of years ahead in time."

I gaped at him. "What are you saying?"

"Ieuan," Prince Dafydd said. "Look around you. Does anything look familiar?"

"Of course not! The land of Madoc is full of wonders, as you yourself said."

"I know I said that," Dafydd replied, "but the reason it's full of wonders is not because I am descended from Madoc, but because when I jumped off the cliff with you, I not only brought you to another land, but I brought you forward nearly seven hundred and fifty years in time, to my world."

"Your world, sire?" Suddenly, I couldn't breathe.

"I have taken you into the future, Ieuan. A future where machines are in every room and used for every conceivable purpose; a future where everyone is literate and educated; a future into which I was born, but neither you nor I belong." He gazed down at his feet. I stared at the top of his head. *Has my Prince gone mad?*

He looked up. "You see my problem, Ieuan. How do I explain to you that you're in the future without you thinking I've lost my mind; while at the same time explain to Bronwen that we are from the past, without her thinking the very same thing?"

Then he smiled. And barked a laugh. "I don't have to explain anything, do I? I'll just let you two convince each other." He clapped his hands.

*Has my Prince gone mad? Have I?*

\* \* \* \* \*

I slept, woke at midday to eat, and slept again. Judging from the light outside, it was mid-afternoon by the time I became fully awake. I was alone in the room. My arse was sore from lying down. I'd never spent so long in bed in my life. Loathe to give in to more sleep, I carefully swung my legs, one at a time, over the side of the bed.

I was tall enough that I could get my left foot on the ground from the prone position, and used the railings on either side of the bed to muscle myself upright with my arms. My ribs *hurt* but I ignored them.

Once seated, I noted that the floor was made of a white rock, but as smooth as sanded wood. I lifted my feet, one at a time and inspected the fuzzy socks that covered them. They were an appealing blue color, but I hoped I wouldn't slip in them when I stood. With my left hand on the railing, also made of a smooth material, though gray, I pushed up to my feet. It made me dizzy

63

and I was tempted to sit down again, but I took a deep breath and released it, and my vision cleared.

An open door lay on the far side of the room: the garderobe, Prince Dafydd had explained. I really needed it now, so I grasped the metal pole from which tubes ran from a clear bottle to my arm, and shuffled across the floor, pulling the contraption with me. By the time, I reached the stone basin that Dafydd said was a 'toilet', I was exhausted. It was too interesting to pass up, however, and I was determined to try it out.

I wore nothing but a thin shirt, open in the back. I managed to relieve myself, but when I stepped back from the toilet, a loud whooshing sound reverberated and the water in the basin disappeared, to be replaced by new water that ran down the inside of the bowl like a waterfall. *Hmmm.*

I stepped forward again, waited through a few heartbeats, and stepped back.

"*Whoosh!*"

More curious implements adorned the room, but I was tired, so I shuffled out of the toilet room and found a chair to sit in right outside. I drifted around in my own mind for a while, trying to get up the strength to try the other door, the one through which Bronwen had marched after her conversation with my lord. I smiled to think of it. *Such spirit!* I was sure that Prince Dafydd had never encountered anyone like her, except maybe his own sister. Of course, he hadn't met my sister yet, either.

Fortunately, all the furniture was constructed with conveniently placed railings, so I pushed to my feet again and shuffled off, my pole in my hand. It was an awkward thing, with wheels on the bottom, and the tubes coming from it that led ultimately to a needle in my arm. The needle was held to my skin with a sticky cloth and Prince Dafydd had encouraged me not to touch it. It itched, though, and I just wanted to rip it out. I didn't.

Instead, I pulled at the handle on the surprisingly heavy door and poked my head into the hall. There was no one in sight. Tugging my pole after me, I exited the room, feeling stronger with each step. The hall matched the room, and I wondered why white was such a favorite color in this land. My home was filled with tapestries woven in beautiful jewel tones of red, blue, and green. Here, the walls and floors were white, along with the clothing of all the people. It was dull to look at. Given the wondrous machines they had, it surprised me that they had leeched their world of color.

I passed other rooms like mine, picking up the pace as I went. In each, a person was in the bed, some with family and friends beside them. It appeared that sick people were comforted the same here as in Wales. The occupant of the room three doors down from mine was a Moor, his skin almost black. I stood in the doorway for a longer look, but when he spoke to me, he spoke English. I tipped my head at him, not understanding his words but not wanting to be rude, and continued walking.

Further on was another door that opened into a small room, perhaps as wide as I was tall and half as deep. A large, brown metal box rested on a red counter, and beside it were a stack of cups (also white!), strange looking sticks, small square packages made of parchment with writing on them, and a pot into which dripped a dark liquid. I studied how everything was set up and then chose a cup. The stack separated easily and I found that the cups were soft and squishy. I squeezed one of them and then patted it back into shape.

The liquid stopped dripping with a final, loud, spitting sound. I picked up the pot. Heat rose off it. I poured the liquid into the cup. It steamed and bubbled. I put the pot back and lifted the cup to my nose. The liquid smelled . . . bitter.

"It's called 'coffee', Ieuan, and it's not good for you." I turned to see Prince Dafydd, lounging against the frame of the door, his arms folded across his chest.

"When Bronwen was in the room, she had one of these cups in her hand, but the liquid was a lighter brown," I replied.

"That's because she filled the cup with cream and 'sugar,'" Dafydd said, using an unfamiliar word. He gestured to the cup. "Take a sip and see what you think."

Hesitantly, I did. It *was* incredibly bitter, but the smell wasn't unappealing. I took another sip. My lord laughed.

"Here," he said. "See how you like it with some cream and sugar." He took two of the parchment packets, and a little pot of cream that I hadn't noticed and poured them into my cup. Then he took one of the sticks and stirred it. I tasted it. Except for the 'chocolate' my lord had given me in that little room in the fort along Hadrian's Wall, I'd never had a taste explode in my mouth in such a fashion.

66

"Everyone likes sweet things," Dafydd said. "Do you remember the candy I gave you from my mother's pack?"

I nodded.

"It was also made of sugar."

"Is it possible to take some sugar home with us?" I asked.

Dafydd hesitated, and then reached across me and took three of the packets. "I'll try," he said. "Come, the nurse is looking for you."

I allowed Dafydd to lead me back to my room.

# 6

*Bronwen*

**D**avid found me that afternoon as I was leaving the archaeology building to get myself a diet soda.

"Do you still have the weapons?" he asked. He'd come around the corner of the building, just as I pushed open the door.

I nodded, still wary of him. He'd not changed his clothes, but oddly, didn't look too out of place. State College, Pennsylvania was a good spot to be in if you weren't quite normal in your dress. There were fifty thousand college students and that made it easy to blend in with *some* group.

"Good," he said. "Are they nearby?"

"Still in my car," I said. "Come with me."

He trailed after me across the plaza to the student parking lot, half a mile away. The night before, I'd miraculously found a closer space. Usually I was lucky to find any parking at all.

Unfortunately, today wasn't my day for cars, either. When we were within a dozen yards of my car, I noticed a man beside it, who wasn't getting into the car next to mine as I first thought, but was trying to get into *mine*!

David put out a hand to stop me, but I was already shouting. "Hey! What are you doing?" I raced forward, leaping across the sidewalk and the grassy median which fronted my car.

As I reached the man he spun around. A switchblade flicked out. My hands automatically came up and I braked, leaning back out of the way before taking a step backwards over the concrete parking block behind me. David had run with me and now stepped in front of me, his arms also up.

"Stay back," the man said. "Turn around and walk away if you know what's good for you."

"That's my car, David," I said.

"I won't let him take it," he said, "not with our weapons in it."

*Well, thanks.* We took another step back, matched by the man's step forward. He was thin, shorter than David, with very dark eyes and pale skin, and wore a trench coat—not exactly usual Penn State summer wear, and looked more out of place than David.

"What are you going to do?" I asked.

"Disabling him would be easy," David said, "if I didn't mind getting cut. But I really don't want to go to the police station and answer a lot of questions, so my best suggestion is that you scream your head off."

I paused, thought a second, and screamed.

At that same moment, David took one step forward and kicked the man's hand. But he didn't just kick his hand, he swung his left foot and hit the man's wrist in exactly the right place so that the man released the knife and it flew across the hood of my car. David moved in, but the man ran and David didn't follow. I stopped screaming. The thief's feet thudded as he retreated across the parking lot, matching the pounding of my heart.

"What did you do?" I asked, trying to get my breath back.

"A crescent kick from karate," David said.

"Where did you learn karate?" I placed my arms on the roof of my car and rested my head against them, feeling my heart slow. "Wales?"

David stood beside me, waiting. When he kicked that man, David had unleashed violence within himself. I could practically see it leaking out his ears in the aftermath as the adrenaline drained off him. Pulling myself together, I stepped to the back of my car, unlocked the trunk, and gestured inside. David looked at the contents with satisfaction. He rummaged through the gear and pulled out a knife with an eight-inch blade.

"My sister, Anna, and I are both black belts," he said. "She's really good, but small," he glanced at me, and then back. "Shorter than you."

"Where's your sister?"

"Still in Wales," he said. He held out the knife he was holding. "Here. Do you think it's possible to sell this for enough money to purchase a vehicle?"

I looked from him to the knife, but didn't move. He held it out to me further, flat across his palms. I wasn't going to let this go. "Weren't you afraid of getting hurt?"

"More for you than me," David said. "You really should know better than to go after a guy like that. If you were alone who knows what would've happened."

Now I was irritated. "And it was okay for you?"

"I'm ten inches taller and weigh a third again as much," Dafydd said. "On top of which, I'm wearing armor, remember?"

I shook my head. David pushed the knife toward me. With some hesitation, I picked it up and weighed it in my hand. *Huh.* More interested than I wanted to admit, I turned the knife around in my hands. It was beautifully worked; hand-crafted and from another era. My fingers itched. Although, like Tillman, my research was in the Roman era, I'd done some medieval stuff. I looked over at David. He stood silently, his hands resting loosely at his sides; not pressing; just waiting. *Who is he? And what is up with his friend?*

"Where did you get this?" I asked.

He didn't answer, and I thought he wasn't going to, but then he said, "From my father."

"Well, it may be very valuable, but it might take some time to value it and find a buyer. I don't really have the resources to do either. Have you tried the museum?"

"We don't have time. We need to get to Bryn Mawr as quickly as possible. If I left it with you, would you give me enough money to rent a car?"

71

"What?"

"We need to get to Bryn Mawr." David repeated.

"Do you expect to rent a car in my name? Do you have any idea how much trouble I would get into if you were caught?" I said.

"My aunt lives there. I think."

I gaped at him. "Why don't you just call her and she can transfer some money into your account if it's that dire. Keep your knife. You don't need me."

I shoved the knife at his chest and he took it. "Take your gear, too," I said.

Wordlessly, he bundled the weapons in his arms. Then, "Please," he said. "Please listen. Please don't be afraid of us. We're lost with no money, no identification, and no way to get home. I have no account into which I could transfer money. My parents aren't in Pennsylvania. I realize that you've already helped us more than you think wise but please don't run away."

I couldn't look at him. I opened the door of my car and got inside, but was shaking so hard I kept missing the button for the door locks. I managed to jam my key into the ignition, and when the car rumbled comfortingly to life, I took a deep breath and shifted into reverse.

Calmer, I pulled out of my space. David stood, arms full, watching me, his face totally expressionless.

I drove home. I found an empty space to park and hoofed the last four blocks to my apartment building, purposefully not thinking. *Come to think of it, I spend a lot of time that way these days.* The entryway was dark, as it usually was, and I grabbed my mail and let myself into my apartment. The door closed behind me and I sighed as I leaned back against it, exhausted.

I hadn't slept for nearly thirty-six hours, as I'd woken up at six o'clock the previous morning. I tossed my keys and backpack onto the floor near the cushions that doubled as my couch, and stumbled into the bedroom to fall face-first onto the bed, or what passed for my bed, since it was comprised of foam pads I'd picked up at a fabric store on sale.

They were soft, though, and I twisted onto my back to stare up at the ceiling. At least my apartment wasn't as Spartan as that of another graduate student I knew—his bedroom lampshade consisted of an old t-shirt stretched around a coat hanger.

I threw my arms up over my head, my thoughts streaking back to that first night in college, alone in my dorm room as my roommate had already found a better offer in some guy's bed. I'd lain there, freezing cold since I'd made the mistake of taking a late shower and my hair hadn't dried. I'd never been so isolated in my life—alone surrounded by hundreds of people, probably many of whom were as lost as I. Overall, the loneliness had lessened as I'd grown older. Or maybe I'd just gotten used to it.

\* \* \* \* \*

In the morning, after fifteen solid hours of sleep, I woke with a nagging feeling that I'd forgotten something. I usually *had* forgotten something; I had just too many late nights and too little sleep. I found in graduate school that there was always more work—another article, another hour on a paper—and when I wasn't working, I felt guilty. Consequently, it was rare for me to have my head entirely clear. I staggered into the kitchen and panicked when I found that I was out of coffee. I grabbed a diet cola out of the refrigerator, took a big slug, and relaxed as the caffeine hit. Then, surfing on brainwave stimulant, I remembered the men.

*That's a pretty big thing to have forgotten.*

I showered quickly, threw my books into my pack, and left my apartment. Before heading back to campus, I picked up my coffee at Mugby Junction, my favorite hangout, and treated myself to an apple fritter while I was at it, rationalizing that I was too stressed for nutrition.

Even though classes wouldn't start for another week, I had a full schedule between my own research and Tillman's. I thought that maybe by evening I could get to the library and research the knife. I had a pretty good visual memory and knew a couple of books that might narrow down its time period and provenance. Maybe that would tell me something about the men. Not that I was ever going to see them again.

I was feeling relatively cheerful and in control by the time I got to the archaeology department. As soon as I walked into the building, however, my ego plummeted into my shoes. It had taken a whole two days for word to spread, but finally, every person in every office knew who had and who had not received a stipend.

At one time, most graduate students worked for professors, either as teaching or research assistants, but that ride had ended two years before. Rather than negotiate with striking students who objected to the abysmal pay, long hours, and slave-like treatment, many universities had done away with the positions entirely. Rich departments like mine created the stipend system, taking only enough students as they could afford to fund. In contrast, many departments required students to pay upfront, just like in college or other post-graduate schools of business, law, or medicine.

In truth, I'd come to Penn State because they had a stipend for me. Now that it was gone, I really didn't know what it meant to work as Tillman's research assistant. *Am I funded by a grant, or is he paying for my work out of his own pocket?* That seemed so unlikely as to be ludicrous, and I worried again about what he might expect from me in return.

Worse, all day, I had to fight off the pity of my fellow students. It was in the way my friends either didn't meet my eyes or gave me an insincere smile as I passed them. It was like batting tenth on a ten-man baseball team. Everyone knew you were left out in the cold, but at the same time, they had to sit in the dugout with you day after day, feigning respect. Of the five of us without funding, three had already cleaned out their desks and were gone. Kate, a (funded) friend, came by about noon.

She plopped into a chair set near where I was standing, examining a pot shard with a magnifying glass. "So," she said. "What's this all about?"

"You mean, 'this,' as in, 'I no longer have a stipend,' or 'this', as in, 'why am I slaving away for Tillman instead of working on my own stuff'?" I said, without looking up.

"Either. Both."

I sighed and looked down at her. "Tillman told me that I am one of the five students to whom the department has chosen not to offer a stipend. Thus, my options are to quit, pay my own way, or work for him."

"But the university doesn't fund research assistantships anymore," Kate protested. "This can't pay your tuition."

I rubbed my forehead with my hand. I'd been so focused on living, I'd forgotten about that little item. This was probably just some campus job, like working in the cafeteria. It would pay my rent, but not my tuition.

"What are you going to do? Are you going to call your parents?" she asked.

I set down the pot, pulled up a chair next to hers, and sat, my head in my hands. "You know what they're like," I said. "I did talk to them yesterday and they offered to rent the shack next to theirs for me."

"No tuition, then," Kate said.

"No tuition," I said. "I'm sure their offer sounded reasonable to them, though within thirty seconds, it was like my mom had forgotten why I'd called. She sent her best to you, though she called you 'Jill,' and asked after 'Mark'."

"You don't have a friend named, 'Jill,' and who's 'Mark'?"

"I don't know," I said. "I dated a guy named Russ for a while during my junior year in college, but it didn't click for us and I don't recall mentioning him to my parents anyway."

Kate looked at me with unmistakable pity. She opened the little white bag on her lap. "Here, have a doughnut."

I took a cream-filled one. *Great.* I was reduced to sponging doughnuts off my friends. So much for improving my diet.

Thus, after a fabulous day, it was nearly midnight before I was able to wave my ID at the guard on duty at the entrance to the library and make my way down into the basement stacks. In the archaeology building, Tillman's lab was on the fifth floor and you knew how well a professor rated by the location of his office. That was fine within our own department, but to the University as a whole, we belonged in the basement. This was about where the funding for projects was too, unless you were a philandering full professor, that is.

I'd come out of the elevator and turned the corner into the stacks, sucking down the last of yet another coffee as I did so, when a familiar figure stopped me in my tracks. *Him.* How did he get in here without any ID? *Probably sweet talked a woman at a back entrance.* I eyed him, uncertain as to whether I should turn around right then or risk a conversation. Every time he opened his mouth, I found myself succumbing to his words, even when they made no sense.

David's sword was on the table beside him and he was well-wrapped in his cloak. Just as well, as it was cold down here. I always wore a sweater or coat to work, even in summer.

"I'm not going to hurt you," he said, without turning around to look at me.

*Does he have eyes in the back of his head?*

"How did you know it was me?" I said, not moving.

"Your fragrance is quite distinctive," he said, turning around now and smiling at me.

I didn't even wear any perfume. Was he talking about the smell of my shampoo? A weird sort of compliment. The violent man of this morning was gone, replaced by the kid who I'd met at first, who only wanted to help his friend.

Trying not to let him know that this was a capitulation of sorts, and that I kind of liked him, I moved to the other side of the table and put my backpack down. His more scary-looking, but incredibly handsome friend was wandering the stacks a short distance away. I was pleased to see him upright and realized that he was over six feet tall too, with the dark hair and blue eyes that screamed "Welsh!" to those in the know. He looked over and I gave him a little half-wave, before quickly putting my hand down. *What am I doing?*

"They let you out?" I asked Ieuan, in Welsh.

"This afternoon," he said. "The wound wasn't deep, just bloody. I'm taking a 'pill' that Prince Dafydd tells me is an 'antibiotic'. He says that is why he brought me to this land, because he was afraid that I would die without it."

78

"Prince Dafydd?" I asked, then covered my ears. "Don't tell me. I don't want to know."

"It's nothing," David said, "just a nickname between the two of us."

I looked at him, and then at Ieuan, who was staring at his feet. Deciding to get down to business, since I was never going to get a straight answer out of these two, I pulled out my laptop, set it down on the table, and opened it. "What are you doing here?" I asked David. "Ieuan shouldn't be on his feet, surely."

"Ieuan says sitting hurts more than standing, so I'm taking him at his word. I'm trying to find a knife similar to mine, so that when I attempt to sell it, I'll already have done some of the work for the buyer."

*Of course. Silly of me to think that I was the only one to have this idea.* "Did you find something?" I asked.

"Here," he said, turning around the book he was reading so I could look at it.

I skimmed the page as he aligned his knife with the picture in the book. They were remarkably similar. The knife in the book was found in a church in Cilmeri, near Builth Wells, in Wales. It was dated to the thirteenth century CE (common era), and purported to belong to Llywelyn ap Gruffydd, the last Prince of Wales.

I looked up at him.

"Is this why you were asking about Llywelyn ap Gruffydd?" I asked. "If your knife is its twin, it's very old."

"I believe it is. As I said, my father gave it to me."

79

"And who's your father?" I asked.

"Um," he said, but again didn't answer. Instead, he reached for the knife and slid it into its sheath.

"Do you know someone who might like to buy it?" he asked. "Dinner at the Salvation Army was filling, but not something we want to do on a regular basis."

I felt bad. They really didn't have any money. I sat down in front of my laptop.

"What's your aunt's name?" I asked. "I'll look her up."

"Elisa Shepherd," he said, and the smile was back.

I searched for her and there she was, with phone number and address and an accompanying map. I pulled out my cell phone and handed it to him.

"Why don't you call her?"

"I can't," he said. "She thinks I'm dead. I can't just call her."

"What? What are you saying? Why is it that virtually everything out of your mouth is a complete sentence that makes no sense at all?"

"I'm sorry," he said. "I just don't think I can call her."

"Back up to where she thinks you're dead," I said.

"My sister and I disappeared in early December, three years ago this coming winter. If I were Aunt Elisa and I called her, I wouldn't believe me either." He shrugged. "My voice has changed since then, so she wouldn't even recognize it."

"But you think showing up on her doorstep will be better?" I said.

80

"At least then she'll see me. She might shut the door in my face, but if I call her and scare her, she might call the police and I'd never get close to her."

"Email?"

"Same thing; and I don't have an email account anyway."

"No email; no money; no phone; no ID. You obviously aren't dead, yet you haven't bothered to let anyone know you're alive. Where have you been living the last two and a half years?"

David looked at me with the same completely blank stare he'd given me in the parking lot, and then looked away. "I really can't tell you," he said, finally. "You wouldn't believe me. Sometimes I don't even believe me."

"Try me," I said, with all the confidence of the congenitally unflappable. I'd lived in a yurt after all. If he was from the frozen tundra, he would find a kindred soul in me.

There was that look again. "My name, three years ago, was David Lloyd," he said. "Somewhere on the internet, you may encounter a record of our unsolved case. If you read it, you would find that my sister, Anna, and I disappeared on the evening of December 11, 2010. Neither the minivan we drove, nor our bodies, were ever found. These last years we've been living in Wales . . . in the thirteenth century."

I blinked. David looked steadily back at me. I opened my mouth, closed it, and then opened it again. *Okay, maybe I'm a little flappable.*

"And Ieuan?"

David sighed. "He was caught up in the time warp that brought me back here. He's one of my men-at-arms."

Ieuan walked over, talking in a flurry of words, only about three of which I understood. *Strike that.* I understood nothing he said.

"Slow down!" I said.

He stopped, and then started again. "As my lord told you, I am Ieuan ap Cynan," Ieuan said, with a slight bow. "We were traveling along Hadrian's Wall when we were captured and imprisoned in Carlisle Castle by the crusader and castellan, Sir John de Falkes. We escaped but English soldiers chased us and one of them shot me in the back. My lord picked me up, ran with me to the edge of a cliff, and jumped. I remember nothing except a black abyss before our feet, and then I woke up in your hospital."

Ieuan pronounced the word in English, as if he didn't know the Welsh equivalent.

I looked at David, who was nodding. "Tell her the rest, Ieuan."

"He tells me that this is 'the future,' though when we were in Wales, he'd spoken of this country as the land of Madoc. I've ridden the vehicle which brought his sister and him to Wales, and it is a wondrous machine, but so is everything and everyone I have seen in this land."

"The land of Madoc?" I asked. I turned to David. "What's he talking about?"

"You may recall the story of Madoc ap Owain Gwynedd. In 1170 AD he sailed from Wales to the New World. Lewis and Clark believed that the Mandan people of the upper Missouri River were his descendants."

"Yes, of course, I know the story."

"Well, it might seem odd now, but it made sense to my father and me to explain the existence of a minivan in thirteenth century Wales, as attributable to Madoc's descendents. It even kind of makes sense."

*If you're demented.* "You're serious," I said.

"Yes, of course. Everything Ieuan and I have told you here is true. My hope is that you can convince him that this is the twenty-first century, and maybe in the process, he can convince you that he was born in 1261 AD."

I coughed. I ran my fingers though my hair and I plopped myself back into my chair. "Okay, Ieuan. Who is David's father? He still isn't telling me."

"Llywelyn ap Gruffydd, the Prince of Wales."

Appalled, I held out my hand to stop him. "That's it!" I said. "Don't tell me anymore." I slammed the lid down on my laptop and stood up. With my hands resting flat on the table, I leaned into David's face.

"What in the hell is going on? Why are you doing this? What's the point? Why do you want to screw with my mind? I actually felt sorry for you for a moment!" My hands shaking, I stuffed my laptop into my bag and threw it onto my shoulder.

David moved to block the exit. I did a side-to-side dance to try to get around him, but then stopped, frustrated, three feet from him.

"Please," he said. "Please listen to me. You speak Welsh and you've helped us, beyond anything I should have asked. I've long since stopped believing in coincidences. Please don't walk out on us."

"You're trying to tell me that two and a half years ago you and your sister time-traveled to the Middle Ages, where you found out you were really the Prince of Wales?"

"Yes," David said. "I know it sounds crazy. Like I said, I would think it was crazy if I weren't living it myself."

"You have men-at-arms at your command, yet you grew up here, with no training or previous knowledge that Llywelyn was your true father?"

David had the nerve to shrug his shoulders. "All Americans behave like royalty, Bronwen. Except for the killing, I don't have to be anyone other than myself."

*Except for the killing.* I stared down at the floor and then at David. Ieuan came up beside me. He stood close, his hand resting on the small of my back. "Tell me when you were born," he said gently. "It would help me very much to know in what time I'm living."

"I was born in 1990. This is 2013," I said. "In your terms, two thousand and thirteen years since the birth of Christ."

Ieuan nodded his head, very slowly, then turned it to look at David. David spread his hands wide. "I'm sorry, Ieuan. I couldn't tell you this when we were in Wales. It's nearly impossible to believe until you live it. I've told very few people, and not even Bevyn. My father has confided only in Tudur and Goronwy."

"Who are Tudur and Goronwy?" I asked.

"Goronwy is my father's steward," said David. "Tudur is the grandson of Ednyfed Fychan, Llywelyn Fawr's steward. Ednyfed Fychan was—"

"I know who Ednyfed Fychan was," I snapped. "His grandson Tudur founded the House of Tudor in England."

"What is she saying about Tudur?" Ieuan asked, his eyes widening. "What has Tudur to do with the English?"

David shook his head and put a reassuring hand on Ieuan's arm. "Nothing, Ieuan." he said. "At least not yet."

"Okay," I said. I turned my back on David and walked the other way, pacing around the table twice before coming to stand in front of him again. "I know I should just walk out of here, but for some reason I'm not going to."

The men had watched my pacing and now Ieuan reached around me and gently relieved me of my backpack. He held it up and inspected it, before slinging it along one shoulder. "This is just like Princess Marged's pack, my lord, though larger, and believe it or not, heavier."

"Argh!" I stomped my foot, then pointed at David. "You have no money?"

"No money," David answered. "I have three packets of sugar that Ieuan made me put in my pocket to take home, if we can, in fact, return home, but they aren't going to get us far."

"All right then.  I have a little.  I know a place that's open all night.  Let's go get a pizza and you can tell me all about it."

Dafydd looked down at me.  "Pizza?" he asked, in an expectant voice.

*Lunatics, both of them.*

# 7

## *Ieuan*

**I** followed Prince Dafydd and Bronwen out of the "stacks," and up the stairs through the library. I admired the many books along the way, and marveled at the number of scribes it must have taken to copy out so many. This calculation alone would have forced me to admit my lord's words were true, but I'd already done so, long before we left the hospital. I'd lain in bed the previous night, staring up at the ceiling, trying to take an accounting of the men and materials needed to create what I saw before me. Prince Dafydd told me that one kind of machine built another kind of machine, which wasn't easy to comprehend, but I also knew that somewhere along the way, a man had to build the first machine.

It wasn't reasonable to think that man had been Madoc, or even his son or grandson. Madoc had sailed from Wales less than a century before I was born. Changes of the magnitude and type in

David's land were not possible in so short a time. I didn't believe it. *But what* had *happened?*

At the time, I'd turned my head to look at Prince Dafydd, who hadn't been asleep either. He was absorbed in a book, written in English so I couldn't make out the title. He'd shown me how small the print was and how thin the pages. It told a story involving a machine that flew to the stars.

"Tell me again, my lord," I'd asked. "How did we come here?"

Prince Dafydd rested the book on his lap. "I don't know, Ieuan," he said. "I wouldn't have thought it possible—but here we are, so it *is* possible."

"How do you explain it?" I asked. "Is it magic? A miracle? A gift from God?"

"I'm not going to deny that, Ieuan," Dafydd said. "I can't sneer at divine intervention or discount the possibility of it."

"But you believe it's something else?" I said.

"Not necessarily," Dafydd said. "Yet, I can't live my life as if I should somehow expect a miracle because I need one. All my life I've learned to operate as if everything has a cause, and if I can't explain something, it's because I'm ignorant. Magic, certainly, is something in which I don't believe."

"So magic to you is not something for which there is no explanation."

"Yes," Prince Dafydd said. "It's simply something for which I don't have enough information to explain. Yet."

I'd faced the ceiling again and thought some more. I'd never felt the need to consider what might constitute the difference between magic and miracles—and that which passed for them. It was remarkable to think about living in a world in which everything had an explanation, as Dafydd seemed to.

To me, magic was pagan: the druids of old whom the Romans, pagan themselves, forced underground. Miracles, in turn, were a gift from God. But now that I was living in the midst of a miracle, I could see how someone could view them as being two sides of the same coin—both events or works that we puny humans were unable to comprehend or explain. I'd never known anyone accused of witchcraft, but I'd heard the stories. We needed to avoid the stain of that accusation at all cost, or jeopardize whatever God had planned for Wales, and for Prince Dafydd.

An image of my castle of Twyn y Garth hovered in my head and a sick feeling settled into the pit of my stomach at how far away it was. "We talked of Humphrey de Bohun when we were in Carlisle," I said. "How worried are you about what's happening in our absence?"

I glanced at Dafydd, the only light from the hand-held lamp—itself a miraculous invention—that he'd clipped to his book.

"I am, quite frankly, terrified to think of it," he said. "I've been driving away thoughts of Wales since we got here. I don't know that I have ever felt as helpless as I do right now."

"Will we be able to return home?" I asked.

"I have some ideas to try," he said, "preferably ones that aren't going to get us killed. I told my father that if I returned to this world, I'd spend the rest of my life trying to find a way back to Wales. I'm just sorry we won't have Bronwen's help."

"She gave you the weapons," I said.

"Yes, but she drove away and left me. I still don't know where we're going to get the money for a vehicle to get us where we need to go."

Prince Dafydd had checked our weapons at the front desk of the hospital. He'd told the woman in charge that we were members of this group—the Society for Creative Anachronism—and had been participating in an event when I got hurt. That she accepted his explanation was not surprising to me—Prince Dafydd had that effect on people as a rule—but what did astound me was that we were the only ones who'd brought swords to the hospital. Or weapons of any kind.

This too brought home to me the vast changes that had occurred between my time and this one. On one hand, in the hospital, families still cared for one another. Mothers sat beside their ill sons' beds while fathers paced the corridors. The mothers looked just like any mother when her child was sick. Prince Dafydd had assured me that women gave birth in one part of the hospital and people died in another part. Every day.

Some people still got married, and some people didn't, *just as in Wales*. A son might rebel against his father and make his mother cry, or follow in his father's footsteps, *just as in Wales*. The sun rose and set, the wind blew, the rain fell, *just as in Wales*.

But the trappings were so different, and I suspected that the meaning behind the behaviors was different too. How was it that Bronwen lived by herself, an unmarried girl?  How was it that a Moor slept in the room next to mine and nobody thought anything of it?  How was it that the only person my lord knew who'd died before he came to Wales was his grandmother, who passed away at the ancient age of eighty-five?  It gave me new respect for the fourteen-year-old boy he'd been, who led an army before he'd ever killed a man.

I brought my head back to the library.  In front of me, Prince Dafydd, with Bronwen beside him, climbed the stairwell, his broad shoulders filling the space.  Bronwen might think him a boy, but in Wales he was a man and he'd done nothing to make us think he didn't deserve the trust we placed in him.  Wales was lucky to have him, but I wasn't sure I was ever going to understand how his mind worked, or the world he inhabited inside himself.

Dafydd pushed through the gray door at the top of the stairs, and led us into the cathedral that served as the university library.  I tried not to gawk, yet at the same time take in the magnificence of my surroundings.  We walked down a wide, central aisle, tables on our right and high bookshelves on our left. Although I intended to keep up with Dafydd and Bronwen, I stopped beside a large book that lay open on a small, raised table. It showed a picture of man on a horse, holding a sword in his right hand.

"From what time is this?" I asked.  His clothes were odd, but the pose was familiar.

Prince Dafydd returned to me and peered over my shoulder. "That's a statue of George Washington. He was the first president of this country."

"I don't understand the word," I said. "What is a 'president'."

Dafydd looked at Bronwen, who answered. "The United States, the country where we are right now, has no kings, Ieuan; has never had a king. All people over eighteen years of age, men and women, of whatever color or religion, with money and without, vote every four years for the person they want to lead our country."

Her words washed over me, but I'd reached the point of acceptance, no matter how strange or impossible the descriptions. "Is there a president of Wales, in this time?" I asked.

Dafydd stilled. He looked across the table to Bronwen, but she didn't seem to share his obvious concern at my question. She shifted from one foot to another, clearly impatient to move on.

"Wales is part of Great Britain, Ieuan," she said. "When Llywelyn ap Gruffydd was killed by the English in 1282, Wales ceased to exist as an independent country. It was absorbed into England. Edward I made his own son the Prince of Wales and the eldest son of the King or Queen of England has held that position ever since. It's only in the last twenty years that Wales has begun to separate itself from England once again. They do vote for their own parliament now, but the real power is still in England."

A chill ran through my body and settled in my stomach. "How can this be, my lord?" I asked my Prince. "We went forward in time to a place that believes your father died at Buellt. But he didn't die. Why don't they know it?"

"Because we're not only in a different time, Ieuan, but in a different world, one that seems to exist simultaneously with our own. This puzzled me when Anna and I first came to Wales. I worried that by changing the history of Wales, I could change the future so dramatically, perhaps I myself would no longer exist. Once we arrived back here, however, and I'd spoken with Bronwen about this matter, I realized that we didn't change this world at all. We left it, and went to another—one whose future *we* will determine. The people here aren't part of our future. We'll make our own future in Wales when we return."

It was impossible, yet here we were. I couldn't look at them, then, nor at the marvelous books and the incredible machines. "So in this world, you never were the Prince of Wales? For the people of this world, the English murdered your father— and then what?"

I glanced up. Dafydd kept his eyes fixed on my face as he spoke words that were like knife strokes to my heart. "King Edward subjugated Wales entirely. My half-sister, Gwenllian, was kidnapped and spent her life in an English convent; Uncle Dafydd's sons were imprisoned in wooden cages at Bristol Castle for their entire lives; and Uncle Dafydd himself was hanged, drawn and quartered, and then dragged through the streets of Shrewsbury. Edward displayed both his and my father's heads on poles in London. This is why Tudur made his peace with England. There no longer was a Wales to serve."

"And when does this happen?" I asked.

"By 1283, Wales was no more."

I stared down at the picture of George Washington. The wonders of this world had lost their beauty. "We need to find a way home, my Prince," I said. "We need to find it right now."

# 8

*Bronwen*

**I** brought Ieuan and David to the pizza place. We wended our way through a surprisingly full restaurant, given that it was one in the morning, to a booth at the back. As we sat down, Ieuan ran his hand over the bright red seats before sitting.

I hesitated. *Who should I sit next to—Ieuan or David?* I chose Ieuan so I could see David talk. It was a trick I'd learned from a psych major friend of mine: in order to watch a guy's face to spot when he was lying. Ieuan slid over to give me room, though there wasn't much, as he seemed to take up three-quarters of the bench without trying. It wasn't that he was that tall, and he certainly was lean, but his shoulders were broad, undoubtedly a product of the hours of sword fighting and archery he'd done in the last ten years. My mind blanked away at that thought. *You believe he's for real, don't you? Where's your objectivity? Why do*

*you want to believe him? Just because you like him . . . a lot?*
*Because it seems he might like you even a little?*

"It's not real leather, Ieuan," David said, sitting across from us. "You'd be surprised at the number of items—even food—that aren't natural in this world. Let's hope this restaurant uses real cheese."

I rolled my eyes at him. "They do, though you can get soy pepperoni if you ask."

A server, a friend of mine—perhaps *former* friend—from the archaeology department who'd refused to catch my eye earlier in the day, came over. Now, she was artificially cheerful.

"Hi, Bronwen!" she said in greeting. "It's great to see you!"

"Hi, Tammy," I said, and introduced Ieuan and David. She took our order, eyeing Ieuan the whole time, and I scooted a millimeter closer to him. I glared at her—he is *so* not available!

She handed us cups so we could get our drinks, along with some sympathy for my predicament. "I heard about the stipend," she said. "I'm sorry. What are you going to do?"

"I don't know," I said, not wanting to talk about it, but at the same time glad she'd dropped the happy act. "Tim, Chris, and Juliann have already quit."

"I know," Tammy said. "I'm moving into Juliann's office tomorrow. It's bigger than mine, and I'll only have to share with two people instead of three."

She smiled at me before turning away, and I stared after her. *Of all the mercenary . . .*

"Are you okay?" David asked, interrupting my thoughts. "What was that about?"

I sighed. "I lost my funding for graduate school the day you got here," I said. "Our server is one of my colleagues."

"Who still has a grant," David said.

I glared at him, then turned to Ieuan. He was watching me openly and his eyes were crinkling at the edges as they smiled.

"This way," I said, grabbing two cups and sliding out of the booth. Ieuan slid out behind me, a little stiffly, a hand to his ribs. He followed me to the soda dispenser and watched me fill my cup with ice and then diet soda. He put his cup under the ice as I had, but when he made to fill it with the same drink I stopped him. "Try the root beer instead," I said, not wanting him to have too much caffeine or corrupt his body with artificial sweetener, if it was the first time he'd ever had it.

Ieuan inspected the dispenser, peering past it to the tanks on the other side of the counter. "Those contain the liquid?" he asked.

I nodded. Determined not to be sucked in, I returned to the booth with Ieuan, sat next to him and sipped my drink. David had root beer too, and made a face after the first sip. "It's sweeter than I remember," he said. "It tastes a bit like cough medicine."

All full-sugar soft drinks were too sweet for me, but I was picky. The old diet soda product Tab tasted to me like Kentucky Fried Chicken handi-wipes, so who was I to complain about David's tastes?

"How long before the pizza comes?" Ieuan asked. Half his soda was already gone.

"About fifteen minutes," I said.

"I can't wait," David said. "I've been trying to create pizza ever since I arrived in Wales, but without success. Pizza dough is the easiest part, but the spices are impossible to find, and without them, it just isn't pizza; that and the fact that there are no tomatoes in Wales, and thus, no sauce."

"You should have seen the face of the cook at Denbigh Castle when Prince Dafydd entered the kitchen for the first time," Ieuan chimed in, laughing at the memory. "She was horrified."

"You liked what I made though, didn't you?" David asked. And then, accusingly, "You said you did!"

Ieuan sucked down more of his drink, but didn't answer, though his mouth was twitching under his mustache. "Anything is going to be better than the food in the hospital," he said. "Why was everything so mushy? Where was the meat?"

"It's called a 'soft food' diet," I said. "Mashed potatoes, oatmeal, gelatin."

"The potatoes were good," Ieuan admitted. "I've never had anything like them before. My lord dressed them up with butter and salt and they tasted delicious."

"They don't have potatoes in Wales?" I asked. "What about the Irish Potato famine and all that?"

"Potatoes are from the New World, Bronwen," David reminded me. "We've got another three hundred years before Columbus brings some back to Spain."

I'd forgotten that. "What vegetables do you have?"

"Oh, lots," David said. "Carrots, leeks, asparagus, Brussels sprouts, mushrooms, onions, peas, parsnips, turnips. Just no potatoes, tomatoes, squash, peppers, or corn."

"What's 'corn'?" Ieuan asked.

*Only the most utilized vegetable on the planet.* I contemplated him while he sipped his drink. I would have looked away, to pretend I hadn't been watching him, but before I could, he winked at me.

"I need some more of this drink," Ieuan said.

"I'll get it," I said. "You sit and let those ribs rest."

Ieuan shook his head. "The more I move, the better. It just hurts getting up and down." Shrugging, I stood and let him pass, and then scooted over to where he'd been sitting. Otherwise, I suspected I was going to be getting up a lot.

A few minutes later, the pizza came. I'd ordered a super-large one with everything on it, and I actually heard the men's stomachs growl as the server placed it in front of us. I ate one piece: *Aha! A new food group!* and they ate the rest.

Watching the men eat pizza was practically obscene they enjoyed it so much, but I was impatient and ready to hear what they had to say. "So are you going to talk?" I asked David after he had consumed his third piece before taking a breath.

"Sure," he said.

Between mouthfuls, David told me how he and his sister, Anna, had been transported to Wales of 1282, rescued Llywelyn ap Gruffydd, who turned out to be David's father, and lived there ever

99

since. David's mother, Marged, had conceived David during a prior trip to Wales, been returned to the twentieth century, and then was sent back again to 1284. From there, the history of his Wales diverged so profoundly from the real history, it was hard to keep track of what was real and what wasn't. David and Ieuan seemed real: their easy camaraderie, coupled with Ieuan's deference was very genuine.

For me, it wasn't David, for all his eloquence and sincerity, that made me want to believe them, but Ieuan. First, there was a wide-eyed innocence to him, despite the gory tales he told me while wolfing down his food. According to Ieuan, David was a man of action, fighting off the English, personally rescuing everyone from stray puppies to damsels in distress, and virtually saving Wales single-handedly. The sub-text that I read, even though Ieuan didn't say it, was that he'd been beside David all the while, protecting and serving him.

Second, Ieuan spoke what had to be an older version of Welsh, and language isn't something you can falsify, no matter how smart you are. It's too elaborate, too complex, to create out of whole cloth just to fool me. Third, his whole being screamed 'Middle Ages', from his completely out of place mustache, to his clothes, to the knife in his boot. It made Peter Jackson's *Lord of the Rings* movies look fake.

Finally, my thoughts kept returning to Ieuan's words in the library, when David had to tell him that Wales was no longer a country, and that everyone he loved had died, some very gruesomely. It forced me to face that either their story was true, or they'd escaped from a mental institution. There was no alternative.

I eyed Ieuan picking a piece of pepperoni off his pizza. David leaned back in his seat, seemingly sated.

"How far is it to Bryn Mawr?" he asked.

"Less than three hours," I said.

*Silence.*

"I know you have a very busy schedule," David said. "Thank you for taking us to pizza, and maybe even believing us a little. We can't take up more of your time."

I said nothing, just fidgeting with my place setting. "You could drive us to Bryn Mawr," Ieuan said. "I would spend more time in your company."

I turned to him. He was studying me, and it seemed that no one had ever looked at me as intently. I racked my brains for one last question; one last thought that would prove beyond a doubt they were not from thirteenth century Wales.

Then it hit me: the newspaper story. There had to be one. Without answering Ieuan, I whipped out my laptop and set it up on the table in front of me. The pizza place had wireless internet, so it was a simple matter to search for 'David Lloyd' and see what came up. Ieuan leaned closer, his arm stretched across the back of the seat. As he coudn't read English, supposedly, it wasn't clear why he needed to see the screen.

And there it was:

> *December 12, 2010, Bryn Mawr, PA.* A Bryn Mawr police
> report was filed today regarding the disappearance of Anna
> Lloyd (16) and her brother David (14). Their mother,
> Marged Lloyd, reported them missing after they failed to
> return home yesterday evening . . .

And then:

> *August 24, 2012, Baker City, OR.* Search and Rescue
> workers, scoured the mountains near Baker City for the
> third day in a search for a downed plane carrying pilot,
> Martin Tesky and his sole passenger, Marged Lloyd, a
> professor at Northern Oregon University. The flight was a
> routine run from Pasco, Washington to Boise, Idaho. Ms.
> Lloyd's children also disappeared in an unexplained
> manner in 2010 . . .

I considered the screen. David could have read about the
disappearances and adopted Lloyd's identity, but to what end?
Just to fool me? I admitted, finally, that it was enough, for now. I
capitulated.

"We can make it by 6 am," I said, "just in time to wake up
your aunt."

David was on his feet so fast he almost overturned the
table. He gathered us up and hustled us out of the restaurant,
back to the parking lot where I'd left my car. Ieuan sputtered a bit,
but he managed to hold onto his last piece of pizza and his root
beer.

When we got to my car, I got in the driver's seat while
David opened the back door to Ieuan and pointed. "You sit there."

Ieuan obeyed, but winked at me as I looked at him through
the rear view mirror. It was very strange to see a sixteen-year old
boy ordering a man around and that man happily obeying him.
David climbed into the passenger side of the front seat and settled
beside me, his sword on his lap. He had a self-satisfied grin on his
face. *Second thoughts, anyone?*

I twisted around to look at Ieuan. He grinned at me too.

# 9

## David

**I** slouched in my seat. I was utterly delighted that
Bronwen was driving us to Bryn Mawr, but I hadn't really slept in
three days and I ached all over. I looked out the window and
watched the lights shift past; then closed my eyes, trying to empty
my mind so I could rest. I dozed off.

>*"My God! No! My lord, no!"*
>
>*Aaron slides off his horse and falls to his knees.
He's stopped fifty yards away, having ridden hard from
the opening in the trees at the top of the cliff. The path on
which he was riding runs east along the cliff edge, 150
yards as the crow flies from where I'm standing, before
curving west to the boat. An arrow can fly that distance
in one breath.*
>
>*I can hear the gulls calling. It almost sounds like
they are saying "No! No!" along with me and Aaron. I've*

had the men ready all day, waiting for my lord's return. As soon as Aaron broke through the trees, they readied their arrows, but it was my lord who appeared, Ieuan cradled in his arms.

"No! No!"

He jumps. Unbelievably, he jumps. I see them fall, and then from one instant to the next, they vanish. The men gasp. We've all seen it—or not seen it—and none of us can credit our own eyes. I run forward, but before I manage ten paces, English riders appear in the space my lord had occupied. It takes me a moment to comprehend who they are. In those seconds, they mill around the cliff's edge, as confused as we are. A breath later, I realize they're easy targets, silhouetted as they are against the trees.

"Fire!"

My eight archers release their arrows. Three of the English and two of the horses go down. We will tally the arrows later and the three men that missed will find themselves chastened.

I lead the chase up the cliff, collecting Aaron on the way. "Mother of Christ, Aaron! What has happened?" I say.

"My God, my God," he replies. "I know what has happened, but I can't believe it. I can't believe I saw it with my own eyes."

*I grab the front of his jersey and pull him to me. "By all that is holy, tell me what has happened to the Prince!"*

*I look into Aaron's eyes, and see first the fear, and then the compassion, and I am chastened myself. I release him.*

*"He has gone to the land of Madoc, Bevyn," Aaron tells me, as we gaze down at the bodies of the dead English soldiers that litter the cliff edge, and the rocks below. "He has taken Ieuan with him. I don't know how, but I can guess why—to save his life, for I heard Ieuan's cry and my lord's shout. An English arrow must have hit him."*

*I hear Aaron's words, but they make no sense. How could the Prince travel to the Land of Madoc by jumping off a cliff?*

*We stare again at the downed men and horses at our feet, and then over edge. The rocks are jagged at the base of the cliff, and two of the Englishmen have fallen on them. Some of my men are slowly picking their way to the bottom, hoping to find the body of their prince to prove what they saw false. I know that at the same time they are hoping not to find him. I'm hoping too, because if he has fallen, he is dead. If he lives, as Aaron says, in another land, he can come back to us; rise again, as another Arthur. . .*

*Arthur, Arthur, Arthur.* I jerked awake, with the name ringing in my head. I glanced around, seeing the car and the darkness outside my window, and realized I must have dreamt as I dozed. Already the dream was fading—it was something about jumping off the cliff? And Bevyn? It was no use. The images were gone.

I came more awake, then, and realized that Ieuan and Bronwen were in the midst of a conversation. Bronwen said, "Would you like to drive the car, Ieuan?"

"No!" I intervened, shooting upright.

"My lord!" Ieuan said. "It's a chance of a lifetime!"

"You can drive the van, once we get back to Wales, Ieuan, once your ribs have healed." Then to Bronwen, "You have no idea what you're offering," I said.

Bronwen looked at me, grinned, and then glanced at Ieuan through the rear-view mirror. They shrugged in unison. Satisfied, I settled back into my seat. It actually felt really great to be moving so quickly, but not be on the back of a horse.

Bronwen spoke. "So, what are you thinking, *right now.*"

I could just *feel* Ieuan shifting uncomfortably at the way Bronwen spoke to me. I kind of liked it actually. She wasn't going to defer to me, and even if someone suggested it, she couldn't imagine why she should.

"I was thinking about the chair I'm sitting in, actually," I said. "I haven't sat in a comfortable chair for three years. The thirteenth century doesn't *have* any comfortable chairs, even for a prince."

Bronwen laughed. "This is a cheap car, too," she said. "I have an uncle who just bought a new one. It's nicer than my apartment. Of course, almost anything would be nicer than my apartment."

Ieuan spoke from the back seat. "I'm thinking about your men, my lord," he said. "The English were chasing all three of us. Aaron was some distance ahead. Did he escape the riders to reach the boat? Did the men see you jump and then vanish, my lord, with me over your shoulder?"

His words made my head itch, as if I should remember something about that. Instead, I said, "I've been trying to imagine what they must be thinking, Ieuan, what they would decide to do. I have to trust that Bevyn will know what is right, but it's frustrating to be so helpless."

"If they sailed on the tide, my lord," Ieuan said, "they still won't reach Wales for another day or two."

"And what will happen to them?" Bronwen asked. "What will they tell your father?" I could hear the worry in her voice and it heartened me.

"Believe it or not, if the men saw us disappear from the cliff face, Father will be less worried than if we're just missing in action," I said. "He knows the whole story, so my family will suspect that what happened is exactly what *did* happen."

"He won't punish Bevyn?"

I turned to look at her, puzzled, but Ieuan understood her question.

"I don't know what you've read about our time in your books," he said, "but we are a civilized people, with a civilized Prince. He wouldn't punish Prince Dafydd's men for something that wasn't their fault." His voice was low, deep, and very deliberate.

Bronwen met Ieuan's eyes in the mirror, and then switched back to the road. "I'm sorry, Ieuan. I didn't mean to malign your prince. It is true, however, that many of the rulers in the Middle Ages behaved just as I described, including King Edward of England, whom your father is fighting."

I turned my head to look out of the window. "Not anymore," I said, under my breath. I hadn't told her at the pizza place about the meeting at Lancaster, because I couldn't quite admit to Edward's death, afraid it might be the last straw that made her walk away from us.

"What?" Bronwen asked.

"Edward is dead, Bronwen," Ieuan said. "He was poisoned in his own tent a week ago."

Bronwen looked at me. "Really?"

"Yes," I said. "He attacked me in his own pavilion, but fell ill before he could finish the fight. That was why we were in England—to meet with him. The Archbishop of Canterbury wanted to encourage peace between Wales, Scotland and England. We weren't gallivanting around the countryside for the fun of it."

"So the English know you were involved?" she asked. "Is that why they shot at you?"

"Well, not exactly," I said.

Ieuan's mouth turned wry. "We don't know, Bronwen," he said. "We weren't involved directly in Edward's death, and at the time thought that by leaving the area immediately afterwards, we'd escaped anyone's attention."

"We heard in Carlisle that the English think I'm dead too," I added, "so we don't know why Falkes cared enough about us to pursue us across Scotland."

"And we don't know what's going to happen now," Ieuan said.

"It's going to be a time of great upheaval," I said. "With Edward dead, who claims the English throne? His eldest son, who is just over a year old, inherits. But you know as well as I that inheriting the throne and claiming it are two entirely different things."

"Hereford," Ieuan growled. He used the same tone every time he mentioned the name. *Everything always comes back to Humphrey de Bohun.*

I leaned my head against the headrest. "Hereford," I repeated. "He won't claim the throne, but while the cat's away, the mouse will play."

"Some mouse," Ieuan said.

"Do I get to ask who Hereford is?" Bronwen said.

"He is a lord of the Marche as well as Lord High Constable of England," Ieuan answered. "His full name is Humphrey de Bohun. The Welsh have suffered for generations under the Earl of Hereford's boot, whoever he may be."

"He'll take advantage," I said. "Edward's death alone is a huge gift to him—but coupled with the deaths of half of the nobility of the Marche, plus mine, will only serve his interests. If I didn't know the true story, I would've guessed that Hereford himself colluded with Jacob to kill everyone."

"Carew will tell your father what happened in the pavilion," Ieuan said. "Even without us there, the Prince will know what to do and how to prepare for it. He is in a much stronger position than he was, even a year ago."

"What will he do?" Bronwen asked, trying to follow along.

David let a breath hiss through his teeth. "Prepare for war," he said.

# 10

*Bronwen*

"**P**repare for war," David said.

No matter how impossible, improbable, and outright ridiculous it was to think it, David thought he was a Prince of Wales. He sat in my car and talked about war with the Earl of Hereford, dead for nearly seven hundred and fifty years, as if it could happen tomorrow. *To him, it could happen tomorrow!*

We drove for a while in silence, each with our own thoughts. Eventually, the sky began to lighten, and I pulled off the highway and into a McDonald's restaurant. We all ordered, and as usual, I paid. I thought they'd eaten a lot of pizza, but I've never seen any men eat as much in one sitting as those two did. Ieuan ordered another root beer and this one was super large. I worried about his teeth. If Ieuan really was from the thirteenth century, he didn't have a lot of familiarity with sugar. But that is probably why both he and David ordered hot fudge sundaes 'to go'. I was surprised they were even on the menu at breakfast, but maybe there was a market for them, beyond my two lunatic companions.

We pulled into the long driveway that led to David's aunt's house a little after 7:30 in the morning. Elisa opened the door to us. She had blonde hair, David's blue eyes, and was dressed professionally in a tailored suit with heels, making her five inches taller than I was instead of three.

"Hi, Aunt Elisa," David said, leaning against one of the porch pillars. He kept a few feet away, so as not to appear threatening. He and Ieuan had also left their swords in the car, which I thought was probably a good thing.

Elisa stood frozen in the doorway, her eyes fixed on David's. She must have seen something in them, because she didn't slam the door immediately.

"Who are you?" Elisa asked.

"It's David, Auntie," he said, "all grown up."

Silence. David didn't fill it. Elisa was immobile as she regarded him. Her eyes traveled from the top of his head, down to his boots, and back again.

"She's not Anna," Elisa said, flicking a glance at me.

"No, Aunt Elisa," David said. "This is my friend, Bronwen Llywelyn."

I stuck out my hand. "Hi," I said.

Elisa's good manners were ingrained, because she took my hand and shook it.

"May we come in?" David asked.

Elisa took a step back, no longer meeting David's eyes. "I have to go to work. Can you come back later?"

A look passed over David's face. Impatience, I thought. "Aunt Elisa," he said, "we have nowhere to go. I have news of Mom and Anna. Please let us in. We won't be any trouble."

Suddenly Elisa's face crumpled. "Is it really you, David? Can it really be you?"

David stepped forward, his shoulder pushing the door open wider, and Elisa moved into his arms. She wrapped her arms around his waist and sobbed into his neck. I couldn't see his face, but he bent his head and rested his cheek on the top of her head.

"I'm sorry to surprise you this way. I didn't know what else to do."

Slowly recovering, wiping the tears on her cheeks, Elisa let us inside the house. As we followed her into the living room, she gripped David's arm so tightly her knuckles were white. Everyone grieved in a different way. Hers was suddenly sharp and new all over again. I didn't know what that was like. I never had any siblings and it wasn't like I was close to my parents.

Elisa pulled David to a seat beside her on her coach. It was yellow, with green and blue flowers, and David looked incongruous there in his war gear. Ieuan and I took chairs opposite but her eyes were only for David. She clutched both his arms. "Why are you dressed this way?"

David put his own hands on her shoulders, but didn't speak, and it occurred to me that he hadn't thought this through further than arriving in Bryn Mawr. *How do you tell your Aunt*

*that her sister isn't dead but living in the Middle Ages as the
Princess of Wales?*

"Auntie," David finally said. "I want to explain, but I can't
think of any good way to do it."

"Just tell me," she said.

David took a deep breath and let it out. "When Anna and I
took your van to pick up Christopher," David said, "we crossed a
barrier into another time, specifically into thirteenth century
Wales. When Mom disappeared a year ago, she also traveled
there. I don't know how it is possible, or why, only that it
happened. We are all well, but living in another world, one I need
to get back to as soon as possible."

Elisa stilled and then released him. She put her hand to
her mouth, her nose pinched and her face white.

"What are you saying?" she asked, anger in her voice.
"Why are you telling me this?"

As her words were painfully similar to the ones I'd fired at
him, I understood what she was feeling, and thought I could help.
"Elisa," I began. "Please listen to him. I know this is hard to hear,
but proof of his words is before you. David *is* here. He has so
much more to explain to you and I believe that he's telling the
truth."

Elisa stood and stepped to look out the bank of windows
that opened to the rear of her house. Two French doors led to a
patio. She leaned her forehead on the glass and fiddled with the
lock with one hand. Then, she fisted the other and raised it above

her head to pound it against the door. The glass didn't break, but Elisa did.

"I can't . . ." she began. "I can't do this." She turned on her heel, both fists clenched at her sides though her anger was contradicted by the tears streaming down her cheeks. "Just . . . just. . . stay here. Make yourself at home." And then she was running from the room, her head down, refusing to look at David again. Her heels staccatoed on the slate in the hall, keys tinkled as she grabbed them off the table by the door, and then the front door opened and closed behind her.

David sat in silence, his head turned in the direction she'd gone. Then he stood and went to the door. I reached him just as he opened it, in time to see his Aunt speed away up the driveway in her car. He turned to us. "I'm sorry," he said. "I didn't know how to tell her, and now I don't know what to say to you."

"Give her some time," Ieuan said. "She's gone to collect herself. She'll be back."

David nodded, shrugged, and closed the door. I looked from one to the other, saddened by Aunt Elisa's grief, but also appalled by the men's complacency. Yet, perhaps they were right, and I hoped, like me, she'd come home willing to listen.

\* \* \* \* \*

*Make yourself at home.* The words resonated in my head. I regret to say, David and Ieuan did make themselves at home, with enthusiasm. I hadn't known that a shower could make a person as happy as the one in Elisa Shepherd's house made Ieuan. He was truly a kid in a candy store. Everything was exciting to him: the food; television; books; floors; cleaning products. He overlooked nothing in that whole house in his explorations. David just let him do what he wanted.

"Ieuan is one of the smartest, most curious men I know," David said in an aside to me. "Let him be. He'll wring from this every possible experience he can, and then return to Wales, grateful for the chance to have seen it."

David, for his part, spent most of the day on Elisa's computer. I poked my head into the office every now and then. He was friendly, but absorbed in whatever he was doing and at first I left him to it. I kept thinking that I should go back to Penn State, but I told myself that I was too tired; that the drive was too long on no sleep. I went back to Ieuan. He was sitting on the couch, his hand resting lightly on his bandages; perhaps his ribs hurt him more than he'd admitted. He held the remote control in his hand and as David had taught him, flipped through the channels.

I sat beside him, finding myself a corner of the couch in which to curl up.

"The colors aren't true," he said, glancing over at me.

"Excuse me?" I asked.

"The green isn't true green; the sky's too blue; and I can stare at the sun in this machine and not hurt my eyes."

He flipped silently through the channels. "Click. Click. Click." I watched him, noting again the solidity of him, how he was so physically *there* in a way in which I wasn't accustomed. He held the remote in his left hand, balancing it in his palm, and it too reflected the arduous nature of his upbringing. Thick calluses covered his fingers, and he had a long scar running across the back of his hand between his thumb and forefinger I hadn't noticed before,.

"What's that from?" I asked, gesturing in the air above it.

"Oh, that." He transferred the remote to his right hand and held up his left, flexing his fingers before forming a fist. "I was skinning a rabbit with a dull knife, so I was pressing harder than I should have had to. The knife slipped and left me this. It took nearly a year to get my full  motion back."

"How old were you?"

"Nine."

"I was ten," I said, holding out my left hand to show a scar on my forefinger, "except I was scaling fish."

Ieuan took my hand to inspect it, and then surprised me by ducking his head to give the scar a quick kiss. "You could have lost the end of it," he said. "You were lucky."

He went back to his television as if our exchange had been the most normal thing in the world and I slowly pulled my hand back, not knowing what to think. He stopped at a soccer game. "I like this," he said. "It's similar to a game I played with my friends as a boy. My sister was always worming her way in, asking to play too."

"You have a sister?"

"Her name is Lili. She's fifteen now and will marry soon. It was my hope that after our trip to England, I would take my leave of my Prince for a time and find her a husband."

He went back to the remote. "Click. Click. Click."

"Prince Dafydd told me that you're not married." Ieuan said.

"No, I'm not," I said.

"You must be widowed, then."

"No," I said. "I've never married."

He looked at me then. "How is that possible? Prince Dafydd says you must be at least twenty-two years old, though I find it hard to believe him. Where's your father?"

"I'm twenty-three, and my father lives in Belize, at the end of a hundred mile dirt road. He doesn't think it's his responsibility to find me a husband. In the twenty-first century, nobody gets married at fifteen and when women do get married, they find their own husbands."

Ieuan turned back to his television, but his eyes had an unfocused look that told me he wasn't watching it. "I don't arrange a marriage for my sister because I want her gone from my house," Ieuan said, "but because I love her and want what is best for her."

"Does she want you to find her a husband?" I asked.

"She wants to join me in Prince Dafydd's service," he said. "Even you must admit that's not possible."

"Not in your time," I said. "In this time, women can be soldiers."

119

Ieuan clicked off the television and gave me his full attention. "Is that what you want?" he asked. "Do you want to fight and kill men?"

"No," I said. "No, I don't. But I support the right of a woman to be a soldier if she wants to be."

"Aah," Ieuan said. "You're talking about choices."

"I am?" I asked, feeling like I was losing control of the conversation.

"It seems to me that you have many choices in this century. That's not true in Wales. For my sister, Lili may become a wife or enter a convent. For me, I had no choice at all. I became a soldier."

"There are other jobs in your world," I said. "Blacksmith, farmer, merchant. Those are all choices."

"Not for me," Ieuan said. "I am my father's only son. He was a knight, so I am also a knight. I have lands and must care for the people who live on them. I have a steward and housekeeper and Lili, who does much of the work of running my estates when I'm away."

"So she does do important work," I said.

"Yes, like mine, but it's not work that she chooses. When I inherited my estate, it became her job to run the household."

"And if either of you chose *not* to do that work?" I asked. "What then?"

"The estate would fall into disarray; we would lose our lands because Prince Llywelyn would object to our lack of husbandry; or worse, the English would see an advantage in our negligence and take our lands by force, harming the people who live on the land and work it. When my uncle died, I swore an oath to Llywelyn, my liege lord, and in turn to the people whom I protect. Doing something different from this, along the lines of what you describe isn't a possible *choice* for us. We have a duty to fulfill, for our Prince and our country, and our children to come."

*Duty.* I certainly knew the word, but it was a foreign concept to me and I wasn't sure I'd ever used it. That and *obedience.*

"Do you never chafe at your restrictions?" I asked. "Do you ever have the urge to just do what *you* want to do?"

Ieuan turned in his seat so he could see my face better. "These questions are so strange, Bronwen," he said. "You're asking if I want to be more selfish than I am? If I want to ignore the needs of my family and those around me?"

I looked away. "It isn't like that, Ieuan. Nobody ever asked me to take care of my family. I feel responsible to my work as an archaeologist, but I can't say that the department feels any responsibility to me. In fact, I *know* it doesn't because my professor made clear that if I left, nobody would care."

"Then why do it?"

"Because I love archaeology," I said. "I feel that it's my life's work."

"And you couldn't have found fulfillment in something else?" Ieuan asked.

"But I *chose* archaeology," I said.

"And that makes the difference?"

I didn't know what to say. A gulf existed between our two worlds that I didn't know how to cross.

"Don't think, Ieuan, that all children in this world are as free as Bronwen." David said. He walked around the couch to a chair.

"What do you mean?" I said. I'd lived a peripatetic existence as a child, but my life wasn't much different than any other graduate student in the department.

"Your parents may not demand anything of you—may not even know or care where you are or what you're doing," David said, "but I suspect that many of your fellow students are fulfilling the dreams and wishes of their parents or running from them, just as they do in Wales."

"Yes," I said. "That's probably true."

Ieuan turned to me. "Do you think your parents love you, for it doesn't look like it to me."

"Yes, of course my parents love me, or . . . well . . ." I hesitated, not knowing if I wanted to say more.

Ieuan jumped all over it. "So, they don't," he said.

"Ieuan," I said, exasperated. "My father does love me, but he and my mother have their own relationship and I've always known that they had little room for me in their lives. I'm their only child, not to mention an unexpected and, at the time, unwanted one. They hauled me all over the planet with them because they didn't have a lot of choice about it."

"They could've left you with an uncle as my father did with Lili and me," Ieuan said. He glanced at David, and then away again.

"Let me tell you a story," I said, straightening in my seat. "When I was eleven, we lived briefly on a ranch in Colorado with some of my parents' friends. On the morning we were to leave, we loaded up the rental car, but as my parents were saying goodbye to their friends, I went into the house because I'd left my book on the kitchen counter. By the time I got back to the front door, my parents had driven off without me. Their friends met me on the front stoop and we stared at each other, horrified."

"What did you do?" Ieuan asked.

"We leapt into their car and chased after my parents. It took us half an hour to catch them, and we managed it only because they pulled off the highway into a gas station."

"Surely they noticed your absence?" Ieuan said.

"Well, that's the question isn't it?" I said. "Did they not notice, or did they actually not care, and see it as an opportunity to leave me behind?"

"You didn't ask them?" Ieuan said.

"No," I said. "Does it matter? Neither answer would have made me happy."

Ieuan was silent beside me, and I crossed my arms across my chest, feeling sullen and cross at the memory.

"As many sons in this world disappoint their fathers with their choices as in ours, Ieuan, even when those choices are the right ones."

Glancing from Ieuan to David, I realized I was missing something. Ieuan stared across the space that separated him from David, but again, he wasn't really seeing him.

"So you know already," Ieuan said.

"Of course, Ieuan. Did you fear I wouldn't trust you if I knew the truth?"

Ieuan got to his feet and paced over to the window, the same one Elisa had looked out that morning. The tree branches behind the house swayed in the breeze, and clouds had formed in what had been a deep blue sky.

"What truth?" I asked. Ieuan stood, his legs spread wide and his fists clenched at his side.

Ieuan answered, his back to us. "That it seems our lot in life to disappoint our fathers." He sighed. "From the moment Prince Llywelyn claimed the throne of Wales, his brother Dafydd plotted against him, with my father at his side. For nearly thirty years, my father served Dafydd faithfully, whether in rebellion or in favor, and then through all the years of exile in England until his eventual return and recent death. My father hated Prince Llywelyn, with the same passion he directed at Hereford. Until I was thirteen, I thought the two men were one and the same. *That son-of-a-bitch Llywelyn; that bastard Bohun; Hereford that lying cretin.* They were all one to me."

"What happened when you were thirteen?"

"Dafydd tried to assassinate Llywelyn. When the plot was discovered, Dafydd escaped to England. My father went with him, forfeiting his lands in Powys. My mother had died the year before, leaving only Lili and me. My father sent us to live with my uncle near Aberedw."

"And your uncle supported Llywelyn?" I said.

"Yes."

"So when you came of age, you joined Llywelyn's men instead of Dafydd's?"

"Yes. At first, my father thought I intended to serve as a spy in his camp," Ieuan said. "When I refused, he cursed me, told me I disappointed him—that I'd always disappointed him."

"You learned something then, though, didn't you?" said David.

Ieuan swung around. "I learned that my choices were my own." Then he smiled at me. "See, I do have choices, just not the same ones you have."

"What haunts you now?" I asked. "Obviously, Llywelyn doesn't mistrust you, or feel that your father's sins should reflect on you, or he wouldn't have assigned you to his son."

Ieuan hesitated, and David answered instead. "I understand, Ieuan," he said. He steepled his fingers in front of his mouth, looking thoughtful. "You feel the shame of your father's betrayal, while at the same time you cannot help feel ashamed at your betrayal of him."

"Yes," Ieuan said.

"We are quite a pair, Ieuan," David said, "though perhaps I was luckier. My father was worthless, but died before I was born so I never knew him. You still have to live with the man who fathered you."

"Now I'm lost," I said. "I thought you said Prince Llywelyn was your father, David?"

"I didn't discover that until we came to Wales, remember?" he said. "Until I was fourteen, the only father I knew was Trevor Lloyd, and he was no prize, let me tell you. He was a couple of years older than my mother when she married him right out of high school. She was only nineteen when she had Anna, but was already fed up with him—he was lazy, a drinker, and treated her badly."

"Your mother told you this?" I asked, surprised that Marged would disparage David's father in front of him.

"Of course not," David said. "Over the years I'd picked up that he wasn't a super guy, but when I was about twelve I overheard Aunt Elisa and Uncle Ted talking about him. They were worried that Mom didn't trust herself to fall in love with someone new, since she'd been burned so badly by my father—or rather, Anna's father."

"Didn't hearing that bother you?" I asked.

David sat still, unusually so for him. We let him think, and as I watched him I thought that this was not a casual conversation to him—that this conversation was one he'd been wanting to have with Ieuan for a very long time, and hadn't known how to begin it.

"It's hard to remember exactly when it all came together for me," David finally said, "but knowing the truth about Trevor Lloyd changed my life. Because of him, I realized that not having him as a father was as much a gift as my facility in math. It was my responsibility to use those gifts to the fullest of my ability."

126

For the hundredth time, I found myself staring at David, not knowing what to make of him. "And now you're the Prince of Wales," I said softly. It was a legacy that left him shouldering the weight of so many responsibilities he couldn't even count them. No wonder he was a little arrogant sometimes.

I didn't tell him that though. Instead, I said, "And you both found new fathers in the Prince and in Ieuan's uncle." I turned to Ieuan. "Is he proud of you?"

Ieuan's face softened. "My uncle died at the battle of the Menai Straits, only a few weeks before Prince Dafydd and his sister returned to Wales. And yes, he was proud of me."

"If I have learned anything about you in the last two days," I said, "I've learned that the word 'honorable' has meaning in your world. I can't believe you were any different as a boy. Admittedly, I'm no expert as far as men are concerned, but what father couldn't want you as his son? Your uncle must have been very thankful when you came to him."

David leaned back in his chair and rested his feet one at a time on the coffee table, clasping his hands behind his head. "I dare you to refute that, my friend. She sees the truth. It's time you admitted it to yourself."

Ieuan looked at me. "And what about you, Bronwen?" he said. "What about your father? Who have you found to fill the void he's left in you?"

I gazed back at him, startled by the sudden change in the direction of the conversation, yet knowing the painful truth. *No one.*

# 11

*David*

"**W**hat are you doing?"

I looked up from some papers that I'd printed out on Aunt Elisa's printer. Bronwen stood in the office doorway.

"I'm trying to think of everything that I might need to augment our knowledge base. It's overwhelming how much I don't know. I don't even know the right questions to ask, so it's making this difficult."

I handed her the sheaf of papers and she thumbed through it. There was information about antibiotics, steam engines, lenses, map-making, navigation, the Black Plague, weapons. It went on and on through several hundred pages. She eyed me over the top of them.

"Are you planning to take these back with you?"

"I'm going to try," I said, typing on the computer again.

She watched me work for another minute. "Why do you want to go back?" she said. "I would think you'd be happier here."

I spun the chair so that I was looking at her, no longer distracted. "How can you even ask that?" he said. "My family's there." And then I swallowed hard because our conversation with Ieuan had revealed that *her* family was no reason to do anything. I tried again. "I'm needed there, Bronwen. It isn't so much that *I*, as an individual born David Lloyd, am important, though as the Prince of Wales, I am. It's more that when Anna and I drove into Wales and saved my father's life, we saved Wales. This is so much bigger than I am; so much more important than I am. I would be a blind man not to see it. There, if I live, I can do great things. Here, maybe not so much."

I turned back to my internet searches. Bronwen found a seat on the couch near the door, the papers in her lap. She read quietly for a time, and then spoke again. "With six billion people on the planet, does any one person ever matter that much?" she asked.

"There aren't six billion people on the planet in the thirteenth century, Bronwen," I said, still focused on the computer. "There are only 300,000 in all of Wales."

"In 1285," she said.

"Yes, of course," I said. "In 1285."

Bronwen rubbed her eyes with her hands. The papers I'd given her represented so much more than it seemed at first glance. *Seven hundred and twenty-eight years of knowledge.* I kept working, and eventually Bronwen wandered out again. I was grateful that she was here. I wanted her to believe Ieuan and me. *To believe* in *us*. She had told Aunt Elisa she did, but I wasn't so sure.

Restless now, I walked downstairs. Ieuan and Bronwen were still in the television room, and, choosing not to disturb them, I wandered into the kitchen for some food. I opened the refrigerator and inspected the contents. *Okay, I miss twenty-first century food. A lot.* Figuring I would clog my arteries while I had the chance, I dug out the ingredients for a ham and cheese sandwich, put it together, and brought it back upstairs. I sat at the computer again and studied the screen. *What next? Ah, I know. 'How to make mayonnaise.'*

\* \* \* \* \*

Aunt Elisa came home around two o'clock, ready to talk. Her face was composed as she entered, and I tried to imagine what she'd been doing all this time by herself. She walked straight to me and reached up to take my face in her hands. "I love you," she said. "I'm sorry I ran away. I'm not going to explain myself to you, but I'm ready, now, to listen."

I kissed her cheek, and then Ieuan, Bronwen, and I sat in the living room together in awkward silence for about five minutes, while she bustled around, straightening cushions and getting us drinks. Ieuan was completely at ease. I was glad we'd had our conversation about our fathers. I'd never known before how to bring it up.

I kept bouncing my knee up and down, making Bronwen nervous. She didn't say anything though, just sat quietly with Ieuan sprawled next to her. Probably my sister would have smacked me. Finally, Aunt Elisa sat down.

"I was listening without hearing, earlier," she said. "Tell me again where you've been and what you've done. I want to know everything."

So I did. I talked for twenty straight minutes. Aunt Elisa didn't interrupt me, and it was as if she'd decided to believe me. It helped that what I was telling her was true and it made me appreciate her in a way I never had before.

"So what will you do now?" she asked. "You may stay here with us, at least for a while. We have a spare room, and your cousins would love to have you around." She paused. "You would have to enroll in school again, though maybe we could just skip the rest of high school and move onto college. Quite honestly, I really can't picture you fitting in with other kids very well."

"Thank you Aunt Elisa, for the offer," I said, "but I need to get back, just as soon as I can."

Her eyes narrowed. *This is the moment. Right now is when she either believes me, or she doesn't.*

"How?" she asked.

"I don't know. I was hoping I could borrow your car and drive there, just like before."

"You want to take another car to Wales?" she asked. "Another one of *my* cars?"

"Sorry, Aunt Elisa. I know it was your van the first time. Did the insurance cover most of the cost?"

"The van was ten years old anyway, and I guess if the beater I'm driving now disappears, it won't be too much of a loss."

"Wait a minute!" Bronwen said. "You're talking about driving to Wales again? How are you going to do that? Drive around until you're magically transported there like before?"

"Um," I said. "That was pretty much my whole plan."

"There will be no wall of snow this time of year," Aunt Elisa pointed out.

"There wasn't for Mom, either," I said. "My theory is that there's something *in* us, in Mom, Anna, and me, that makes world shifting possible. The worst thing that can happen is that it doesn't work."

"The worst thing that can happen," Aunt Elisa said sourly, "is that you wreck my car."

"Do you have a better idea?" I asked her. She pursed her lips, but shook her head.

"What do you think of this, Ieuan?" Bronwen poked him with her elbow.

"Think of what?" Ieuan asked. We'd been speaking in English, and Bronwen must have forgotten that he didn't understand what was being said.

"Getting back to Wales," Bronwen said in Welsh. "Do you have an idea?"

"Whatever Prince Dafydd thinks is right is fine with me," he said.

Bronwen wrinkled her nose as she studied him. "Just like that. Whatever he wants?"

"Yes," Ieuan agreed.

Bronwen turned to me. "And who is going to drive the car?"

"I am," I said.

"You don't have a license. You can't drive."

"How hard can it be?" I asked, looking at Aunt Elisa and speaking English again so she could understand. "I've driven the van a couple of times since we arrived in Wales. It was easy."

"My car is manual transmission, actually," Aunt Elisa said. "It's a little more difficult than the minivan."

I shrugged. "I don't see an alternative."

Ieuan spoke up, having missed the specifics of our exchange but not the intent. "Bronwen could drive her car."

I shook my head before Bronwen could answer, speaking again in Welsh. "No, I'm not taking her to the thirteenth century, Ieuan. There are too many difficulties, too many barriers. Believe me, either Anna, Mom, or I have lived through all of them already."

"Wait a minute," Bronwen said. "You don't have the right to decide that for me. Ieuan has a point. I could drive."

"You have no idea what you're saying," I said. "You don't want to be an unmarried, father-less, property-less girl in the Middle Ages, even if you're good friends with a prince. You're arguing with me only because you don't really believe we're going to be driving to Wales tomorrow and because you don't like to be told what you can and cannot do." Bronwen opened her mouth, and then closed it. "I'm right," I said. "Don't try to deny it."

We were all silent after that, none of us knowing what to say, or how to say it.

Then Bronwen spoke again. "No, I don't think you are right, David." She looked at Ieuan. "I would be willing to travel with you. It's been in the back of my head all day; all the while you've talked about who you are and what your purpose is. I'm an archaeologist. I live in the past in my head. Why do you think I've never cut my hair?"

She put her hand to her hair and undid the bun that she always wore. Her hair cascaded past her shoulders to her waist and Ieuan reached out, almost touching it, and then seemed to think better of it. Bronwen laughed and answered her own question: "Because as a girl I had dreams of being transported to the past and swept off my feet by a knight in shining armor. As I grew older, I knew those dreams for the fantasy they were, but the little girl in me never forgot."

"Everything that has happened to me up until now, forces me to believe that who I am and what I am comes with a purpose." I said. "How can I look at Ieuan, sitting there, whole and well, and think that I shouldn't have brought him across the abyss? Having saved his life, I can't help but think that I'll be able to take him back—that I'm meant to take him back."

"With great power comes great responsibility," Bronwen intoned.

"Don't laugh," I said, "not when it's true."

"I'm not laughing," Bronwen said.

"Anna wondered once if she were to jump from the highest tower at Castell y Bere, if she would vanish half-way to the ground, or fall with a sickening thud to the earth," I said. "Are you willing to take that kind of a chance with *your* life, Bronwen, especially when you don't have to?"

"Who says you're the only one who has responsibilities?" Bronwen said, a little more starch in her voice. "You take so much on yourself, yet you deny the same right to others. What if you met *me* because I'm meant to help you. What if, as you said back in the courtyard at Penn State, there's no such thing as a coincidence?"

Now it was my turn to open my mouth, and then close it. I could hear Anna in my head: *She has you there, kiddo—you're not the only one who can argue logically.*

Then Ieuan spoke. "Will you come with me?" he asked, his voice so soft I almost couldn't hear it. "My armor has dulled over the years, but I am a knight. I would have you as my wife."

Bronwen froze, her fingers threaded through her hair. "Ieuan," she said. "You can't mean it. I can't be your wife."

Ieuan smiled, more with his eyes than with his mouth. "I've never met a woman such as you. No one like you exists in Wales."

"Your wife." Bronwen shook her head. Ieuan hadn't taken his eyes off Bronwen's face. I held myself still, projecting calm, but I knew, even if there was no way Ieuan could, that she wouldn't say 'yes' She couldn't say 'yes'.

Bronwen shook her head again, looked at the floor, and then back at him. "You can't ask me to marry you, Ieuan," she said. "You don't know what you are asking. You don't know me."

"Yes, I do," said Ieuan. "I learned everything I needed to know about you the first day we met. Are you saying that you have secrets that would make me like you less?" He had curled a lock of her hair around his finger, and now tugged it.

Bronwen raised her hands, and then dropped them into her lap in a despairing gesture. "That's not how it works in this world, Ieuan," she said.

"Then people in this world have it all wrong," he said.

Bronwen's eyes met mine, "I don't know what to say."

Ieuan brought her attention back to him with a finger to her chin. "Don't say 'no'. I don't want you to say 'no' before you take some time to think about it."

"What's happening?" Elisa asked. She spoke no Welsh and we'd forgotten her for the last five minutes.

"Apparently, Ieuan thinks it's a good idea to have Bronwen drive us to Wales," I said.

# 12

## *Bronwen*

Near dinnertime, Aunt Elisa's husband, Ted, arrived—red hair, as tall as David but incredibly skinny—bringing their two children with him. Christopher was a miniature of his father at ten years old. The baby, Elen, was not such a baby anymore at nearly four.

David and I were waiting for them in the kitchen. "Elen won't remember me but Christopher surely will," David said, and sure enough, when Christopher walked through the kitchen door, he ran to David and threw his arms around his waist.

"David!" Christopher said.

"Your Aunt Elisa called me before I left work," Uncle Ted said. "This is a little hard to take in, David."

"Hard for me, too," David said.

Christopher released David and knocked on his stomach with his knuckles like he was a door. "What are you wearing, David?" he asked. "It feels like armor."

"It is armor, Christopher," he said. "I have a sword, too."

"David!" Aunt Elisa said.

"Can I see it?" Christopher said.

Before Aunt Elisa could protest again, David said, "Do we admit the truth, or not? Do we lie to him, or not? Tomorrow I'm leaving here and may never return. How are you going to explain that to him? I think he deserves the truth, and someday, when he grows up, he might find a way to explain it. If all goes well, I'll be in Wales, and will never get the chance."

Elisa and Ted glanced at each other and though Elisa's heart was surely still shouting "No!" Ted nodded. "You're right," he said.

David, Christopher, and I went out to the car and I opened the hatchback. David took out his sword. Despite having driven with it and housed it for three days, I'd never seen it unsheathed.

"You can hold it," David said.

"Whoa," Christopher said as David let go of the blade. "It's really heavy."

"Compared to a baseball bat or a tennis racket, sure," David said. "Those are weighed in ounces. My sword weighs a little over two pounds, which is just right for me." He took the sword from Christopher and stepped away from us, into the center of the driveway. "Most of the time, I do well with only one hand on the sword, particularly on horseback because I need a shield in

138

my other hand." He brought the sword up and slashed down to the right and then the left.

"If I were to fight you, however," David continued, bringing the sword above his head with two hands in preparation for slashing downward, "I would hold it like this."

"Just like in the movies!" Christopher said.

"I think you've seen some movies maybe you shouldn't have seen, young man," David said, with a smile. He reached over and tousled Christopher's hair, and then bent to one knee. "Understand, Christopher. This is a weapon. Throughout history, real people have died at the end of a sword."

"Have you killed people, David?" Christopher asked.

I held my breath.

"Yes, Christopher, I have," David said. "Too many."

"Oh," Christopher said. He looked at the sword that David had rested across his thigh.

"It's not so fun when you think of it that way, is it?" David said, standing up again. "Probably, it would be best if we kept this conversation inside the family. You can talk to your parents, but perhaps talking to the kids at school about your cousin who lives in medieval Wales and kills people is not the best idea."

"They wouldn't believe me anyway," Christopher said. "It'll be our secret. Yours and mine."

David sheathed his sword and picked Christopher up to hug him. "I'm sorry I won't see you again," David said. "You're a great kid."

Christopher held on, his head resting on David's shoulder.

\* \* \* \* \*

We spent the rest of the evening organizing our things. Elisa built stacks of sandwiches, accompanied by wonderful twenty-first century cookies and chips. As a special gift, she gave Ieuan a six pack of root beer that she had in the pantry. David borrowed—or rather, took—a backpack for his papers. We behaved as if we were really going to travel to the thirteenth century. When I confronted David with this, he refused to even consider the alternative.

"I'm going back," he said.

"David," I said, keeping my voice reasonable. "What if you can't?"

"I will entertain the possibility only when it becomes one. For now, I'm going to assume I can—and will—return to the thirteenth century tomorrow." His face was a little gray, indicating how tightly wound he really was. I let it go. If he was wrong, we'd know soon enough.

As we bustled around, I tried not to look at Ieuan, tried not to be alone with him. I couldn't believe he'd actually asked me to marry him. I shouldn't have left it hanging, but somehow I couldn't just tell him 'no' and be done with it. We had nothing to talk about; no common interests; and vast differences in cultural experience. *I am completely, totally, and incontrovertibly out of my mind to even consider it.*

Forgoing Ieuan's offer to watch a movie with him, and thinking I was exhausted enough to sleep, I closed my bedroom door and climbed into bed. I'd just gotten settled when someone knocked. "It's David. Can I come in?" he asked.

"Yes," I said.

He pushed open the door and hesitated awkwardly when he saw me under the covers. I wore some of Elisa's pajamas—shorts and a tank top. Not indecent, but . . .

"Sorry," he said. "We need to talk."

I pushed myself up and plumped a pillow behind my back. "Where's Ieuan?"

"Already asleep," David said. "I made sure he took his antibiotic and his painkillers and they knocked him right out before the movie was half over."

I felt bad. I'd almost forgotten he was even hurt.

"That's what I want to talk to you about," David said.

"Ieuan?" I asked.

"Marrying Ieuan," he said. "You need to decline his offer, get in your car, and drive back to Penn State."

"That would be the smart thing to do," I said.

"The right thing to do," he said. "Ieuan wants to give you his heart—maybe he already has—and you need to give it back to him and let him go."

I fidgeted with the edge of the comforter on the bed. It was handmade, pink and white flannel. "You're afraid I'm going to hurt him," I said. "That I've already hurt him."

"Of course," David said. "I'm his liege lord. I do have the right to deny him a wedding if I don't approve of the bride."

"You wouldn't!" I said.

"Watch me," he said. "It's better for him to walk away now than for you to hurt him later when he realizes you don't love him."

"Who says I don't love him?"

David tipped his head to one side. "You do love him?"

I threw back the covers and climbed out of bed. I paced around the Persian rug on the floor, trying to get my thoughts in order. "You coming here has changed my life, David. All of a sudden, I don't know what's real and what isn't," I said. "Despite my parents' careless existence, I had my life planned out from a very early age. Unlike them, I would work hard at one job; I would be successful; I would achieve great things. But the last few years have been more work than I think they should've been. The last few days have shown me that I don't know what I want anymore. I don't have the answers for my life and I don't know where to find them."

"Coming with us to thirteenth century Wales isn't going to help, Bronwen. It'll make your path clearer only because you won't have any choices."

"Is my life so great that there is something better here to live for? I've not been happy for a while—not sleeping well, not eating right. It feels like my life isn't my own, despite what I said to Ieuan." I stopped pacing and looked at him, my hands on my hips. "No man has ever looked at me the way Ieuan does. At *me*, as *me*. He cares about totally different things than any man I've ever met. He *is* a knight in shining armor. We could be friends; we could be more than friends; but if I don't go with you, if we don't try, then I'll never know, will I? Everyone wants someone to love them, David. It's intoxicating to have someone as amazing as Ieuan think he loves me. *How do I walk away from that?*"

"You're from the twenty-first century, Bronwen," David said. "You have no idea what Wales is like, how hard it is, what it takes to survive there."

I sat down on the bed across from him. "And if I don't come with you, I'll never know that either."

"He fell for you the first time he saw you," David said. "He looked at you from his hospital bed, and after that, you're all he's seen."

"That's what I mean, David. You think I don't deserve him?"

"I didn't say that," David said. "I think you're a good person, and I think everything happens for a reason, including meeting you. I just want to know that you are thinking this through, okay?"

"Okay," I said.

David stood to leave, but just as he passed through the door, he poked his head back around the doorjamb. "One other thing. You do realize that women of the Middle Ages generally obey their husbands? If you accept him, Ieuan will expect it, though I suspect," he grinned, "that obedience has never been your strong suit." I glared at his retreating back as he pulled the door closed.

*I have never obeyed anyone in my life.* I pictured Ieuan's eyes. Then my cell phone beeped, interrupting my thoughts to tell me it was ten o'clock. Suddenly, I knew the answer to my dilemma, epitomized by the bright light shining from the screen. David was right. I was a woman of the twenty-first century and always would be. I had a life, a career. Tomorrow I would return to Penn State and commit to it.

Still restless, even though I felt relief that I'd made a decision, I stared at myself in the mirror above the dresser. *What did Ieuan see in me?* I leaned closer. If I went to Wales, how long before I no longer recognized myself? David spoke of his role as Prince as a duty, a responsibility, but there was more than that in his voice. *He loves Wales.* I could hear it when he talked of returning. *What is it that I want for me? And how do I find it?*

# 13

*Ieuan*

**P**rince Dafydd entered the room. His clothing rustled as he removed it and slipped into his bed on the floor. I turned onto my back.

"Ieuan?"

"I'm awake, my lord," I said.

"I was hoping you'd stay asleep. We have a long day tomorrow."

"I was asleep, but my dreams woke me."

"What did you dream?" Dafydd asked.

I sighed. "The same as you."

"Oh," he said. He knew what I meant. Each man learned to live with battle, with killing, in his own way, but our dreams wouldn't let us forget what we put aside during the day.

"That raid last year haunts me," Dafydd said, and I heard the rustle of the sheets as he rubbed the scar that marked his leg where the English soldier had struck him. "I see the man shift, knowing that I am too late to counter him. In my dreams, Bevyn isn't there to save me and I fall from my horse."

"You dream he kills you?" I asked. That was an omen every knight feared.

"No," he said, and I relaxed. "I wake before I hit the ground."

"I've been falling in my dreams," I said. "A black abyss opens beneath my feet."

"I know what that dream is," Dafydd said.

"You've had it too?" I asked.

"No," he said. "I've seen it awake—twice. It's the abyss we crossed when we came from Wales to this world."

"And you hope to see it again tomorrow."

"Yes," he said. Silence fell between us. Then David spoke again. "I talked to Bronwen. Perhaps I shouldn't have. Your love life is none of my business, but I couldn't help myself."

"What did you talk with her about?" I asked.

"About marrying you."

"I didn't speak with you before I asked her to marry me. That is my lapse, not yours," I said. "I apologize for assuming you would accept my choice."

Dafydd sighed. "It's not that I don't accept your choice, Ieuan. All things being equal, she is a great choice—if she weren't a twenty-first century woman who we're asking to come with us to the thirteenth century."

"You think she will say 'no'; that she will leave me and return to her university?"

"I told her to say 'no'," he said. "I told her I had the power to deny you the right to her."

I felt like he'd punched me in the gut. "My lord," I said. The words came out strangled in my effort not to shout them. "What . . . what . . . why?" I threw off the covers and got to my feet, my hands and teeth clenched. "How could you?"

David's voice came out of the darkness. "Because I don't want to take her to Wales only for her to find that loving you can't make up for what she misses here. I don't want her to suffer as my sister and mother have suffered. They didn't have a choice about coming to Wales, and she does. Bronwen has no idea what it's going to be like for her.

"You don't know how it is, Ieuan. We grew up as Bronwen has—not as well-traveled, but sheltered and safe. We were free then, as she is now. Soft."

David had sat up. An outside light shone through the window, illuminating his face. He hugged his knees and rested his head on them, his hands tugging at his hair as if he would tear it out. "Anna cried the first time she sent me away to battle. She didn't think I saw her tears, but I did. My mother tries to hide her fears—for me, for my father, and for Anna, but I've heard her in the night. Here, in this world, anything Bronwen wants to do or be is hers for the taking. All she has to do is reach out and grasp it. In Wales, she becomes your wife—nothing less than that, but nothing more either. She'll live in fear—for you, for herself, for your children."

147

Suddenly, I felt sorry for him. *He honestly thinks that people in his world don't live in fear?* I'd spent the afternoon watching his television. Program after program showed his people, running from their lives, drowning their fears in alcohol and sex, instead of acknowledging death and embracing the truth of it—and living as free people.

"It's not your place to make that choice for her, Dafydd," I said. I squatted down beside him and on impulse, wrapped my arm around his shoulder. "Nor for me. I knew when I asked her to marry me that the chances of her accepting were slim. *I* accepted that. Her choices, though, are hers alone. We can't ever have all the information we need, or want, in life. God hasn't given us that kind of control. In your world, you think you have it, but you don't, anymore than we do in Wales."

Dafydd put his face into my shoulder. "God, I'm so sorry, Ieuan. I'm a sixteen-year old idiot and I was wrong to talk to her. You have every right to be angry with me. Please forgive me."

"You carry the future of your entire country on your back, my lord. But this—this burden is only for Bronwen and me."

\* \* \* \* \*

I didn't feel as forgiving the next morning, however, when Bronwen didn't put in an appearance at breakfast and her car was gone.

"She left?" I asked Dafydd. "Without even saying goodbye?"

148

"I'm sorry, Ieuan," my lord said. "I can only say it again, even though I know it doesn't make it better."

Further recriminations were useless, so I gathered my belongings—including my root beer—and tossed them into the backseat of Aunt Elisa's car. Discarded items—old clothes, single gloves, empty bottles—had littered the floor and seat, but Dafydd had gathered the refuse in a large white sack and left it in the garage.

Dafydd kissed Elisa goodbye and said something that I didn't catch, as it was in English. She hugged him, and then pushed him toward the car. Before I opened the door, I bowed. She raised her hand. We settled ourselves in the front seats.

"Give me a second," Dafydd said. "I need to figure out the stick shift." Dafydd started the car. I watched as he pressed the 'clutch' and shifted through the gears. "Ready?" he asked.

I nodded. "Yes, my lord."

He hesitated. "You called me 'Dafydd' last night," he said. "The first time, I think."

"And the last, perhaps," I said, "though if we stay in this world, I can't go around calling you 'my lord' in front of others. Every time I've said it in Bronwen's presence, a smile forms around her mouth." I fell silent at the thought. Dafydd eyed me, and then shifted into first gear. *Not a happy topic.*

Slowly, Dafydd raised the clutch and pressed the gas peddle. Knowing I was interested, Bronwen had explained how the gears and clutch worked during the drive to Bryn Mawr, and I peered under the steering wheel to watch Dafydd's attempts. The engine revved, Dafydd released the clutch, the car jerked forward twice, and then died. I sat back in my seat.

"Sorry," he said, shifting into neutral and starting the car again. "I'll get the hang of this eventually. I saw my mom do it often enough."

Again he revved the engine and released the clutch. The car jolted forward but this time it caught. We eased forward, at not more than five miles an hour. Elisa had a long driveway and Dafydd was about to shift into second gear when a car appeared in front of us. Dafydd slammed the brake, stalling the car.

*Bronwen.*

Bronwen had braked hard too, skidding into the dirt beside the driveway in order to stop in time. She shoved at her door and leaped out of the car. Her door slammed behind her. "What are you doing?" she demanded, her hands on her hips and her chin pointed at the pair of us.

Dafydd had his hands up in the air, defensively. "We thought you'd gone!"

"You thought I'd gone," she said. "You think so little of me that you assumed I would leave without saying goodbye!"

"There was no note!" Dafydd tried again.

"And you!" Bronwen turned on me, coming around to my side of the car and poking her finger at my chest through the open window. "What did you think?"

"You hadn't given me an answer," I said. "I didn't know what to think, but when my lord said that he'd spoken with you last night . . ."

Bronwen interrupted me. "Your lord," and the way she said it was not complementary, "tried to convince me not to come with you. That I didn't love you. Well—" She put her hands on either side of my face, ducked her head into the car, and kissed me hard. "So there," she said. I put my hands on her shoulders and pulled her closer. David cleared his throat. We released each other, and we all laughed.

"Where did you go?" Dafydd asked.

"Elisa was out of coffee," Bronwen said. "If you can bring all those papers with you, I can bring coffee." She stalked back to her car, bent in through the open door and brought out a cup and a small brown sack. "See," she said.

"We almost left without you," Dafydd said.

"I got lost," Bronwen said, putting the coffee back in her car. "These roads are confusing."

"Yeah, no kidding," David said, under his breath. He looked at me. "Are you ready for this?"

"Is Bronwen going to drive?" I asked.

"You!" Bronwen stood impatiently by Dafydd's door. She pointed at him. "Out!"

"Yes, madam," my lord said, and opened his door.

She climbed into his seat and worked the gear shift, much more agilely than Dafydd had. Satisfied, she started the car, looked at me, grinning, and backed the car down the driveway to Aunt Elisa's door.

"Get your stuff," she said as she reached for the door handle. "I want to put my stash of coffee in the backpack."

"Wait," I said, and reached for her. I caught the back of her neck and pulled her to me for another kiss. I could have sat like that all day, but Dafydd opened the door to the rear seat.

"Let's go, love-birds," he said. "Aunt Elisa filled her tank for the drive, Bronwen. How about yours?"

"Just now," she said, and tugged away from me. "You, sir, look entirely too pleased with yourself."

I hadn't let go of her and now pulled on her thick braid that fell half-way down her back. "That would be because I am," I said.

# 14

*Bronwen*

As I climbed into the front seat of my car, my stomach had that unsettled, excited-sick feeling that I often got before a test or, when I was younger, before the airplane taking us to another country took off. *This is impulsive. This is crazy. This is absolutely right.* And yet, I hadn't been impulsive as all that—I'd left letters for Elisa to mail to my family and friends if we didn't come back, though not ones, of course, that told the whole truth.

David had trudged back and forth from Aunt Elisa's car to mine with their things, before plopping himself into the front seat. Ieuan was in the back. David looked over at me. "Shoot," he said.

"What?"

"I wasn't prepared for you to come with us. You're not dressed right."

I inspected my clothes. I wore jeans, a t-shirt, and a cardigan; the very same clothes I'd worn the day before, as a matter of fact. David turned to Ieuan who'd already popped the top of a bottle of one of those fancy brands of root beer that Aunt Elisa had given him, and was taking a sip. "We're going to have to find her a dress," he said.

Ieuan swallowed. "I like her the way she is," he said.

"Ieuan," David admonished. "Be reasonable."

Ieuan laughed. "We've been here long enough for you to forget who you are? She's no different in this from your sister and your mother. After witnessing their arrival, is anyone going to think ill of my beloved?"

*His beloved.* I looked at him in the rear view mirror. He winked.

David turned back to the front and buckled his seat belt. "Okay, fine. Let's go."

Shaking my head at my crazy men, I started the car. I pulled out of the driveway, turned right as David indicated, and started driving. After a few minutes he stopped giving directions and just sat, his arms folded across his chest, looking out the window. I drove and drove, up one winding road and down another. Except for the slurping, Ieuan was silent in the back seat. Every time I reached a more populated area, or one of the main streets through the Main Line, David had me turn around and go back the way I'd come.

Finally, after forty-five minutes of this, I pulled to the side of the road. "What exactly are you looking for?" I asked.

"I don't really know," he said. He ran his hand through his hair. "It's been nearly three years and it was snowing. The terrain looks completely different today. The trees have leaves and the roads are lined with flowers instead of snow. How far are we from my aunt's house?"

"A couple of miles," I said. "I'm not really sure."

"Good. Just keep driving."

Fine. *He's an escapee from an insane asylum and I'm just as bad for humoring him.* I started the car again and pulled into my lane. I went up one hill, down another, up again and was just heading down another, following it as it curved to the left, when David tensed and leaned forward, anticipating something that he saw but I didn't.

"What?" I asked.

He didn't answer. We took the curve at a higher rate of speed than I normally might, and I braked, before straightening once we were on the other side of the hill. David turned in his seat to look behind us.

"Pull over and turn around," he said.

I did as he asked, driving through someone's circular driveway before heading back the way we'd come. We drove back up the hill and when I was a hundred feet past it, straightening the wheel, David asked me to turn around again.

"What are we doing?" I asked.

"I'm trying to figure it out," David said, without really explaining. "Pull over again."

I did so, about fifty feet from the curve, and he got out of the car. David walked away from us and stood at the corner, on the right side of the road, looking ahead to the part of the road I

155

couldn't see. He stood, watching who knew what, while four cars passed us.

Then, all of a sudden, he turned and came running toward us. "Start the car, Bronwen!" he said. "Let's go!"

I was already accelerating forward as David threw himself into his seat. As before, we crested the small rise and were taking the downhill curve to the left when a large truck came lumbering up the hill in our direction. David leaned over to grip the wheel. He turned it hard into the truck and then pulled it back just before we hit it.

"Are you insane?" I screamed, slamming on the brake and wrenching the wheel from him. In doing so, I overcorrected. In five seconds we went from perfectly safe and normal to totaled. I skidded sideways into the truck. *And then through it.*

A black gaping maw encompassed us. "Hang on!" David said.

In a moment we were bumping and jerking over a grassy field near a small stand of trees. A turf wall loomed ahead and I managed to twist the wheel hard to the right so as to avoid hitting it. We stopped.

David reached over and turned off the engine. "Excellent," he said. He looked back at Ieuan who was sprawled in the back seat, his long arms stretched from door to door to hold himself steady. "Except for the fact that I don't know where we are. This isn't where I thought we should end up."

"That was quite invigorating, my lord," Ieuan said. And then to me. "You are not injured, *cariad*?"

I shook my head but couldn't speak. I was listening to my heart beat, feeling the car settle, breathing the sweet air coming up from the meadow through the open window. The grass was green and still dew-covered, with a foggy layer near the ground. Trees shimmered in the distance, with mountains beyond. Birds sang, accepting our existence.

I wrapped my arms around my waist and leaned forward, my eyes closed, almost in tears. The doors opened on either side of me and a second later, Ieuan had replaced David. He leaned towards me across the gear shift, wrapped his left arm around my shoulders, and pulled my head into his chest. I tried to breathe deeply. "You told me the truth," I said, stunned. He was from the thirteenth century. *I am in the thirteenth century.*

"He did," David said from his post on the other side of the driver's side door. "I've lived with lies all the years I've been in Wales. For better or for worse, we told you the truth. I thought you believed us."

He strode away from me, clearly angry. Ieuan brought my chin back around with his hand to look at him. "Don't worry about him," he said. "He carries the weight of the world on his shoulders and sometimes feels too alone. I think, in a sense, he was as lost in your world as I was, more so perhaps, because he thought he should understand it."

Together we gazed at David, who stood on the turf wall, staring over the meadow. Ieuan spoke again. "When I asked you to marry me, you didn't think I was serious, did you?"

*Was he right, after all? Was David?* I looked down at my hands.

"So, now do you say 'yes?'" he asked.

*Did I? How could I know?* "Yes," I said.

Ieuan flashed me that fabulous grin and squeezed my shoulders. "Good, because the tide has turned. You're in my world and we have a journey ahead of us. *You* are going to have to trust *me*."

\* \* \* \* \*

We got out of the car. "Where are we?" I asked.

"In England, it looks like," Ieuan said. He climbed onto the turf wall to stand beside David.

"Guys?" I said, to their backs. "What's going on?"

"We're near Offa's Dyke," David said.

I squealed. "Offa's Dyke?" I clamored up next to Ieuan.

Offa's Dyke was a turf wall that ran the full length of the border between the present-day England and Wales, or at least it did in the Middle Ages. Over the centuries, many English rulers had feared the Welsh and felt the need to contain them. The commonly held belief was that the Dyke was built in the eighth century by Offa, the Saxon King of Mercia—before England *was* England.

The Dyke consisted of a rampart twenty-four feet high and twenty feet across, which towered over a ditch on the Welsh side of the border and allowed the English to gaze into Wales from a great height. I followed David's pointing finger, and there it was, less than a mile away.

"We're in the no-man's land between England and Wales," I said.

"And there lies Huntington Castle," David said, pointing northeast.

Ieuan spit on the ground. "Hereford. Again."

"Tell me about Hereford," I said. "Now that we're really here, I need to hear it one more time." I looked from one to the other.

"Huntington belongs to Humphrey de Bohun, the third Earl of Hereford," Ieuan said. "We spoke of him earlier. It could easily be Bohun's heir who leads here, while his sire has bigger fish to fry."

"His heir is only ten, Ieuan, but the wife could command in her husband's absence," David said. "I would like to avoid them all, if possible. Despite my father's recent victories, the Bohuns are lords in this land. Only last month they laid siege to Buellt Castle. My father and the men of Powys drove them away. Bohun also controls Brecon castle, a stronghold in Wales to the west of here, and Caldicot Castle to the south, among others."

"They control all the lands in this region," Ieuan said.

I saw the problem. "Hereford is more than a place and a man," I said. "He's an institution."

"More importantly," Ieuan said. "He'll have patrols throughout the countryside."

David nodded. "I'd say that's one there."

159

To the east of where we stood, a road ran from Huntington Castle heading south, and on it were more than a dozen riders, fortunately not looking our way. David jumped to the ground and trotted back to the car. He popped the trunk, removed his backpack so he could rummage through it. He took out a small, black box. Then, he climbed onto the wall again with a small pair of binoculars in his hand.

"Where did you get those?"

"Uncle Ted," he said.

"Uncle Ted didn't care?" I asked.

David took the binoculars from his eyes and looked at me, his brow furrowed. "Uncle Ted believed my story after a five minute summary over the phone from Aunt Elisa," David said. "I think *he* would have come with us, if I'd asked."

"Somehow I don't think that Aunt Elisa would have been in favor of that," I said.

David laughed. "No, she sees him little enough as it is. He's a political analyst of some sort and is never home. Quite frankly, the only time I've ever seen him take a day off is on Christmas, and that's only because nobody else is working so he can't talk about work. He bought these, Aunt Elisa said, because he lists his hobby as 'bird-watching,' but he has two more expensive pairs that he uses if he ever goes out. Which is rarely."

"What do you see in these 'binoculars'?" a clearly impatient Ieuan asked.

"Riders. They wear Hereford's colors, about twenty of them." David swung his binoculars further south.

"And there are another ten, belonging to the Tosnys."

"The Tosnys hold Castell Paun, or Painscastle as the English called it, which lies on the main road into Wales. The road we can see here leads into it," Ieuan explained.

"Then we'll have to avoid all of them, won't we?" David said. He jumped off the wall. "Okay. Let's move. We need to hide the car and get out of here."

"You would be quite a prize, my lord," Ieuan said, joining David beside the car. "What the English wouldn't give for a chance to get their hands on you, roaming around free in their country."

"I don't know of any Englishmen who will recognize me on sight, not even Hereford. Until our trip to England, I'd never left Wales. Still, as in Scotland, patrols abound. I'm loathe to be caught up in one again." David stowed the binoculars and reached in through the open window of the car to release the brake.

"How is it that Hereford thinks you're dead if he doesn't know what you look like?" I asked.

David grunted, the muscles in his arms bulging as he and Ieuan pushed the car into some bushes. "In my fight with Edward, he tore my surcoat from me. My colors are the red dragon of Wales on white."

"The Welsh flag," I said.

"Close to it, yes," he said, "but not in the Middle Ages. In this time, that flag hasn't been seen since the mid-7th century when Cadwaladr ap Cadwallon was high king."

*That's a little strange.*

"What?" David asked, noticing my furrowed brow.

"Do you know how it became the Welsh flag?"

"No."

"Henry Tudor—Henry VII—flew it when he marched across Wales to Bosworth Field to unseat Richard III from the throne of England," I said. "And do you know why?" I didn't wait for him to answer. "Because Welsh legend says that the man who carries that flag is the redeemer of the Welsh people who will lead them to victory against their enemies. He has a name, too."

"Arthur," Ieuan said.

"Yes indeed," I said. "Arthur."

"You're kidding me," David said.

"You didn't know?" Ieuan asked.

"Of course I didn't know," David said. "You're telling me that since I began flying that banner, everyone has looked at me as if I am the return of this Cadwaladr? Of Arthur?"

Ieuan studied David through a couple of heartbeats. "Yes."

"That's just what I need," David mumbled under his breath. He tossed each of us a sandwich, made sure the rest of the food was in his pack, and then locked the car. He tossed me the keys.

David continued to mutter while he and Ieuan pulled their swords from their sheaths and hacked at some of the nearby branches. "The green blends in well," Ieuan said. "At least in the summer."

Then Ieuan noticed how stiff I was and came over to me. He put his hands on my shoulders and bent down to look in my

162

face. "I don't know what the next hours will bring," he said.
"From this moment on, you need to follow my direction. Your
ability to do so might save your life."

"Obey you," I said.

"Yup." That was David, shooting me an *I told you so* grin.

"Can you?" Ieuan asked, still looking into my eyes.

"Like you obey David?"

The corners of Ieuan's eyes crinkled as he smiled. "Well,
maybe not exactly like that." He threaded his hand through the
hair at the back of my head and kissed me.

When he let go, I staggered back, a little shocked. "Okay.
Fine. I'll obey you," I said.

"Good." Ieuan took my hand and nodded at David. They
checked their weapons, and Ieuan slung his great bow on his back.
David wore the twenty-first century backpack. We climbed over
the turf wall and began to walk.

"Do you have any water in that pack?" I asked.

David pulled a water bottled from a side pocket. "Here," he
said.

"What else do you have in there besides my coffee and the
food?" I asked.

"Lots of stuff," he said, shouldering the pack once again.
"Some things I've missed that I think we can duplicate pretty well,
like a good pair of scissors, and some things we can't, like
medicines. Aunt Elisa and I went to a drugstore after you were in
bed. I couldn't sleep and neither could she. We filled the cart with
everything I thought might come in handy, including fifteen tubes

of antibiotic ointment—we bought out their entire supply, in every brand they had available."

"You have your papers, don't you?" I said.

"Yes, along with some maps of Wales I downloaded from the internet and a detailed geological survey. Wales is rich in minerals; we just have to know where to find them."

David really did have plans for Wales, just as he'd said. "Can I ask where we're going?" I asked.

"You can ask," David said.

"But you're not going to tell me."

"I actually don't know where we're going. My intent is to find a holding where I can buy clothes for all of us. You need a dress, and Ieuan and I need some plainer clothes. Then, we must find some way to cross the border into Wales without the English capturing us."

If I weren't walking across this grass, hand-in-hand with Ieuan, under sunny skies without a power line, airplane, or automobile in sight, I wouldn't have believed it. I stopped. Ieuan, who'd been striding forward, tried to tug me with him, but I dug in my heels.

"This is just so not okay, David," I said. "This can't be real. I can't be in the Middle Ages."

He stopped too and met my eyes, and I could see something in his face that looked like pity. "We can only go forward now, Bronwen. It's too late to turn back. Believe me when I tell you that it's best not to think about it. When we're safe,

I'll get you to my mother and sister who can talk you through this. Right now, I need you to walk."

Looking down, I brushed tears from my cheeks with the back of my hand. I'd thought Tillman had blown my world apart when he denied me a stipend to continue graduate school. *What a laugh. This time, I've blown my own world apart. I've nothing left—no family, no friends, no career, no possessions—beyond these two men and the clothes on my back.* Hiding my face and the tears with my hair, I walked.

# 15

## David

"There, my lord," Ieuan said.

I nodded. We'd been walking for forty minutes, heading south, away from Huntington. The countryside was relatively flat, with meadows and fields to cross and copses of trees here and there. The hills of Wales rose up to our right and I was impatient to lose myself in them.

We crossed a creek, leaping from rock to rock without getting wet, and came through a stand of trees. Then Ieuan spied a small farmhouse, inhabited, as smoke rose through the center of the roof.

"Okay," I said. "You two stay here and I'll attempt to negotiate with whoever is at home."

"Will they speak Welsh?" Bronwen asked.

"Maybe, maybe not. And even if they did I wouldn't risk using it in England. *Aye speeke Englisch*," I said.

"Is that Middle English?" Bronwen asked.

166

"Historically, we are in a time of transition," I said, shrugging. "You'll have to ask my mother if you get a chance. She knows stuff like that."

"How are you going to pay them?" Bronwen said, hitting upon a key point.

"With this," I said, pulling the small sack from my waist in which I stored my coins.

Bronwen looked at me. Her expression clearly said: *idiot!* "Why didn't you produce that gold back at Penn State?"

"I thought the knife more valuable in your world, but the gold more valuable in mine," I said. Bronwen opened her mouth to speak, but I forestalled her. "I knew we'd make it back and then I would need the coins."

Ieuan tugged at her and she allowed herself to be dragged away. It was becoming a trend—Ieuan didn't like her to question me and tried to protect her from me and me from her. I needed to let him know when I got a chance that his concern was needless. I reached the door of the hut, and knocked. A moment later, the door opened.

"What do you want?" The woman who answered asked, looking at me with suspicion. She looked old, though in this era it was often hard to tell how old a person was. Living the kind of life this woman must have led, she could've been forty or sixty. Either way, the lines on her face were pronounced, her hair was grey, and her shoulders hunched, whether permanently, or out of fear of me, I didn't know.

I could understand her apprehension. Her farm wasn't exactly located in an auspicious spot. The land was beautiful, but comprised some of the most fought over territory in England, if not the world. American law, even if imperfectly applied, protected both high and low alike. That wasn't true in the Middle Ages. The common folk were always the ones who got caught in the middle in war. At the same time, they didn't always care who won, as long as they didn't lose their livelihood—or their lives—in the process.

"Madam," I said. "My horse went lame some distance from here. If you have a horse and wagon to sell me, I have gold in exchange."

"Gold! Aren't you fine?" Then her eyes narrowed. "Let me see it."

I showed her one gold coin but didn't let her touch it. It could have been the first coin she'd ever seen. In time of war, gold is the most portable and useful of goods. She weighed her options. I could have taken from her what I wanted by force and she knew it, so I wasn't surprised when she grunted, "I've a cart and a horse."

"I need also need clothes for me and my companions."

"I have few to spare," she said.

"Perhaps you've a neighbor who'd like my money instead," I said. I took a step back from the door.

"No, no!" she stopped me. "I'll take the coin."

I handed it to her and she brought me inside. The hut was as I expected, furnished with a table and two stools, with a cooking pot centered over the fire in the middle of the room. It was hot and stuffy, as she had no windows. She went to an alcove in one corner of the room and dragged a wooden box from the end of the sleeping pallet. Opening it, she removed a small stack of clothes and gave them to me.

"The dress was my daughter's," she said, with a sniff. "She died last year. The others belong to my husband. He won't miss them either."

The woman threw some food in a sack, even though I hadn't asked for it, and gave me a blanket as well. She did have a horse, surprising really, given her poverty, but he was a sad fellow who couldn't be ridden. He came with saddle bags, though no saddle, and was capable of pulling the cart. I thanked the woman, placed the sack in the cart, and clip clopped my way back to where I'd left Ieuan and Bronwen.

Bronwen wrinkled her nose at the clothes and I opted not to tell her that the previous owner had died. "Leave on your t-shirt and jeans," I said. "They're cleaner than these and you might want them for warmth tonight. Put the dress over the top."

Bronwen did and transformed herself into a medieval woman, except for her shoes.

I turned to Ieuan. "She should be barefoot."

"She can't," he said. "She'd never make it."

Bronwen lifted the hem of her dress and all three of us inspected her feet. She wore brown leather slides and matching socks. Anna would have swooned over them.

"All right," I said. Bronwen let go of her hem. "If we see anyone, keep your feet under your skirt and we should be okay."

I shared Bronwen's aversion to the smell of the clothes. We wrapped our weapons and my backpack in the blankets, rolled the fine clothes into a ball, and piled everything in the back of the cart. I rummaged in the pack of food the woman had given me and pulled out a small loaf of bread. Medieval food didn't have preservatives in it and we should eat it before the chips from Aunt Elisa. Ieuan and Bronwen climbed to the seat and I broke the bread and handed Bronwen two-thirds of it. I would walk beside the horse. It was little matter to me, but social strata in England was rigid. Nobody would suspect that I was more than I claimed to be.

* * * * *

We followed a trail south, hoping all the while to find a track leading west into Wales. I wanted to put Huntington Castle behind us as quickly as possible, but the Dyke was a formidable obstacle in this area of Herefordshire, and we couldn't take the cart across it unless there was a road that cut through it. We could have easily walked along the top, but that might call too much attention to us.

My intent was to head directly for Aberedw, my father's castle south of Buellt. He'd held it for many years and Ieuan's holdings were close by. The road rose steadily ahead of us and for a mile was free from soldiers. That didn't last long, however. Our track intersected a larger one, coming southwest from Huntington, just short of the Dyke.

"You there!"

Ieuan stopped the horse and allowed the English soldiers to overtake us. I didn't have to tell Ieuan what to do. His bright eyes watched me for a moment before he looked down in feigned submission. I followed suit, waiting for the soldiers to canter up to us.

"You there!" the lead soldier of four said again. "Out of the way!"

Ieuan obeyed. He twitched the reins and encouraged the horse to pull the cart as far off the road as it could. We held still after that, heads bowed. I kept mine down until the soldier poked me with his lance.

"What say you?" he asked. "Don't you know trouble's coming?"

"My mum is sick," I replied. "We're for Hay-on-Wye."

The soldier grunted. "Mind the river, then," he said. "If you cross it, you may find yourself on the wrong side of a good fight!" Then he laughed and spurred his horse forward, with the rest of the troop of twenty men following.

"Those were Hereford's men," Ieuan said, as the last of the riders passed us.

"Yup," I said. "They were pretty cheerful about the possibility of war, too. What does that tell us?"

Ieuan shrugged. "Nothing good. But nothing we didn't already know."

SARAH WOODBURY

# 16

## *Bronwen*

I exhaled a held breath, my shoulders sagging. I'd never been so scared in my life as when that soldier spoke to David. My heart had thumped so loudly I was afraid everyone could hear it. Ieuan had placed a hand on my thigh, trying to make sure I knew to be quiet. He needn't have worried. I understood only one word in three that the man had said, but was too scared to talk anyway.

"Never fear, *cariad*," Ieuan said as the soldiers rode away. "Prince Dafydd and I kept our knives close. We wouldn't have let them harm you."

David walked to my right foot and looked up at me. "It takes you by surprise, doesn't it?" he asked. "The fear, I mean."

"Yes," I said, pulling my cloak closer around me. The rush of the adrenaline was fading, leaving me exhausted. "And this was nothing."

"Not nothing, Bronwen," David said. "The danger was real. The soldiers could have killed us and taken you for the fun of it with no repercussions."

"That violence is always under the surface, isn't it?" I asked, looking from David to Ieuan. Ieuan put an arm around my shoulder. "I see it in you two. You take it on and off like a cloak."

"It's one of those things you learn to live with," David said. And then to Ieuan he added, "Let's move on, before they come back. I say we cross the Dyke right here and not wait for the road to turn across it. Other soldiers at the crossroads will be watching."

"Peasants would stay on the road," Ieuan said. "They'll expect it."

"Can you see us withstanding a thorough search? You're Welsh, and for all intents and purposes, so is Bronwen. They might just run you through once you open your mouth, rather than bother with questions. I don't want to risk it."

Ieuan examined the country through which we were traveling. We were alone, all sane people who were not soldiers having already hidden themselves in their crofts or retreated to a safer spot. It was very quiet. "Right," Ieuan said. "I've not been here for many years, but my uncle's lands—my lands—are ten miles from here as the crow flies."

"Can you lead us there?" David asked.

"Yes," Ieuan said. "But not with the cart."

"We'll turn this beast around and send him back the way we came," David said. "He helped convince the soldiers we were common folk, but he'll only hinder us from here on."

"We shouldn't, my lord," Ieuan said. "If soldiers see an abandoned cart and horse they'll wonder why."

"Then what do we do?" David asked.

"We hide the cart, as we did Bronwen's car, and bring the horse with us. He can carry our belongings and should have no more trouble walking than we do."

David nodded. "You're right, Ieuan. Let's do it."

I turned on the bench and climbed into the back. I couldn't wait to cross into Wales. "Here," I said, handing Ieuan his sword and quiver. "What shall we do with the clothes?" David had climbed into the back with me, and tied a blanket to disguise his backpack.

"The horse will carry it all," he said. "We'll leave nothing in the cart for anyone to find." Then he grinned wickedly at me. "Your fiancé is a smart man, even if he's a Welsh barbarian."

"Wha—?" I managed, before Ieuan laughed. He put his hands at my waist and lifted me from the cart. I handed him his bow, which I clutched in my hand.

"Should she have a weapon?" David asked him.

Ieuan stiffened, but then looked down at me and nodded. "I would there was no need, but if anything happens to us, I'd prefer she could defend herself." He took a knife from his belt and showed it to me, before tucking it at my waist.

"Show me how you grasp it," he said.

I pulled it from its sheath and held it out like it was a very short sword.

"Not that way," David said. "Reversed. If someone comes at you, hold the knife in your right fist as if to stab, but don't raise it high. You want it down at your side, right arm bent, a little behind you. Keep your left hand out in front, holding your opponent at bay, and then swing the knife up and across to slash him. Your fist should end up to the left of your head. Then you can bring the knife down and to the right to stab him again. You're much stronger that way."

I practiced the motion a few times.

"I wouldn't have thought to teach her thus, my lord," Ieuan said, watching, his brows furrowed.

"Karate again," David said. "In general, a woman is at a disadvantage even with a knife, but this will give her a chance, especially if she can surprise him."

Ieuan took my chin in his hand. "If you have to use the knife, you use it," he said. "Don't hesitate, don't think. You use it and run. Do you understand?"

"Ieuan . . ." David said.

I slipped the knife back into its sheath. "It's okay, David," I said. "I can take it. It isn't as if he isn't right."

"You'll need to have a talk with Math, Ieuan," David said, working on the ties that held the horse to the cart.

"Anna seems biddable enough," Ieuan said.

David rolled his eyes. "Not likely. That's just an act for the benefit of guests. She has opinions about everything and she tells him what they are."

"And he doesn't object?" Ieuan asked. He held one of the handles to the cart that had stuck out to one side of the horse. David handed the horse's lead to me and took the other cart handle. They rolled it forward into a copse of trees to the left of the road.

"He's learned that she's perceptive and smart and things go better if he listens to her," David said. "She's his most trusted adviser because she always tells him the truth and isn't afraid of him. Think of William the Norman and his Matilda. They had that kind of marriage."

David's words faded and were the last I heard, for the men had gone out of earshot. I stood alone with the horse, listening to the silence until my ears rang with it, but then Ieuan hurried back across the road.

"I didn't mean to leave you alone, lass," he said. "It's not safe, not even for a moment."

"I wasn't worried," I said.

"That's only because you don't know better," he said. "You'd be as fine a prize for the English as Prince Dafydd . . . though for different reasons."

"You live with a constant threat of danger, don't you?" I said.

"Yes," said David, coming up behind Ieuan, "but not like this. I'd never set foot in England before last week for that very reason. In Wales, we are surrounded by my men at all times. I can't go anywhere alone, even to a stream to wash."

"You did that once and look what happened," Ieuan said, taking the horse's reins from me.

"What happened?" I asked.

"I was kidnapped by Welshmen, one of whom was a man from my guard," David said. "They meant to sell me to Edward."

"But they didn't succeed," I said. "Obviously, you got away."

"And had to kill two men to do it," David said, starting to walk away.

I looked after him, not moving. Ieuan took my hand and pulled me forward. "He did what he had to do," Ieuan said. "This world is not like yours."

Ieuan's hand warmed mine. I felt cold; the tears from before were gone, but the fear settled in, maybe to stay. Every bush, every hillock could hide some new threat which we would have to counter. *How can they live this way all the time? How am I going to live this way?*

I wasn't allowed to see much of the Dyke, much to my regret. We scurried over it like mice, running up and down again to lose ourselves in the trees on the other side. And that's what I saw mostly: hills and trees. I didn't recognize the kinds of trees, botany never having been my forte, but they were deciduous and green, and many of them would have been great for climbing, if one were so inclined.

"We aren't really in Wales yet," Ieuan explained as we walked along, talking under our breaths in case anyone was close by and listening. "We've at least three miles of open country that Hereford controls before we can breathe more easily."

"And even then," David said, "there's no telling how far into Wales Hereford has sent his patrols. He could be gathering his men behind the Dyke in preparation for a strong offensive, or he could be sending patrols deeper in our territory in an attempt to determine where our weaknesses lie."

"I thought you said that Hereford would have gone to London or wherever Edward II resides at the moment?"

David and Ieuan glanced at each other. *Okay, yes, I'm an idiot . . . again.* David answered. "Look, Bronwen," he said, "when you spoke of Hereford as an institution, you were right. Every great lord has a number of lesser lords who serve him directly, and hundreds of lesser knights and men-at-arms, all of whom have sworn loyalty to him. Any of the lesser lords could command here, and who it is might tell me how to defeat him, but the one pulling the strings would be Hereford."

"This may not even be some hasty campaign, instigated since King Edward's death, Bronwen," Ieuan added. "Hereford knew of the conference in Lancaster long in advance. With Prince Dafydd and Prince Llywelyn distracted in England, Hereford could have been laying his plans for weeks instead of days, preparing for the optimum moment to attack. The only new information from Bohun's point of view is Edward's death, along with the death of many of his rivals."

We moved through the woods, the land rising steadily. Ieuan led, as he knew the area, with me in the middle and David leading our horse, whom I'd dubbed, 'Fred,' so I could stop calling him 'the horse.'

"Will we make Aberedw tonight?" I asked at one point, when we stopped to rest near some scraggly bushes.

Ieuan shook his head. He wasn't really paying attention to me, instead peering through the growth, looking for intruders. "No, it's too far."

"And Painscastle is too close," David said. "My father has hemmed the Tosnys in, but they're still powerful and aligned with Hereford."

"We should seek shelter for the night at the chapel at Bryngwyn," Ieuan said. "It's been a while since I was there, as I've been numbered among the Prince's men since I was fifteen, but the priest is a childhood friend by the name of Merfyn."

"Not English, then?" David asked.

"No. He's Welsh, and for the Welsh. Or at least he was," Ieuan said.

David and Ieuan looked at each other and Ieuan nodded, as if David had spoken. "I'll go alone to scout the area," Ieuan said. "Once we have the chapel in sight, we can hide ourselves and rest until dark."

"We could travel at night," I said. "You said your land was only ten miles away. Surely we can walk that in a few hours." As soon as I spoke, I could tell once again I'd said something idiotic and they were trying to figure out how to tell me so, without insulting me.

"What?" I asked.

"It's about to rain, *cariad*," Ieuan said.

"And when the clouds come in, you will be astounded by how dark it is," David added. "Night is not a time to travel, unless the need is very great."

"Which we hope it's not," Ieuan finished. "I don't want to stumble about in the dark so close to English lands."

"Okay," I said, shrugging. "Whatever you say."

David looked at me closely. "We don't mean to dismiss your ideas. It's a different world we brought you to, with different rules."

"I know it, David, or at least I am beginning to understand," I said, exasperated. "It's fine. I'll catch up eventually."

"Another mile, then," Ieuan said, "and we'll stop." He set off, with us following as before.

A mile is hard work when there's no discernible trail. As far as I could tell, Ieuan maneuvered entirely by dead reckoning. It was up this hill, around another, through this stand of trees, along that creek for five minutes, across it, getting our feet wet, and then up a hill again. A mile turned out to be more than an hour's journey, with the darkness overtaking us before we stopped again.

I crouched with the men in a ditch on the edge of a field, abutting the church lands. The church was a pretty thing, made of whitish stones, with a real roof, not just thatch. The priest's house stood off to one side. It was of simple construction, like the farmhouse we'd found in England: wattle and daub walls and a thatched roof.

"I'll be back," Ieuan said. He headed toward the house, skirting the church and keeping to the trees until he could approach it directly.

"Do you think this will be okay?" I asked David as we waited, a few raindrops beginning to plop on the ground around us.

"If Ieuan thinks so, then so do I. I don't know these lands and my father's rule has only occasionally extended this far. The people here have been under the English thumb for two hundred years. Many have forgotten who they are."

After fifteen minutes, Ieuan returned, circling around to us again. "I think it's safe," Ieuan said. "One of us must still watch through the night, but I believe him to be the friend I remembered."

"Let's hope so," David said.

"I told him that you were another knight in the Prince's company, and . . ." Ieuan paused and looked at me. "I told him you were my bride."

"Quite an assumption you're making there, aren't you?" I teased.

"It's better this way," David said. "You shouldn't be traveling with us unless you're a wife or a sister."

We approached the door of the hut and it opened to reveal a short, scruffy man in his twenties, with a full beard. He held up a lit candle so he could see us better. Ieuan and David towered over him, so he had some difficulty, but I was just his height and his eyes met mine. His widened when I stepped forward into the light, and I touched my hand to my hair, suddenly afraid that we'd gotten it wrong.

But no. As he ushered me past him, I heard him say under his breath to Ieuan, "You have done well for yourself, old friend, but why did you bring her out here in her condition?"

My shoulders must have jerked at his words, because David's hand pressed on the small of my back, pushing me forward, while he whispered in my ear. "Just go with it, Bronwen," he said. "Merfyn need not know any more about us than this."

I glanced back and wrinkled my nose at Ieuan, who grinned from behind his friend. *Great! Not only married but pregnant too! What else has he told Merfyn? But then, maybe I don't want to know . . .*

We huddled in Merfyn's house as the rain pounded on the roof. Leaks formed in the thatch, which Ieuan assured me was unusual and meant that either Merfyn hadn't been taking care of his home, or his parishioners hadn't been taking care of him. I rested beside Ieuan on a bench while Dafydd and Merfyn sat on stools around the fire that sputtered and guttered in the middle of the room. We'd eaten the rest of the bread and some cheese from the farmhouse, supplemented by roasted meat that Merfyn shared, along with a jug of mead (a honey wine). We didn't dare get out Aunt Elisa's cookies. The rain fell so heavily that it came through the hole in the roof for the smoke.

"Tell us a tale, then?" Ieuan prompted Merfyn.

"Oh, aye," Merfyn said. He didn't say anything right away, however, and I wondered if he'd fallen asleep or forgotten the question. Ieuan made a motion as if to prompt him again, and then Merfyn began:

> *When Arthur ruled*
> *The people of Cymry*
> *Possessed wealth and peace*
> *Before their sovereign king.*
> *The people of Cymry*
> *Found tranquility at his table.*
> *But what is this?*
> *Commotion in every land.*
> *The men who ride at Arthur's side:*
> *Cai, Bedwyr, Ieuan, Rhys, Gruffydd.*
> *They ride towards us,*
> *Riding out of tales*
> *From another age.*
> *Strapping their swords to their waists,*
> *Setting their pikes in their rests,*
> *Spurring forward,*
> *Protectors of a ravaged country.*
> *When Arthur passed*

# PRINCE OF TIME

*Into Avalon,*

*The Cymry lost their bounty,*

*Choosing alliance with their enemies.*

*The ambitious man raised his head,*

*The jealous man rose from his knees,*

*The righteous man lifted his hands in prayer,*

*Begging for deliverance.*

*Our enemies ride against us*

*To lay waste to our lands*

*And to ruin Gwynedd,*

*Powys,*

*Debeuharth,*

*To demand our pledge*

*in trade for peace.*

*The people of Cymry*

*Live as slaves*

*Until the day*

*Ynys Afallach,*

*the realm of Avalon,*

*Awakens Arthur in his mountain.*

*He will come,*

*No longer hiding,*

*The dragon banner raised high,*

*Submitting to no one,*

*Whether Saxon or Norman.*

*The land will be red*

*With battle and strife.*

*None will stand against him.*
*All will fall to their knees before him.*
*The Cymry will rise,*
*When Arthur returns.*


Entranced, I hardly noticed when he finished. The song ran like one of the poem's of Taliesin, a sixth century bard who many have confused with Merlin. David had his head up and was studying Merfyn.

"Where did you hear that?" he asked.

"In the north, this past spring," he said.

David shook his head. "Don't sing it again." He stood and went to the door, looking out at the rain, as the fire crackled and sputtered behind him and we stared after him.

# 17

## *Ieuan*

**I** awoke from a pleasant dream, my arm wrapped around Bronwen for warmth. It had been a long time since I'd slept with any woman. I'd enjoyed wrapping her up in my cloak with me, even if six layers of clothing separated us. I'm not sure how much she enjoyed it, as she was still angry with me for telling Merfyn we were wed and expecting a child. I confess, the notion wasn't the least bit unpleasant to me.

I turned my head at movement near the door. Dafydd stood in the open door, his back to me. The rain had stopped and the moon was out, playing hide and seek with the clouds. It was brighter outside than in because the fire had gone out. At least it was August, and we weren't cold.

"Merfyn's gone," Dafydd said.

"Did you see where?" I said, hoping it was simply to relieve himself.

"I feigned sleep for a time because I didn't trust him, and he took advantage of my supposed inattention to slip out. I heard him in the stables and then he disappeared."

"How long has he been gone?" I asked.

"Ten minutes; no more. I would have shaken you awake in another minute. I've been listening."

"And what have you heard?" I asked, getting to my feet and joining him at the door.

"Listen," he said.

I listened, but there was nothing to hear, which didn't bode well for us. We should've heard something, whether birds, the movement of animals, or other small noises of the night. Instead, only a slight breeze blew through the trees around the hut.

"I'll get Bronwen," I said.

Leaving Dafydd, I placed my hand gently on her mouth and shook her awake. She awoke with a start, eyes wide, but then relaxed when at my "it's me." I took my hand away.

"What's happening?" she asked.

"We need to leave, now," I said. "Merfyn has disappeared and Prince Dafydd and I are worried about where he might have gone."

"I thought you trusted him," she said.

"I did. Come." I helped her to her feet and we rolled the blankets back into a bundle and joined Dafydd at the door.

"The horse is gone," he said, when I reached him.

"No question, then," I said. "Merfyn has betrayed us."

"Maybe," Dafydd said. "It's also possible he had no choice."

"There's always a choice," I said.

Bronwen slipped her hand into mine and I squeezed it. If ever there was a moment to regret bringing her, this was it. Somehow, I couldn't.

"What now?" she asked.

"Back across the road to the ditch," I said. "If we make it alive, we'll try for Aberedw."

"Whatever happens," Dafydd said, "you two stay together. If we get separated, we will meet there."

"My lord . . ." I said.

Dafydd gripped my arm. "Just a precaution, Ieuan. We can't know what will happen."

I nodded. "Let's go."

In single file, we ducked back into the hut and through the door that separated the human quarters from the stables, and then hurried across the floor to the far side of the building. Dafydd peered through a crack in the wall.

"Anything?" I asked him.

"Not that I can see," he said.

"I should go first," I said.

"You've got the bow," Dafydd said. "I'll go first. If someone shoots at me, you can cover the rest of my advance. Once I reach the trees, I can circle through the woods until I find them."

"I don't like it, my lord," I said.

"Why can't we stay here?" Bronwen asked. "We could hold them off until morning, surely."

"An idea, but not our best option right now," I said, regretfully rejecting yet another of her ideas.

"I'm only a burden," she said. "I hate that."

"We're not dead yet," David said. He glanced at me. "Ready?"

"Ready, my lord," I said. I moved out the doorway and stood to one side, but still in the shadow of the roof. Bronwen crouched on the ground beside me, out of the way. I brought my bow up and knocked an arrow. I could press and loose at least ten arrows in a minute. I hoped that would be quick enough.

"All right, then," Dafydd said, and was gone, running in a crouch across the grass in a zigzag pattern. If he'd not been moving, I would've lost him immediately. He stirred the air, however, and I tracked him that way. Unfortunately, someone in the woods did too.

*Thwtt!* An arrow hit the ground somewhere in front of us. There was no accompanying grunt from Dafydd, so he wasn't hit. I couldn't tell precisely from where the arrow had come, but loosed three arrows in the general direction anyway, hoping to keep the archer honest. One thudded into a tree on the other side of the field.

I listened to the night. A man shouted in English. Then Dafydd gave a call. He claimed it was a barking dog, but it always sounded like a dying pig to me. "That's the prince," I said. "He's telling us to come to him."

I grabbed Bronwen's arm and together we ran along the path my lord had taken. Twenty heart beats later, we entered the trees. Dafydd slipped out of the shadows.

"Are you all right?" I asked.

"Yes," he said.

I tried to read his face, but couldn't make out his expression in the dark.

"How many?" I asked.

"None, now." He touched my shoulder as he passed me, and I pulled on Bronwen to follow.

"What did he mean?" she asked.

"He killed them; that's all," I said.

Bronwen shuddered, but she didn't speak again, not even when we discovered 'Fred', a quarter of a mile on, cropping the grass in a clearing near a stream.

"It would've been a shame to lose my pack after coming this far," Dafydd said. No one had disturbed the bags and Dafydd tugged Fred's reins. The horse followed us, his feet thudding gently on the moss-covered trail. The sky had begun to lighten when I stopped.

"We're less than three miles from Twyn y Garth, my home," I said. "I've led you more south than I realized. These are my lands."

"Is there a safe place to rest?" Dafydd asked, hollow-eyed.

"There's a cave a little ways in front of us," I said. "Lili and I discovered it when we were children. It's probably smaller than I remember, but it will hold us all easily, even Fred."

"Good," Dafydd said. "Lead on. Bronwen can barely put one foot in front of the other."

My lord was right. She looked at me, and tried to smile, but her heart wasn't in it. "I'm fine, Ieuan. We can rest if you want, but I can walk another mile or two if you need me to."

I shook my head. "The cave is just ahead," I said.

I led them to the opening, and pulled aside two branches that had grown across the entrance. Dafydd and Bronwen ducked inside and I was about to pull Fred in after me, when Dafydd shouted. Dropping Fred's reins, I bounded into the cave behind Bronwen. Dafydd had his hands up and was standing in front of a young boy, who held Dafydd at bay with a knife. I froze, took a moment to take in what I was seeing, and then laughed. I stepped in front of Dafydd and pushed the knife away.

"Prince Dafydd ap Llywelyn," I said, "may I introduce to you my sister Lili. Lili, this is your Prince."

"Ieuan!" Lili dropped the knife and launched herself at me. She wrapped her arms tightly about by neck, like she used to when she was little and scared. This time, however, she held onto me for only a second, before she loosened her grip and wiggled out of my grasp. She stepped back, and though her face was whiter than usual, her eyes were clear. She looked from me to Prince Dafydd, and then she curtsied.

"I apologize, my lord, for my initial greeting," she said. "I feared you were English."

PRINCE OF TIME

"No apologies necessary, my lady," Dafydd replied, bowing. "Your behavior was completely understandable under the circumstances. I would want my sister to do as you did."

"But why are you here?" I asked. I waved a hand at her. "Dressed like that?"

"I was practicing, if you must know," Lili said.

"Practicing what?"

"The bow, as you yourself taught me," she said.

"Alone?"

"I'm not stupid," Lili said, her own voice rising. "Geraint accompanied me to the butts yesterday evening and I dressed as a boy so as to not call attention to myself."

The English are everywhere," I said.

"I *know* that, Ieuan," Lili said. "Three of them came upon us unexpectedly yesterday evening."

"By all that is holy, Lili, tell me what happened!"

"Geraint went down with an arrow in his throat," Lili said, a hitch in her voice. "I loosed an arrow at one of the soldiers. It hit him and he too went down, but by then I'd turned to run. I lost them among the trees. I couldn't risk returning to Twyn y Garth alone, so I came here."

In one stride, I caught her in my arms again.

# 18

## *David*

Ieuan was squeezing Lili so hard, it was a wonder she could even breathe. Lili said something, but it was muffled in Ieuan's cloak.

"What?" he asked, releasing her.

"I'm fine now," she said, taking a step back. "Spending the night alone in this cave is not something I ever want to repeat, but I survived it. The only demons here were my own. At the moment, I'm just sorry about Geraint, and anxious about what the English are planning."

"As are we," I said.

Lili turned to me, her chin jutting out stubbornly, perhaps fearing criticism from me as well Ieuan. Despite her clothing, I'd not been fooled for more than a second into thinking she was a boy. She'd braided her hair in a long plait down her back, which wasn't unheard of among men, but rare. If we were in the twenty-first century, I wouldn't have mistaken her for a boy at all. Like Ieuan, she had nearly black hair, but her features were finer and she was small and lithe, like a gymnast or a dancer. I was having a hard time imagining her pressing an arrow into any bow, much less the one across her back, which had to be as tall as she was.

Ieuan had a hand on Bronwen's arm and tugged her forward. "This is Bronwen," he said, "my betrothed."

Bronwen appeared to be recovering. I didn't know if she'd been so quiet during the night because she was afraid, upset, or angry—or a combination of all three. That I'd killed three men without appearing to think twice about it had shaken her. The key word, of course, was *appearing*.

I had worried about her as we trudged through the woods in the dark. She'd not spoken more than two words in hours. Ieuan hadn't seemed to notice that anything was amiss, but it was out of character for Bronwen, and I'd waited for her to either rage at us or fall apart. At the same time, I was proud of her for holding it in, and for doing neither.

Now, as Ieuan introduced Bronwen to his sister, Lili stepped forward and embraced her. "Ieuan has told me nothing of you!" she said, smiling. "I'm so happy you're here, even if under somewhat trying circumstances."

"It has all been rather sudden," Bronwen said, returning Lili's hug. "I've so many questions for you."

"Oh no," Ieuan said, stepping between them. "Not now; maybe not ever."

The two women gazed at each other with one of those looks that sends men running. Ieuan could be in trouble very, very soon. I turned to him.

"What now, Ieuan," I asked. "Are we safe here?"

He glanced at Lili, and she answered. "Twyn y Garth should be safe," she said. "Your man Dogfael is capable. He would have secured the defenses whether or not I'd returned. I hope we didn't lose any more men in search of me."

"Did you see any other English on your way here?" Ieuan asked.

"No." She shook her head.

"Lili saw three; we saw three more. That sounds like patrols," I said.

"Looking for what?" Bronwen asked.

"Perhaps they seek Prince Llywelyn's army," Lili answered her. "It's no secret that the Prince has spent the summer in the south. Last I heard he was at Buellt, less than ten miles from Twyn y Garth."

"Hereford has plans, and once again, we are in the center of it," Ieuan said.

"Hereford!" Lili said, and I wouldn't have been surprised had she spat on the ground. "The English I encountered weren't wearing his colors."

"Nor were the ones we saw at Bryngwyn, come to think of it," I said. "Admittedly it was dark, and I didn't linger."

"I thought Hereford was in the north, anyway." Lili said after a pause.

"He was," Ieuan said shortly, "though from what we saw before we crossed into Wales, his men are not."

Lili nodded, but her brow furrowed. "I thought you were in the north too! The council with Edward was set to begin only a week ago! How is it that you are here? Did all not go well?"

"Not exactly," I said, "or at least, it didn't go well for King Edward. He is dead."

Lili blinked. "That is news indeed and the first that has reached us here."

"I wonder if my father knows?" I said.

"How did he die?"

"Poison," Ieuan said, "though this information is for your ears alone. We'll explain more another time. Our first concern right now is finding safety for you and Bronwen."

"I can take care of myself, Ieuan," Lili said.

"But I can't," Bronwen said, flatly. "I've learned that in the last twenty-four hours. I wish I could say differently, but I don't know how to use either a bow or a sword, and without either, I'm only a burden."

"I thought we determined that wasn't true," Ieuan said. "Everyone has different skills. Yours do not include warfare for which I, for one, am grateful."

"What do you propose?" Lili asked. "I should go home, for everyone will be worried about me."

"We will go to Twyn y Garth, if you are agreeable, my lord," Ieuan said. "I'd like to confer with my men and ensure that all is well there."

"I agree," I said. "The road leads from there to Aberedw and then Buellt and I have a burning need to see my father."

Ieuan moved to the cave entrance and poked out his head. "The sun is fully up," he said. "Now is the time to move, in case the English are early risers too."

Ieuan led the way out of the cave. I'd forgotten that we'd come there to rest, but we'd stood talking for so long that we'd lost our chance.

Lili made almost no noise as she walked. Ieuan had obviously taught her well, and then she must have practiced what he'd taught. She held her bow in her left hand, and her quiver bobbed up and down on her back. I had my sword out, prepared as I could be for whatever we might encounter.

We threaded our way along a trail that was barely evident to me, but Ieuan managed confidently. We stayed within the wood for at least a mile before coming upon the River Wye. Our path to Twyn y Garth led south, and Ieuan took it, following the course of the river. To reach Aberedw, we would have turned north.

Fifteen minutes later, Ieuan held up his hand. "My lord!" he whispered, and gestured that I should come forward. I handed Fred's reins to Lili, and brushed past her to crouch beside Ieuan. A hill with a fort on it rose before us, a hundred feet above the river and surrounded by a defensive ring work. English soldiers camped to the east and south of the fort's walls.

"Why are they here?" asked Ieuan.

"Your castle commands in a beautifully defensible position," I said.

"That might be why they want it, but is also why they'll never take it," Ieuan said. "Not for weeks."

"Maybe they think they have weeks," I said. "If Hereford intends to challenge my father openly, then he knows my father won't have the men to relieve Twyn y Garth."

"What's happening?" Lili had tied Fred to a tree and had pushed her way forward. She stopped. "Those are Clifford's men."

"It was the Clifford heir at Bronllys," I said. "We took his castle. Is he here for revenge?"

"He can only be here at Hereford's bidding," Ieuan said.

I glared at the English soldiers, sick of seeing them in my way all the time. "So we must turn north and find my father," I said. "First Aberedw, and if he's not there, Buellt."

"I assumed you would be safe once we reached Wales, my lord," said Ieuan. "This is worse than Scotland."

"Not quite," I said. "Not as long as we remain free."

We didn't bother to look any closer, but turned back the way we'd come and headed north along the river to Aberedw. The four miles took us nearly three hours, as we were careful about the noise we made and the terrain was difficult. By the time we reached Aberedw, a larger castle than Twyn y Garth, but not set as high above the countryside, Ieuan's shoulders revealed his tension at the effort of keeping quiet, and keeping us safe. No more important people existed in his world than the three of us, and it showed.

This time we crouched in a thicket to the south and east of Aberedw castle, and perused the distance across the field to the gatehouse. The tower high above still flew the four lions of Gwynedd and the bustle in and out the entrance looked normal to me. A man with a wagon loaded with oddments entered through the open portcullis. The driver tipped his hat to the guardhouse soldier who barely looked at him as he waved him through.

"Right," Ieuan said. "I'll go ahead. You three stay here."

"If you go alone," Lili said, "you will have no one to watch your back. We are both known here. I will come with you."

"No, Lili," Ieuan said. "I won't risk you if the castle is not as it seems."

"Lili is right, Ieuan," Bronwen said. "You shouldn't go alone, but I should come with you, as I'm the most expendable of all of you."

"No," the three of us said in unison.

"I will go with you," I said. "You cannot gainsay me, Ieuan. If all is well, Lili and Bronwen will be alone for only a few minutes, and if all is not well, they're far safer outside the castle than within it."

Ieuan nodded, forced to accept my logic. We stepped out from the screen of bushes that hid us from the castle. We had nearly three hundred feet of space between us and the castle and crossing it felt like walking to the gallows. We passed the ditch that cut around the edge of the mound, and crossed the wooden bridge that led to the gatehouse. The portcullis was up. The soldiers on the battlements watched us the whole way without a challenge and allowed us to enter the castle.

"Lord Ieuan!" A man crossed the bailey at a trot to intercept us. "It's an honor to have you with us, my lord." He and Ieuan grasped forearms and Ieuan gestured to me. "Cadoc ap Morgan, this is . . ."

"—Dafydd ap Bran, my lord," I interrupted, before Ieuan could give my real name. There was no reason for me not to admit who I was, except that the English had surrounded Twyn y Garth, and there was no sign of worry or heightened defenses here. *Why?* "I'm one of Prince Llywelyn's men," I added.

"I'm glad you're here," Cadoc said, and gestured that we should come with him. "I have food and drink for you, and I would have your news of the Prince."

We followed Cadoc as he led us up the stairway into the wood and stone keep that dominated the courtyard. The entrance to the keep was one floor above the ground, and we'd not gone three paces inside the hall when we discovered why Cadoc didn't fear the English. The door slammed shut behind us, our host spun on his heel, his sword in his hand, and a smile lit his face. Neither Ieuan nor I were able to pull our swords half out of their sheaths in time to counter him.

"Gently, sirs," Cadoc said. "We can't have that, can we?"

"What is this, Cadoc?" Ieuan asked. "You're a traitor, now?"

"One man's traitor is another man's patriot, young man, though I have to admit that the English gold went a long way in determining my loyalties." He laughed, as did the dozen men who surrounded us.

"Do you mean to kill us?" Ieuan asked.

I wanted to kick him—*thanks for reminding the man!*

But Cadoc laughed. "I don't see why. A few more days and there'll be no need. I will have my reinforcements, Prince Llywelyn will be dead—along with his son—and Edward will be ruler of Wales."

"What are you saying?" Ieuan asked.

"Edward intends to put an end to Llywelyn's bastard in Lancaster, if he's not done so already, and even now Prince Llywelyn lies ill with a fever from a wound he received at Buellt, and from which one of his men assures me he will not recover."

"Which one of his men?" I asked, forcing out the words even as they choked me. "Who?"

"Tudur," the man sneered. "It is always those we trust most that are most likely to betray us. That's why I don't trust anyone—perhaps not even myself." Cadoc laughed again, and gestured for his men to take us away. With our arms screwed up behind our backs, we stumbled between the men. They forced us down a stairway to a room near the kitchens that must normally have been used for storage. They stripped us of our weapons and closed the door behind us.

Ieuan and I gazed at each other across the small, dark space. "I suppose we can't count on little Thomas to set us free, can we?" Ieuan said.

"And no help from Buellt, even if they knew Tudur stands against us."

I stared at the wall, which I could see only dimly in the light coming through the bottom of the door. Tudur was the grandson of Ednyfed Fychan, seneschal to Llywelyn the Great. In his late twenties, he owned estates near Aber and on Anglesey, and was one of the wealthiest landowners in Gwynedd.

Ieuan pushed on the door, shoving his shoulder into it, and when it didn't give, began to pace about the room. As in Carlisle, we were well contained—better contained, actually, because we couldn't kick down these walls. The stone floor and wooden walls were much thicker than at Carlisle. I leaned against the far wall and watched him.

"What next, do you think?"

Before Ieuan could answer, the door opened, revealing three men. One of them, an older fellow with the full mustache typical of a Welshman, gestured to me. "Come," he said.

Ieuan started forward, but one of the men transferred his sword to his left hand and shot a fist to Ieuan's jaw. Ieuan fell sideways, striking his head on the wall as he went down. I crouched beside him and grasped his hand. "Ieuan," I said.

"Go," he said. "I'm well enough." He put a hand to the side of his head and came away with blood. Our eyes met, and I nodded, glad to see his eyes were clear, and released him. I followed the old soldier out of the room, knowing without them saying a word that Ieuan was a hostage to my good behavior.

\* \* \* \* \*

The men led me up two flights of stairs into Cadoc's study. I surveyed the room. It was light and airy, with a desk and bed, and a beautiful blue and red tapestry on the wall between the windows. They sat me in a wooden chair and pinioned my arms behind my back.

"Well, Dafydd ap Bran. I'm so glad you and Sir Ieuan decided to join us today," Cadoc said. He smiled at me, as if I were a friend meeting him for afternoon tea instead of his prisoner. He walked around his desk, slipping a glove on his right hand as he did so. "I have a few questions for you. I thought perhaps you might be more willing to answer them than Sir Ieuan."

Before he asked any questions, however, he backhanded me across the face. I tasted blood on my lip, but the soldiers prevented me from moving my arms, so I sat there, the blood dripping down my chin.

"Why are you here?"

I didn't answer immediately, and Cadoc didn't wait another second for me to try. He hit me again; my head spun.

"We . . .we were . . . ." I stumbled over the words as I tried to clear my thoughts and think of what to say.

"You hit him too hard, my lord," one of the soldiers said. "He cannot think."

"I'll give him a minute, then," Cadoc said, and leaned against his desk, his arms folded across his chest. "Try again, boy, and I'll see if I like your answer."

"We came from Twyn y Garth, Lord Ieuan's castle," I said. "He was hoping to visit his sister there, but the castle is surrounded by English. We traveled here in hopes of finding men to relieve it."

Cadoc studied me. My eyes ran tears and his shape was a blur through them.

*Thwack!*

"There is more, surely. Where are your horses? Your men?" he asked. "I have my soldiers scouring the forest but so far they've found no one. Where have you hidden Prince Llywelyn's men?"

*Thwack!*

*O God. Bronwen. Lili.*

*Thwack!*

"Speak!"

I didn't have the mental stability to speak by then, even if I wanted to. I fell forward in the chair, and the last words I heard before my eyes darkened were from one of Cadoc's soldiers.

"Where shall we put him, my lord," he asked, "until he wakes up and you can try again . . ."

*She is standing on the battlements, looking for her son. I've been watching her for a mile now, the entire time we've ridden, more slowly than perhaps we could have, up the road to the castle. I look up at her and our eyes meet. She knows the truth. He has not come.*

*I've spent the last four days between desolation and jubilation. My lord is alive, but yet he is not. When Aaron and I stood at the edge of the cliff, I understood how close to death the prince and Ieuan were. If the* choice was between traveling to his foreign land and death, then I understand why he jumped. But part of me cannot forgive him for leaving me with the uncertainty.

And what do I tell his mother?

"The truth," Aaron says, as we ride under through the gatehouse and into the courtyard of Dinas Bran.

Math and Marged gather at my stirrup. Math grasps my horse's bit to steady him as I dismount. He knows I must see to my men, but the impatience in his eyes cannot wait. Aaron and I follow Math into the keep. Marged hurries ahead to Anna who stands at the top of the stairs, Cadell cradled in her arms. I cannot meet her eyes either.

A servant brings meat and wine and Math dismisses her with a wave. He settles Anna into her cushioned chair, and then Marged. He finally seats himself, leaving Aaron and me standing. The symbolism is not lost on me. Unless I can explain Dafydd's absence, he will have my head.

It is Aaron who speaks. "He has gone to your land, Marged," he says. "We saw him jump."

At his words, all three lean forward, their eyes wide. "Gone back?" Anna asks. "You are sure?"

"As sure as we can be, my lady," I say. "Ieuan had taken an arrow in his side, and your brother threw him over his shoulder and jumped off a cliff. We saw them vanish."

"And the men?" Math asks.

"All of us saw him vanish," I say. "Like me, they've spent the past days in an agony of anticipation and despair."

"What are they saying?" Marged asks.

"They do not say witchcraft, at least," Aaron says. "They've been with him too long for that."

"All he needs is a magic sword, and they will call him 'Arthur' openly," I say. "The Prince borrowed Cadwallon's sword before he rode away from us, and now Cadwallon cradles Dafydd's sword in his arms as if it's a holy relic. The countryside already tells stories about him, but now his own men create them. It started with the vehicle you brought to this country . . . then the banner he carries . . . now this . . . no one will be able to contain the stories now."

* * * * *

. . .the scene shifts and I stand behind my queen, Marged, as she lays out her possessions that Aaron brought, one by one. She weeps and I know her well enough by now to realize how rarely she allows herself her tears.

"Excuse me, madam," I say, starting to back out of the room.

"No, stay, Bevyn," she says. "You of all people may stay."

*I gaze at the items, and cannot begin to discern what most of them are. The red bag rests to one side, empty. Aaron sits in a chair in the corner of the room. He has retreated inside himself. Perhaps he thinks Dafydd's absence is his fault. Perhaps it is.*

*Marged turns. Tears glisten on her cheeks, but her eyes are clear as she looks at me.*

*"My lady," I say, uncertain and uncomfortable with her vulnerability. I wish the Prince were here instead of me.*

*"You were with him in Lancaster," she says. "You know what mood he was in when he sailed from Poulton. Tell me, will he come back to us?"*

*I am astonished that she would need to ask, and then upon reflection, perhaps less so. A mother's fears are not always well-defined, but she should know her son better than that.*

*"He will come back, my lady," I say, and suddenly I am sure of it myself. "He will come back, if he can."*

# 19

## *Bronwen*

Lili and I had watched the patrols come out of Aberedw for longer than we should have, still waiting for Ieuan and David to return.

"They're not coming," I finally said. "Something's wrong."

"I know it," she said. "I knew this wasn't a good idea. Why didn't I say something?" She'd been worrying at her lip, which was chapped, and a spot of blood appeared where she'd bit it. It was her only outward sign of concern, but I felt a warmth for her to see it.

My initial impression of a waif-like nymph had given way to admiration for her grit. She was small but sturdy, and I figured I was about to be grateful for that. I was older than she, but useless and lost, and here she was, fifteen, and the burden of our quest lay entirely on her shoulders.

"Would Ieuan have listened?" I asked. He and David had listened to me every time I'd offered a course of action, but had never taken any of my suggestions.

"Yes," she said. "He's learned to trust my intuition."

I eyed her and Lili stopped in the act of backing out of the bushes in which we'd been hiding. She dropped her head to look down at her feet. "And why didn't I say anything this time, you ask? Because I feared Prince Dafydd would think me foolish."

She turned from me, grasped Fred's reins, and tugged him along with her. I followed and we walked quickly up the trail down which we'd come earlier that morning. Her confession made me feel awkward, uncertain of what to say—*Did she think this was her fault? If she did, she was worse than David!*—so I changed the subject.

"What do we do now?" I asked.

"First, we find a place to hide the pack off this horse. It hinders us. I gather it contains valuable items or you wouldn't have brought it this far?"

"Prince Dafydd needs what's in it," I said.

"Then we'll keep them safe for him," she said, "somewhere."

We walked another hundred yards, with Lili veering off the path every twenty feet to check a rock or bush. At one point, she crouched by the river and dug up a plant. She broke off the root, wrapped it and some leaves in a cloth, and stuffed it into a pocket at her waist.

"What is that?" I asked.

"Hemlock," she said. "We may need it."

*Dear God.* I didn't question her further however, not sure I wanted to know what I was getting into. Finally, after some more forays off the trail, Lili found something else she was looking for: a bush, fronting a rock, under which an animal had lain, but abandoned. She went to Fred and unbuckled the pack. It fell heavily to the ground.

"What is this?" she asked, stopping in surprise. David's navy blue backpack had come out of its bundle.

"As I said, it's Prince Dafydd's," I said. Lili stood still, looking at the pack, and then at me. I didn't waste time but knelt beside the back and unzipped the pockets, quickly going through them for anything that I should take with me immediately. I grabbed two pieces of beef jerky and one of the four small baggies of coffee at the bottom of the main compartment, underneath David's sheaf of papers. I lifted up my skirt to stuff them into the back pocket of my jeans, so desperate at this point I was almost ready to pour the coffee grains down my throat. Then, in one of the backpack's front zipper pockets, I discovered Ieuan's antibiotics.

*Damn that man—he hasn't been taking them!* There were at least twenty left. For good measure, I took an antibiotic tube too, in case his wound had opened again. I made to slip them into my jeans as well, but Lili stopped me, grabbing them from my hand.

"What is this?" she asked. "What is the writing on this? Where did you get it?" She narrowed her eyes at me. "Who are you really?"

"I am your brother's betrothed, and we don't have time to discuss this. The English are coming and I think you have a plan for getting Ieuan and the Prince out of Aberedw?"

"I do," she said. "But . . ." she paused, looking again at the pills in one hand, the tube in the other, and then back at me. "These are from the land of Madoc, aren't they? Ieuan told me all about it when I saw him last."

"Lili," I began.

"Are you from the land of Madoc?" she asked.

"Lili," I tried again.

"Don't try to deny it! I saw the clothing you wear under your dress, and this pack, and this vial." She held up the pills.

"These items are the Prince's, yes, and yes, they come from the land of Madoc. Can we talk about this later?" I grabbed the pills and stuffed them into my pocket. "Shouldn't we hurry?"

Lili seemed to shake herself. "Yes," she said. She shoved the pack and blankets under the rock and spread the bush back on top. We threw handfuls of fallen leaves around the space and backed out of the area to the trail.

"Can you remember the place?" I asked.

Lili gave me a withering look. "Of course," she said.

She tugged Fred's reins and we walked another half a mile until Lili turned east, off the trail. I plodded along beside her, feeling more and more exhausted with every step. My feet hurt, my head hurt (undoubtedly lack of coffee), I was thirsty despite sharing the last of the water in David's pack with Lili before we left it, and I figured if I sat down I would never stand again. I was *not* used to this much physical activity, especially on half rations and little sleep.

We left the woods and crossed several open fields before reaching a thatched hut. An old man in a faded brown jacket and a hat pulled over his eyes stood in the yard, hitching a horse to a wagon full of hay.

"Hello, Lili," he said as we approached him. "What are you doing out with so many English about?"

"English soldiers have passed by here?" she asked.

"A dozen or so," he said. "They didn't bother me, for they were moving fast and not interested in razing the countryside, or setting fire to it, just yet. A good thing too, with a barn full of crop for the winter."

"My guess is that you're delivering that hay to Aberedw," Lili said.

"You guess right, luv," the man said. "What of it?"

"Give us a ride?" she asked.

The old man surveyed us, and I saw intelligence in his blue eyes, even as they crinkled at me from under his hat. "Introduce me to your friend and I'll consider it," he said, and winked.

Lili smiled. "This is Bronwen ferch . . "

"Llywelyn," I supplied. Then stopped, afraid I'd made a mistake, but the old man smiled and nodded.

"The name's Cawrdaf, but you can call me Daffy. Everyone else does."

"Thank you, Daffy," I said.

"What about your horse, there," Daffy said. "You want to bring him along?"

"I thought I'd leave him with you, in exchange for the ride," Lili said.

Daffy studied Lili, his head canted to one side. "You in some kind of trouble, girl?" he asked. "Something old Daffy ought to know about?"

"A little," Lili admitted, "but none that should involve you. We just want a ride to Aberedw. I'll help unload your hay in the stables and you can be on your way."

"Humph," Daffy said. "Don't know what I think of that. I gather you don't want it known you're a daughter of the manor, so to speak?"

"No, Daffy." Lili looked down at her jerkin and trews. "I think it best if I stay a farm boy."

Daffy nodded, still not convinced, but put Fred in his barn. After a minute, he returned and climbed onto the wagon seat. Lili stuffed her quiver and bow into the hay and we climbed into the wagon to sit at the back, our feet dangling over the edge. We jerked forward. The road unfolded behind us, rough and uneven, with deeply rutted wagon tracks. We bounced along, but for all that, I leaned against the hay and found myself relaxing for the first time in days.

Lili sat beside me, her hands composed in her lap, her head forward, her chin resting on her chest. I peered at her, thinking she was asleep, but then she straightened. "Has Ieuan said anything of me?" she asked. "I could tell he was embarrassed for you to meet me for the first time, dressed as I am."

"I think he was too worried to be embarrassed," I said. "I wasn't concerned in the slightest. In my country, women dress as men all the time."

"They do?" Lili asked. "And do they know the bow, as well?"

"No," I said. "Don't tell me you're embarrassed yourself? These clothes fit you well and I suspect you wear them often."

"Whenever I can." Lili laughed. "Ieuan thinks to find me a husband. There's a little chance of that as long as I look like this." She grinned.

"You don't want to marry?" I asked, in truth, thinking more of myself than of Lili.

"Marriage would be all right, if Ieuan could find me the right man. It's babies I don't want. Unfortunately, you can't have one without the other."

I thought I understood. "Your mother . . ."

Lili jerked her shoulders. "He has told you? My mother died with my little brother, Owain. They survived the birth, but not the fever that followed. That will not be *me*."

"I'm sorry," I said, at a loss for what else to say.

"And you?" Lili asked. "You don't fear the childbed?"

"I hadn't thought that far ahead," I admitted.

"Well, it isn't too late, though I wouldn't be sorry if you married Ieuan," Lili said. "In all the hours we've traveled today, you haven't complained once. I wouldn't have expected that of any woman, other than me, of course. You're far better than any of the fools at court."

"For whom you have no patience," I said, not as a question.

Lili snorted. "Not that it's their fault. My uncle taught us to read and write—and once he learned, Ieuan taught me to shoot and track through the woods. None of them have a brother such as I, the worse for them."

It was past midday—of what was becoming a very long day—before we reached Aberedw again. I woke from a nap as Daffy rolled the cart through the gatehouse and turned toward the stables. All my anxiety at the thought of how we were going to get inside the castle was for nothing, as I'd slept through the danger! The castle walls enclosed a space a hundred feet on either side, with a keep centered at the very top of the hill that the walls encompassed. The bailey housed the stables at the bottom of the hill, and when Daffy pulled his horse to a stop, we jumped down.

"Now, you know what you have to do, right?" Lili asked me for at least the third time. I didn't mind. Her love for Ieuan drove her, and she wasn't alone in her fears.

"Yes," I said. "I enter the keep through the kitchen entrance and say that the steward sent me to help with the evening meal. I find where Ieuan and Dafydd are being kept and meet you at dusk outside the stables. If they are in danger, you and I will figure out how to release them."

"It will depend on where they are, you see," Lili said. "They'll be harder to free if they're in the tower than if they're stored somewhere more accessible." Lili gripped my shoulders, standing on her toes to look into my eyes. "You need to be smart and careful. Their lives depend on what you can accomplish."

"I know," I said. "I don't know how I'm going to do this, but I will."

Lili released me, she went off to help Daffy unload the hay, looking very much like the stable boy she very much was not, and I turned towards the keep. A stairway led to the back side and I followed it, huffing and puffing, to the top. The keep was fifty feet square, maybe less; Lili had told me the great hall took up the whole of the second floor. The castellan, Cadoc, would have his apartments above that, with the kitchen and storage below.

My heart was in my throat by the time I reached the kitchen door. I took a deep breath and remembered that throughout my childhood, I'd walked into more unfamiliar places than I could count, and the best policy was always to act if you knew what you were doing. People saw what they wanted to see, and rarely did anyone question someone behaving obviously and normally.

The door to the kitchen was open and I peeked inside, squinting because it was much darker inside than out. And hotter. At least fifteen people bustled about, some even running.

"Don't just stand there!" a voice said. "Grab that pitcher and bring the water to the master's room. He's waiting to wash."

"Yes, sir, yes, sir," I said, hurrying into the kitchen. I reached for the pitcher and had picked it up before the man really looked at me. My eyes still saw spots, so he was merely a dark bulk to me.

"Wait," he said. "Who are you?"

"Bronwen, sir. The steward sent me to help."

"Oh, well," he said. "Good. We need the help, what with three of the scullery maids retching their guts out every morning. They'll be good for nothing now. Hustle along then."

*Three!* "Yes, sir," I said, and hustled.

A door opened onto a wide hallway on the far side of the kitchen. I trotted along it, past several closed doors before I reached the stairway leading up. A guard lounged at the bottom of the stair and he pinched my rear as I passed him. I would've kicked him but thought that 'Bronwen the scullery maid' probably wouldn't have complained, so I refrained. I followed the stairs to the great hall, but kept going up another staircase to the third floor, to what I assumed were the castellan's rooms.

I knocked. Nobody answered. I was about to knock again when I heard a moan and heavy boots crossing the floor. The door opened inward and I stepped back. Two men shoved their way past me, with a third man hung between them, his eyes closed.

*David.*

I knew it was he, less from his face, which was so swollen and puffy it obscured his features, than from his clothing, now stripped to his cream-colored jersey and dark brown breeches.

Reddish stains—blood—covered his front. His feet dragged behind him as the men maneuvered him past me and down the stairs.

I stood frozen in the doorway and came to myself only when Cadoc called to me. "You wanted something?"

"My lord. Your water, sir." I hurried inside and poured the water into a basin set on a table near the door, my hands shaking so badly I was afraid I'd spill the water all over the floor. The room smelled moist and musty—of sweat and blood.

Cadoc sat behind a table littered with papers. A bed dressed with heavy curtains was positioned against the far wall. I finished pouring the water and made to leave, but Cadoc spoke again. "You won't stay, eh?"

"I'm sorry, my lord," I said curtsying. "We're very rushed in the kitchen. I must get back."

"Later, then," Cadoc said, and I turned away before he could see my shudder and the sweat dripping off my brow.

I hurried down the stairs and reached the ground floor in time to see the two soldiers coming out of one of the doorways in the hallway near the kitchen. One of them locked the door, and then turned to the guard who sat at the bottom of the stair. He swung his arm and the key sailed across the space between them. The guard caught it, looking satisfied, and the other man waved, before turning to enter the kitchen.

I nearly tripped as I passed the door, I was focusing so hard on *not* looking at it. Once back in the kitchen, the cook proceeded to run me off my feet for the two hours it took to serve and clear the evening meal. Every now and then I poked my nose out the kitchen door, hoping for some fresh air and to check the location of the sun, which by the end of my shift was obscured by clouds. While I watched, rain began to fall.

Finally, as it began to get dark, the cook gave me permission to relieve myself in the outhouse near the stables, as the garderobe inside the castle wasn't for servants. I hurried down the hill, soaked before I'd gone twenty feet and slipping on the muddy steps. Lili met me at the stable door. She had sticks of straw in her hair but a smile on her face. Most of the soldiers and servants were still in the hall and we were alone.

"I found them, Lili, I found them, but Dafydd is badly hurt. They beat him up." I couldn't contain my distress any longer and the words burst from me.

Lili put her hands on my forearms. "It's all right, Bronwen; it's all right. Are they in the tower?"

"No," I shook my head. "Cadoc's keeping them in a room off the kitchen, guarded, but accessible."

Lili squeezed my arms. "Good," she said.

"We have to save them, Lili," I said. "I overheard in the kitchen that Prince Llywelyn is ill and not expected to live! We've got to get them out of here!"

"I know, Bronwen. I heard that too, but the stories are too vague to be absolutely true. By tomorrow morning we'll be at Buellt. We must face what is before us tonight, not what happens tomorrow."

"Okay, okay," I said. "Tell me what to do."

Having transferred the pills earlier to her scrip, Lili handed me the plastic vial that had contained Ieuan's antibiotics. "The hemlock juice," she said. "This is all we have. It has a noxious smell, so you may have to coax the guard to drink it."

"Coax him?" I asked. Lili raised her eyebrows at me, and I realized what she meant. *Oh, coax him.*

"Do *not* allow him to kiss you after he's drunk it," Lili warned. "I don't know that his breath will harm you, but you can't be sure that a drop of the liquid wouldn't remain on his lips."

I was starting to get angry—not at Lili—not at Ieuan—not at David, though God knows I could come up with a good reason for it—but at myself. "Lili," I said. "I've been in your country for fewer than two days, and in the last twenty-four hours I've been betrayed by a priest Ieuan thought was a friend, shot at by the English, pinched by a guard while masquerading as a scullery maid, propositioned by the castellan of Aberedw, and now you're telling me I could have the pleasure of being poisoned as well, while playing temptress?"

"Are you saying you won't do it?" Lili asked.

My anger ebbed. "Of course not. Ieuan and Dafydd are in danger and we can help them."

"I would go myself, but Cadoc will know me, even if I'm dressed as a boy."

"I understand," I said. "I'll do it."

I didn't linger with Lili longer, as I didn't know how quickly the cook would miss me. Braving the rain, I ran up the stairs, but came to a halt once I reached the kitchen, surprised to find it empty. I lowered myself to a stool by the fire, my clothing steaming. A minute later, the cook returned. "The master is looking for you," he said. "If you don't want to end up like those three girls you replaced, I suggest you make yourself scarce. I'll tell him I couldn't find you."

"Thank you," I said. I leapt to my feet and was practically running by the time I reached the kitchen door. I hugged the side of the keep, trying to avoid the wind and rain, and ran into a lean-to a few steps from the kitchen door. I slipped inside. It smelled of herbs. I stubbed my toe on a box, and reaching out, blind in the dark, I felt for it and settled myself onto it.

I don't know how long I sat shivering, but eventually the pitter-patter of rain on the roof and the dripping inside my shelter slowed, and then stopped. Thinking it had to be late by now, I returned to the kitchen, hoping it would be empty but the cook was still here.

"I was hoping you'd left for home, young lady," he said. "The master has gone to bed—with someone else, mind you, so you've a reprieve for today, as long as you stay out of the way of the men in the hall. Where's your father? You'll not be safe as long as you stay here. Aberedw has been without a mistress for too long."

"I will be gone by morning," I said.

The cook nodded. "I've left some wine by the fire," he said. "It's not fine, but at least it's warm. You may pour some for yourself. I'm going to sleep."

"Thank you for your help," I said.

"Don't waste it," he said, and left the kitchen.

I looked after him, not knowing exactly what he meant by that last statement, but having every intention of doing as he suggested. I peered into the hallway. A single torch lit the space and a lone guard—a different one from earlier—slouched at the foot of the stairs. He was about my height, so not very tall, with light brown hair and a wispy mustache that must have annoyed him a great deal, since in Wales a male's manliness was measured at least in part by the luxuriousness of his facial hair.

I ducked back into the kitchen, grabbed a cup, and poured wine into it. I took in a deep breath and tipped in the hemlock liquid. Then I braced myself to do something that was *so* unlike me and sashayed into the hallway. The guard noted me immediately and straightened.

"Some wine for you, sir?" I asked, swinging my hips in a parody of Marilyn Monroe, someone whom the guard had fortunately never seen.

"Baby," the guard said. "Come sit with me."

I tried not to smirk. *You'd think that seven hundred years before my time, they'd have come up with something different to call me!* I reached him, handed him the wine, and found myself pulled onto his knee with his arm wrapped tightly around my waist. "Drink it while it's warm," I said. "It's better that way."

"To you, baby." The guard raised the glass and downed the liquid in one breath. Some of the wine seeped out from his lips and oozed down his cheek. It reminded me of what Lili had said, and I pulled away from him.

"I'll get you more," I said, reaching for the cup.

"But I just want more of you," the guard said. He tried to grab me, but I skipped away.

"Don't go away," I said. "I'll be right back." I reentered the kitchen. I didn't know how long the poison would take to work, so I took my time refilling the cup, my hands shaking the whole time at what might be happening to him.

"Girl!" the guard called. "I'm coming after you."

*Just what I need.*

I'd hoped the guard was required to stay at his post, which didn't include the kitchen. The guard appeared in the doorway.

"Just a moment," I said. "I've biscuits too."

"I'm not hungry for anything but you," he said. "Get over here."

I took another minute to stoke the fire before turning back to the guard. His face was pale and his breathing shallower.

"Girl," he said. He grasped the doorframe with one hand, trying to hold himself up, and then slumped to the floor.

I dropped the poker and ran to him. My own breath came in short gasps. I pushed aside his tunic and found the key to Ieuan's prison on a string at his waist. With one jerk I pulled it free.

I ran down the hall to their door and jammed the key in the lock. I didn't know how long we had before a change in shift or someone came looking for the guard. I tried not to think of anyone but Ieuan and David. *This can't be real. This isn't real. I can't have killed someone.*

I tugged the door open. The light from the corridor illumined the two men on the floor: Ieuan, with David's head cradled in his lap.

"Hello, *cariad*," Ieuan said. "I hoped to see you again.

# 20

## *Ieuan*

Bronwen fell to her knees beside me.

"It's all right," I said. "Neither of us are badly hurt."

"I saw the soldiers bring him out of Cadoc's room hours ago," she said, stroking a stray hair out of Dafydd's face. "He looks worse than he did then. How can you say it's all right?"

"You're here, aren't you?" I asked. "And Lili too, if I guess right. He looks bad, but I don't believe he bleeds inside, which is the worst fear."

"His face," Bronwen said. "Your face."

"Ach, I'm fine. One of the soldiers caught me off guard with his fist."

"But Dafydd!"

"I pushed the teeth they loosened back in. If he doesn't eat anything hard for a few days, they'll set. They broke his nose and I straightened that too. It might even add an air of mystery to his

226

face that will attract the ladies. Just think about getting us out of here. You and Lili have a plan?"

"Lili has a plan. Can you stand?"

I nodded and shook Dafydd gently. He'd been awake on and off since they brought him back the second time. They'd given us a candle for the evening meal, but it had long since burned out. I'd not eaten what they'd brought, and neither, of course, had Dafydd, but the light had given me a chance to address his wounds. Bad as they looked, they could've been worse. They'd not broken any of his fingers, nor pulled his nails.

"Wha—?" Dafydd asked, through puffy lips.

"Up you go, my lord," I said. I pulled him to his feet, wrapped my arm around his waist, and threw his left arm over my shoulder. Bronwen took his other side, though she was so much shorter I wasn't sure that we weren't more awkward that way. We had to angle ourselves to get through our prison door and then stumbled toward the kitchen.

"Oh . . . the guard," Bronwen said, stopping. A body blocked the doorway and Bronwen ducked away from us to grab the man's feet and haul him further into the kitchen. Fortunately, he wasn't a big man, or I would've had to help, and Dafydd would have fallen without me.

"You killed him?" I asked her as we followed her into the kitchen, Dafydd taking two steps for every one of mine. I wanted to hold her but she was acting very purposeful and I didn't want to distract her.

"Bonwen," Dafydd said. "He beb?"

227

"Yes, he's dead," she said.

"Bonwen," Dafydd said again, "welcome to Wales."

"Was that a joke, my lord?" Bronwen asked. And then she made a face. It was the first time she'd called him that and I suspected she hadn't meant to.

"He's not been quite right in the head since they brought him back from his last beating," I said.

Bronwen pulled open the kitchen door and we went through it, breathing the fresh air, but instantly soaked from the rain that poured down.

"Great," Bronwen said. "I thought it had stopped."

"It will impede our pursuers," I said.

I gripped Dafydd tightly as we navigated the stairs, trying to keep him upright and walking forward. It was so dark we had to move by feel. When we reached the bottom of the hill, Lili appeared out of the darkness of the stables, leading two horses.

"You're a miracle worker," Bronwen said.

Lili grasped my free arm. "I poisoned the guard at the postern gate, and the two at the gatehouse are getting steadily drunker on mead I found hidden under a pile of hay in the stables."

"You've done well," I said. "Let's not stop now."

Lili led us along the wall from the stables and around the back of the keep until we faced north. She opened a door in the wall, and we went through it. Dafydd laughed beside me. "De poste'n gate; De poste'n gate; wemind me neber to buil' a castle wib a poste'n gate," he said.

"Sssh," Lili said. "We must get clear before we speak."

"Lili!" Dafydd replied. "Bootiful girl, Ieuan. Sharp mout' on her, dough. I don' envy de man you choose for her husban'."

"My lord," I said. "We need to be quiet."

"Okey dokey, Ieuan. I alway li'en to Ieuan," Dafydd said.

The river trail that we'd followed from Twyn y Garth picked up again north of the castle. We reached it and stopped to readjust in the shelter of the trees.

"Is he drunk?" Lili asked. She couldn't see his wounds in the dark, or much of anything for that matter. "You've carried him the whole way here."

"They tortured him, Lili," Bronwen said. "He's not himself. He probably has a concussion."

"Dey hi' me a lo'," Dafydd said. "Los' coun'. Dad is ill. Mus' save him." His head fell forward, and I shook him gently, not wanting to touch his face to wake him up.

"Dafydd; my lord Dafydd," I said.

"Wha—? Wha—?" Dafydd woke again. "Dad is ill. Mus' save him." Dafydd took a step and would have fallen if I hadn't stepped with him.

"Can he ride?" Bronwen asked.

"We can't see to ride anyway," Lili said, "but if you can get him on the horse and lead it, Ieuan, I'll ride behind Dafydd and hold him up."

"I ca' ride," Dafydd said.

"Of course you can, my lord," I said. Lili had saddled the horses, which would help Dafydd stay seated, but meant that Lili would have to work not to slide off the back of the horse. Good thing she was so small. It was a flatter saddle than some at least.

I forced Dafydd to the horse. With Bronwen and Lili holding him on either side, I took his foot in my palms.

"One, two, three," I said, and miraculously, Dafydd understood enough to push off me as I lifted him. He ended sprawled on his stomach across the horse's back.

"Bee' here, befo'," he said, as we shoved him up further, fitting his foot into the stirrup to allow him to claw his way into a sitting position. "Traitor then, too."

"We will deal with Tudur as soon as we get to Buellt, my lord," I said. "It's only five miles from here."

I boosted Lili up behind Dafydd and she wrapped her arms around his waist. That prompted another comment from Dafydd.

"Oh," he said, "a girl," as if he hadn't acknowledged her earlier. "Do you t'ink she likes me, Ieuan?"

"Of course she does, my lord," I said.

"What abou' my nose?" he queried. "B'oken nose, now. Look funny."

"You look fine, my lord," Lili assured him. "Not to worry."

"Okay," Dafydd said. "We go?"

"Now," I said. I took the horse's reins and led him down the trail, Bronwen following with the other horse.

"Wha abou' guards?" Dafydd asked. "Shou'd I sing?"

"There are no guards here, my lord," I said. "You don't need to sing."

"Like to sing," Dafydd said under his breath. "Good at singing."

"Yes, my lord," Lili said.

I kept everyone moving. As I walked and she rode, Lili and I conferred as to the exact location of the ford across the Wye. Twyn y Garth and Aberedw were on the eastern side of the river, while Buellt Castle sat on the western bank, ensuring that we'd have to cross it eventually. I preferred to do it sooner rather than later to elude our pursuers.

We came upon the ford a mile north of Aberedw and crossed it without incident. It must have been nearly three in the morning. I wondered if the guards had changed just before Bronwen released us such that no one would discover our absence until morning. By then, we'd be at Buellt.

We walked into the early morning. Once the sky began to lighten, I boosted Bronwen onto the second horse. If Dafydd had been more cognizant, I would have ridden with her, but as it was, I didn't dare leave him. Lili was such a little thing, I wasn't sure how long she could hold him up. It did seem as the hours passed, though, that my lord became more aware and coherent.

Finally, we approached Buellt. Taking the risk that all was well, at least in the castle the Prince of Wales defended, I led the horses onto the road and right up to the front gate. Buellt Castle sat atop a motte—a high, rounded hill—which supported a great round keep. The English had built two Norman baileys, an inner one and an outer one, and surrounded them by a curtain wall with six towers, all accessed through a twin-towered gatehouse. Inside the walls lay a kitchen block, the great hall, a chapel, and quarters for a hundred soldiers.

My spirits rose as we approached. The familiar blonde head of Sir Nicholas de Carew looked down at us, meaning he, at least, had come home safely from Lancaster. Now that he was on our side, he wore a surcoat sporting Prince Dafydd's red dragon of Wales, but his stance and attitude remained the same: *My blood is purer, my arm stronger, my heart more honorable than that of any other man.*

As we approached, I waved at him, and he returned the greeting but then froze with his hand above his head. "Mother of God!" he said. He left the battlements, moving pretty quickly for an old fellow, and was through the gate with another dozen men before we'd covered the last ten yards.

"How—how—how did you get here?" he stuttered when he reached us, and then was distracted by Dafydd's face. "By the saints!" he said, "what happened?"

Together we reached up and helped Dafydd off the horse. He was able to stand, though he swayed, and we held him up between us.

"Carew," Dafydd said, "how is my father?"

I silently thanked our Savior for my lord's coherence and realized that the prince must have been working hard to speak so that Carew could understand him.

"He's much fevered my lord. According to Goronwy, a single arrow caught him in the midst of his men as he rode on a routine patrol last week. No one thought the English were within ten miles, and the culprit was not caught."

"Perhaps he wasn't English," I said. "It has happened before."

"So Goronwy suggested, but Tudur isn't convinced."

"Tudur betrays us," Dafydd said. He laid one foot in front of the other, carefully pacing across the bailey, making slow but steady progress as we supported him on either side. Dafydd hadn't spoken loudly enough for other men to hear, but I cringed, thinking that the prince wasn't strong enough to confront the man.

"What?" Carew said. "What did he say?"

"The castellan of Aberedw says that he's Tudur's man," I replied.

"He's responsible for my wounds, for he administered them to me personally," Dafydd said. With each step he enunciated more clearly and his voice became stronger. "He named Tudur as the traitor—as the one who will ensure my father never rises from his bed again. Cadoc knew of Edward of England's attempt on my life, although he doesn't know that Edward is dead, and I certainly didn't tell him."

"I don't know the man at Aberedw, but I can't believe Tudur would betray our cause," Carew said.

"I also didn't tell Cadoc my real name," Dafydd added, his eyes focused on his feet.

"When did you arrive here, Lord Carew?" I asked.

"Last evening, Sir Ieuan, late. We encountered a storm in the Irish Sea that delayed our return to Wales. Fortunately, we survived it without losing the ship or our lives. We rode hard from Rhuddlan, stopping only at Dinas Bran where I spoke with your mother and Lord Mathonwy. I've only had a chance to speak with Goronwy, Tudur, and Gruffydd ap Gwenwynwyn of Edward's death, as your father is too ill to hear it."

"Did anyone say anything of me?" Dafydd said.

"Rumor only, that you'd perished in Lancaster. I assured them it wasn't true."

"Did anyone send word to my mother that my father is ill?"

"Not that I am aware, my lord," Carew said.

"Take me to him," Dafydd said. He gritted his teeth. "The wound is infected?"

"Yes, my lord," Carew said, "and the poison spreads."

"Ieuan," Dafydd said, "your pills."

"They were in the pack," I said, dismayed. "Where are my lord's things, Lili?"

"We brought the pills," Bronwen said, speaking for the first time. She'd dismounted, along with Lili, and had followed silently behind. "I kept them out. At the time, I was mad at Ieuan for not taking them as he should."

I felt the urge to kiss her. *Come to think of it, I am going to kiss her, just as soon as I can.*

Another few steps and we reached the bottom of the stairs to the keep. We looked up and my lord's mouth twisted wryly. He took a deep breath and we began to climb. "It's not my legs that hurt," he explained when we paused, half-way up, "but my ribs ache and my stomach muscles scream at me every time I move. We're quite a pair, Ieuan, are we not?"

"As you say, my lord," I said. My ribs were much better, in part because I'd become accustomed to their constant ache. After my shower at Aunt Elisa's, Bronwen had retaped them and wrapped an 'elastic' bandage around my entire torso. No doubt Dafydd needed the same treatment.

The keep loomed ahead of us. Goronwy met us at the door. His face blanched when he saw us.

"My lord," he said, his eyes riveted on the disaster that was Dafydd's face.

"Goronwy," Dafydd said. "Send a rider, right this moment, to my mother. Tell her that I'm alive and that I need her. No one else is to leave the castle. *No one.* Is that clear?" He put out his hand and gripped Goronwy's arm, making sure that he was paying close attention and there would be no mistakes.

Goronwy nodded. "Yes, my lord."

Dafydd released him and then allowed us to lead him to the staircase at the rear of the hall, from which we could reach the offices and bedrooms on the floor above.

"No sign of Aaron?" Dafydd asked Carew. We stood at the bottom of the stairs, looking up them. Again, a look of resolution crossed Dafydd's face.

"None," Carew said. "I thought he was with you."

"We got separated," Dafydd said, without explaining further. "Who has cared for my father since he fell ill?"

"I don't know, my lord," Carew said, "but I will find out."

235

Tudur met us at the door to the apartment that normally held the castle's castellan, but now housed the Prince. Before last year the castellan had sworn loyalty to the Mortimers, but now Gruffydd ap Gwenwynwyn ruled here. I liked the man, though he was another we didn't know if we could trust. The list of the Prince's enemies, and former enemies turned friends, was long.

"You!" Tudur took a step back.

"How is he?" Dafydd asked, and I marveled that he could keep his anger in check.

"Not well," Tudur replied. "We've tried everything."

"Not everything," Dafydd said. He turned to the company who crowded the stairs behind him. "Carew, Ieuan, with me. The rest of you return to the hall."

Tudur bowed, but didn't follow the others. "You too, Tudur," Dafydd said. "Please leave us."

"My lord," Tudur protested. Dafydd stared at him hard. Tudur returned his gaze, puzzlement in his eyes, but backed away.

Dafydd didn't wait. He shook Carew and me off and strode towards the room behind the office in which his father rested. The room was hot and musty, and the smell of the Prince's sickness turned my stomach.

"How could they allow this?" Dafydd asked.

"I was unable to see the Prince until now, but all looks in order," Carew said.

Bronwen walked to the window and pushed open the wooden shutters. Fresh air flooded through the room. Dafydd had already gone to his father and pulled back the covers. The smell of rotting flesh hung in the air. Dafydd lifted the cloth that covered the Prince's ribs where the wound seeped pus.

"You see before us, Ieuan, what I feared for you," Dafydd said. "We'd better not be too late."

# 21

## *Bronwen*

David switched to English, perhaps so his father wouldn't understand, though I wondered at Sir Nicholas's ability to keep up. David didn't appear to care. He directed his attention to me.

"Okay, what do we do?"

"This is a little outside my range of experience," I said. "But I saw enough wounds in Nepal to know that we need clean it first. I don't know what is available, but pure alcohol would be best, though it'll hurt like hell."

"He's past caring," David said. "I think that's what my mom would do too."

"Then the pills," I said. "He's of a similar size to Ieuan, with a similar wound. He should take them in the same quantity as Ieuan, just like it says on the bottle."

"Will Ieuan be okay without them?" David asked.

"He got IV antibiotics in the hospital, didn't he? These pills were probably precautionary. Ieuan's wound looked fine three days ago and I taped it really well. I know it's not ideal, but your father needs them more than Ieuan now."

"I agree," David said.

He turned to Ieuan and switched back to Welsh. "I need a bowl of really hot water, clean cloths, a knife, and the most powerful alcohol you can find on short notice. We also need a pitcher of drinking water and a cup."

"Yes, my lord," Ieuan said.

"I'll help you," Lili added. They left the room at a run.

I sat next to the Prince and held his hand. He was a tall man, though thin, perhaps thinner than he should've been now that he was ill. He'd once had black hair, but it was graying. I put a hand to his forehead. He was burning up—the fever of which the castellan at Aberedw had spoken.

"He needs a cool washcloth," I said.

Dafydd leaned over a washbasin and sniffed the water. "Smells okay," he said. A cloth lay on the table beside the basin and he soaked it, squeezed it out, and brought it to me. I laid it on the Prince's forehead, and he surprised me by opening his eyes enough to look into mine.

"Dafydd's here," I said in Welsh. "We're going to help you."

"Who?" he asked, which I interpreted to mean *who are you?*

"Bronwen. A friend from the land of Madoc," I said.

239

Llywelyn's eyes brightened before closing again. "Good," he said.

Meanwhile, David had been talking earnestly with Carew, and I picked up the last of their conversation:

"I need you to speak with Goronwy, Gruffydd, and Tudur. All three know that Edward is dead, but none of them are aware that I've been to Aberedw. Only the traitor thought I should be dead instead of here, and knows that the English have increased their patrols on either side of the border in preparation for my father's death."

"You suspect Goronwy instead?" Carew asked.

"I would as easily mistrust myself," David said. "It's easier to suspect Gruffydd than Tudur, but the castellan at Aberedw was very sure of himself. Now that we're here, I see that any one of them could have orchestrated my father's illness."

"But you trust me?" Carew said. "Not long ago you said that you didn't."

"Maybe I shouldn't trust you; maybe you're playing a *very* long game," David said. "Given the events at Lancaster, not trusting you seems foolish."

A ghost of a smile hovered around Carew's lips. He nodded, bowed, and left.

A minute later, Lili appeared with a pitcher and a jug, followed by a maid with a basin of hot water and fresh cloths. Ieuan hurried after them with a knife and a flask. I held my hand out to Lili and she put two of Ieuan's pills into it. I turned to

Llywelyn and got him to open his eyes. I held up a pill between my thumb and forefinger.

"I'm going to put two pills, one at a time between your teeth. Hold the pill there while I tip water into your mouth. When your mouth is full of water, release the pill and swallow it along with the water. Do you understand?"

The Prince nodded. I looked at David. "Can you sit him up?"

David got his arm underneath his father's shoulders. "We've been here before, haven't we, Dad?"

Llywelyn smiled, then, just a little, and swallowed the antibiotics. When he'd finished, without choking once, David laid him down. David continued to hold his hand, with Llywelyn holding on tight.

"Son," Llywelyn said. "You're alive. Heard voices . . . speaking in the next room . . . said you were dead."

David leaned closer and spoke in his ear. "It's Edward who's dead, Dad."

Llywelyn turned his head, his eyes full of questions. "You?" he asked.

David shook his head. "I wasn't to kill a royal cousin, remember? One of his servants poisoned him."

Llywelyn turned his head and looked up at the ceiling. "I need to live," he said.

"You will," I said. Then Dafydd and I looked at each other, asking the dreaded question *who is going to do it?*

Not David; not to his own father. *It will have to be me.*
"Can you heat the knife in the fire, Ieuan?" I asked.

While Ieuan did as I asked, I knelt on the floor beside the
low bed with what passed for medical equipment spread out
around me. The wound was still open, not having healed at all,
oozing and, quite frankly, gross. Purple bruising and red, angry-
looking striations spread out from it on all sides. I soaked a cloth
in hot water and dabbed at Llywelyn's wound, squeezing at the pus
and trying to get most of it out. Then, I soaked a different cloth in
alcohol and taking the knife, lifted the flap of skin that half-
covered the wound. I squeezed the alcohol into the wound, and
then gently scraped around the inside of it.

It had to hurt, but Llywelyn lay still. When the pus no
longer seeped, I took another deep breath, and poured more of the
alcohol over the wound. I was screaming inside my head, my teeth
gritted, but Llywelyn lay still with his eyes closed. He gripped
David's hand on one side, and held onto Lili with the other. David
whispered to him constantly, and I could just hear his words,
repeated over and over again: *The Lord is my shepherd, I shall
not want. . .*

Finally, I dried his torso and unscrewed the tube of
antibiotic ointment. Upending it, I squeezed the tube and
smeared the entire contents in and around the wound. I was glad
Aunt Elisa had bought the kind that had a pain reliever built in,
though I didn't know how powerful it really was. *Better than
nothing.* David lifted his father so I could wrap a clean cloth
around and around his torso. By the time I was done, I was

dripping with sweat and as David pressed the end of the bandage into place, I started to shake. Ieuan released Llywelyn's legs, which he'd been holding still, and pulled me onto his lap. I buried my face in his shoulder.

"Trial by fire, eh, lass," he said, brushing my hair with his hand.

"How long will it take for your mother to get here?" Lili asked David.

"She's at Dinas Bran, last I heard," David said. "If the messenger has already left, he can be there in two days; it will take twice that for her to reach us. By then, hopefully, my father will be on the mend."

"Having you here has made him better already, my lord," Lili said.

"Having Bronwen here, you mean," he said.

I looked up and Lili met my eyes. She nodded.

*Maybe I have something to offer this world, after all.*

# 22

## *David*

*Oh Lord, do I hurt.* I sat beside my father as he lay in bed, trying not to think. *But I have to; someone has to and Dad is lying here, asleep.* I wished I could sleep. Even if I had the time, my catalogue of injuries might have prevented it. My face ached and I'd never felt such pain behind my eyes before. *Broken nose: check; blackened eyes: check.* I suspected I had a couple of broken ribs and even a bruised kidney as well. I needed to do something about those soon. When Ieuan had straightened my nose the evening before, I'd screamed and passed out. Oblivion sounded kind of nice.

"We need to keep watch on the Prince, twenty-four hours a day," I said.

Ieuan looked up. "Yes, my lord," he said. "And not alone either; two at a time."

Every muscle in my body screamed at me as I carefully stood up. "You and Bronwen stay here for now. Lili," I said, turning to her, "will you come with me? I need your help again."

"Certainly, my lord," she said.

She came around the bed to help me hobble out of the room. I put a hand on her shoulder, trying not to drive her into the ground since my weight could have been twice hers. We managed to navigate the stairs without falling down them.

"I didn't really mean that I needed your help to walk, Lili, though I appear to," I said. "I need you to help me enact a little drama in the great hall. Will you follow my lead and do what I ask without questioning?"

"You don't need to ask that, my lord," she said. "Of course, I will."

"I know that, in theory," I said. "But I've the sense that you have little patience with men and their machinations at court, and thought it would be better to ask."

We reached the bottom stair, and Lili turned to look up at me. "Yes," she admitted, "in that you are correct. However, I think I'm willing to make an exception in your case."

"Oh," I said. *How about that?* "Good. Well, once more into the breach, then, shall we?"

Lili smiled, forgiving my reference to Shakespeare, whom she couldn't know as he wouldn't be born for nearly three hundred years. Once in the hall, I made a great show of limping and staggering to my father's chair. I hadn't planned to use it, but suddenly there it was, the perfect stage. I fell into it, grateful that it was well-cushioned.

"My lord!" Carew sat at the high table with Goronwy, Tudur, and Gruffydd ap Gwenwynwyn. I raised my hand to them. Another twenty men, a few of them my own, were scattered throughout the room, some eating and drinking, others talking or playing chess. "The Prince?" Carew asked, rising to his feet.

"He will be well," I said.

"Sir knight," Lili said. "He needs bandages and warm water so that I may tend his wounds."

"Of course, of course." It was Gruffydd who responded, signaling to a serving maid who hustled from the room.

"Was that right?" Lili asked under her breath as she knelt beside the chair.

"Perfect," I said. "Now let's get this jersey off me . . . slowly, slowly . . . ahh, it hurts!" I didn't have to dramatize my pain as I struggled to free myself from the ragged piece of linen. Lili pulled the shirt over my head, revealing for the first time the mottled blue and purple bruises that covered my torso from breast to waist. I slumped in the chair.

All four men were on their feet now, their expressions ranging from horror (Goronwy) to bemusement (Carew), whose eyes twinkled at me. He knew there was no reason for me to expose myself this way if I didn't choose to.

"Who did this?" Gruffydd asked. He was always the most likely to speak to me as the boy I was, without the formal designation of 'my lord.'

"I will tell you in a moment," I said. "We've more important things to talk about first. Let me tell you what I've discovered, and then we can make decisions about what we must do next."

Gruffydd subsided, and I began to tick off the points one by one on my fingers. "One, King Edward of England intended to bring about my death in Lancaster. He cared not at all for convention or protocol in this, but revealed his unquenchable hatred for me and my father. Before he could accomplish his goal, however, he was poisoned by one of his servants, to which my men and Sir Carew were witness.

"Two, Hereford arrived too late to witness Edward's death, but is under the impression that *I* am dead as well, thanks to a forgotten surcoat in the pavilion where I met Edward. This, coupled with advance notice among some of Edward's confidants that he intended to kill me at Lancaster, is the source of the rumor you may have heard that I was dead."

Carew nodded slowly. He too had forgotten the surcoat amidst everything else.

"Three, Hereford has had time to make his own plans, none of which can be good for Wales. As of two days ago, Hereford had increased his patrols along the border. Whether under Hereford's orders or for his own ends, Clifford's men are right now besieging Sir Ieuan's castle at Twyn y Garth.

"And four, the castellan at Aberedw, Cadoc, who administered my injuries personally, is in Hereford's pay."

Goronwy stood with his hands on his hips, his eyes narrowed. "You've learned all this first-hand?" he asked.

"Yes," I said.

"You've been busy," Gruffydd said.

"I'm the Prince of Wales," I said. "It's my job to know what's happening in my domains."

"Yes, my lord," Gruffydd said, giving me a slight bow, probably hoping I didn't see the smirk that accompanied it.

I went on, shifting forward so that Lili could begin wrapping the bandages around my ribs. "What we don't know is: one, how soon Hereford arrived in Lancaster; two, where he's gotten to in the intervening days; three, what Hereford intends to do with his men; and four, who among my father's men has betrayed him to Hereford."

"My lord!" Goronwy, Tudur, and Gruffydd protested. I forestalled them again. "Cadoc named Tudur traitor," I said.

The hall fell silent, for I'd allowed my voice to carry to everyone in the room. Goronwy found his chair and sat heavily into it. Tudur himself stood, feet apart, his eyes blazing as he looked at me.

"You believed him," he said, not as a question.

"I did," I said. "At the time, anyway."

Tudur raised his hands and let them fall helplessly. "You take the word of a man who did *that* to you?" he asked.

"I have withheld judgment, Tudur, for that very reason."

"You have no proof, then," he said. I let the silence lengthen, until he realized that was exactly the wrong thing to say.

248

"Do I need it?" I asked.

"I'm no traitor," Tudur said, his voice soft. "Cadoc lies."

I nodded. "Possible. Perhaps, then, you should be the one to go to Aberedw and find out the truth. You would be clearing your own name, finding our traitor, and unseating my wayward castellan at the same time. Take the men you need, though I would hope that none of your men would find their way into England to get word to Hereford in the meantime."

Tudur stared at me as my gift to him sank in, and then bowed. "You have my word, my lord."

As he walked away, I called to his back. "When Cadoc beat me, he didn't know who he had in his hands. He recognized Ieuan, but I called myself Dafydd ap Bran."

Tudur stopped in mid-stride and turned back. "Now that is interesting." Just the way he said the words showed me the intelligence and humor in the man. "This is information I can use. Thank you, my lord," he said, and bowed again.

He left the hall. Carew sat in his chair, his chin in his hands. Goronwy had risen to watch Tudur leave and now stood, his arms folded across his chest, contemplating the space where Tudur had been. Gruffydd studied me.

"Will he run?" Carew asked.

Gruffydd shook his head. "You are more devious than I gave you credit, my prince," he said. "You've forced him to choose."

By now, Lili had nearly finished doctoring my wounds. I sat very straight as she tugged on the strips of cloth she'd wrapped around my midsection. I was having trouble breathing, so I just nodded.

"He will choose Wales," Goronwy said. "I knew his father and have known Tudur his whole life. His defection, if there was one, was a temporary aberration."

"In my house, he would pay for it with his life," Gruffydd grumbled.

"He still may, Gruffydd," Carew said, "but the prince goes about things a bit differently from you and me."

"True, true," Gruffydd agreed. "Cadoc is dead, regardless."

*Another dead man on my conscience.* I decided this one, out of all of them, would weigh the least.

\* \* \* \* \*

As Gruffydd had surmised, Tudur returned three days later. Lily and I were on duty, though Lili was out of sight, through the door behind me in my father's room. I was sitting in his study, literally contemplating my navel whose color had bloomed a purple I'd never quite seen before, when Tudur walked in and dropped a dirty, woven bag on the desk in front of me.

"Cadoc's head," he said. "He died during my interrogation of him regarding the traitor among your father's men. He did not reveal a name."

I looked at the bag with distaste. "Set that in the corner by the door and pull up a chair, Tudur."

"Don't you want to examine it?" he asked.

"I'll have Goronwy look at it when he wakes up," I said. "I trust that you wouldn't bring me the wrong head."

"Even if you don't trust me in other matters," Tudur said.

"Even so," I agreed. "I think you would've found a place for yourself in Edward's Wales, if he'd lived to create it. I wonder that you chose so early, and so wrong, if in fact you did betray my father."

"I did not betray him."

"Then tell me what you did do," I said.

I didn't know Tudur well. As a man, he was intimidating, not because he was tall or a great warrior, but because of the power he wielded. He also *knew* about Anna, my mom, and me, knew we were from the future, and his possession of that knowledge always made me feel at a disadvantage with him—*like he's just waiting to use that knowledge against us if he can.*

That was one of the reasons why my choice had been between executing him on the spot or giving him a chance to repent. I absolutely didn't want to drive him into Hereford's arms.

"I rode to Aberedw with fifty men as you instructed," Tudur said. "There, we entered the castle unhindered, subdued the garrison, and questioned Cadoc. Upon his death, I gave his men a choice: follow the Prince of Wales, or die. They chose to live. I left twenty of my men in possession of the castle and departed, retaining the thirty men who'd served under Cadoc. We then rode to Twyn y Garth. That is a perfectly positioned castle for reconnoitering the English, by the way."

I nodded. "What did you find there?"

"I found the upstart Clifford lad, thinking to take the castle as a means to assuage his dignity at the loss of Bronllys. He had only forty men. What he was thinking, I don't know." Tudur shook his head. "Anyway, he lost half his men in the first three minutes, and the rest we sent packing. Twyn y Garth is yours again, my lord, or rather, Sir Ieuan's."

"Thank you, Tudur. It relieves my mind considerably to have the Wye in our possession again."

"Am I back in royal favor now?" he asked, with a mocking smile.

"Tell me what happened with my father," I said. "His condition when I found him was unforgivable."

Tudur started up from his chair. "We did all that we could! We changed his sheets and bandages daily, with clean water as your mother would have demanded. Once we removed the arrow, we could do nothing but wait."

"A poultice perhaps, to draw the pus?"

"We tried that three times before you came, but once the fever sets in, there's little anyone can do," he paused. "Except you . . . you have cured him, have you not, with your futuristic miracles?"

We contemplated each other across the table. His expression wasn't friendly, but it didn't show hatred either, and I wondered if perhaps he feared my mother and me. Perhaps that was why he'd not sent for her, rather than an intent to betray.

"Tudur," I said. "Has my father or mother spoken to you of what you were in that other world? Who you became?"

Tudur fixed his eyes on a point above my head. "No, my lord," he said. "And I've not asked."

"I didn't know myself until my mother told me," I said. "In my old world, you make your peace with Edward after my father's death. Consequently, you retain all your lands in Wales and your descendents ultimately found the House of Tudor, which counts among its members in the coming centuries some of the greatest kings and queens of England."

Tudur said nothing, but continued to stare at the wall behind me.

"That is what Edward offered; what alliance with Hereford could offer," I said. "What my father and I give you is merely our trust, our love, and the hope that Wales can survive those same centuries intact."

Tudur still didn't look at me. "You speak of this as if it's a Sisyphean task. Wales is stronger than you think."

"We are stronger when you are with us, Tudur, than against us," I said.

"I am with you, my lord," he said.

I nodded. "You may go, Tudur, and may God go with you."

He stood and bowed. "My lord," he said, picking up the sack containing Cadoc's head as he left the room. The door shut behind him. I closed my eyes. *Tired.* I forced myself to my feet and walked to the door that separated the office from my father's room.

I poked my head around the doorframe. Lili sat beside my father's bed, his hand in hers. They both gazed at me, their eyes bright.

"You heard?" I asked.

"Yes," my father said.

I leaned against the frame, and studied them. "You can't believe everything you hear," I said, "especially while eavesdropping."

"I'll take my chances," said Lili.

I entered the room and sat down on the bed next to Dad, opposite Lili. His face was gaunt, but he'd been awake since dawn and the fever had gone.

"You told Tudur you are from the future," Lili said. "Your father confirms it."

"*A* future," I said, "not *our* future."

"What does that mean?"

I shrugged, giving in. "It means, Lili, that the choices we make today are still our own. What we do today, we do for the first time, and no matter what happened in the world in which I was born, it has no bearing on what happens in *this* world."

"Which is why you let Tudur go," Dad said. "Whatever he did in that other world, he doesn't have to do the same here."

"No," I said. "And it appears he knows it too."

"I trusted him," Dad said. "His father was like a brother to me—closer, in fact, than my own brothers, who routinely betrayed me."

"We all trusted him," I said. "I still don't know if that trust was misplaced. We may never know, provided he continues to work with us."

"You walk a narrow rope across a canyon, my lord," Lili said. "Any misstep and you, and all of Wales, plunges to our death."

Dad patted Lili's hand. "It's not as bad as that," he said.

I wasn't interested in exploring that topic any further. *I'm so tired of that topic.* "What happened when you got shot?" I asked.

Dad sighed. "I needed the exercise and you know how important it is to mingle with one's men, so I rode with a patrol. We hadn't gone far, having stayed on the western side of the Wye, when an arrow flew from the woods and hit me in the ribs. That's all there is to it."

"But you, Tudur, or Goronwy sent men to find the culprit," I said.

"Goronwy led the search personally, following the trajectory of the arrow. He found no one. If it was a lone man, however, he could've easily slipped through our fingers and been a mile away within a few minutes of shooting me. The Welsh have used 'guerilla warfare' as you called it once, to great effect for a thousand years. It's impossible to guard against a lone assassin."

"And he probably *was* Welsh," I said.

Dad turned to Lili. "Would you fetch me some wine, my dear?"

"Of course, my lord." Lili stood and sketched a wave to me, before leaving the room.

I looked at my father, waiting.

"I almost died," he said. "Are you ready?"

"I'll never be ready," I said. "And you didn't die."

"How many close calls can one man survive?" Dad asked. "I've already lived longer than most men."

"Mom will not be happy with that kind of talk," I said, "especially because where she comes from, many people live well into their eighties."

"Save me from such a fate!" Dad said, and actually laughed, though he cut it short abruptly with a hand to his side. I eased him down further in the bed and grabbed another pillow to hold against his ribs. "I would rather die before I lose all my teeth and am bent double with age, barely able to stagger from the bed to the dinner table and back!"

He sobered and held out his hand to me. I leaned forward and he kissed my forehead and then each cheek. "You are my beloved son," he said. "Whenever my end comes, you will be ready, whether you realize it or not."

His words made me lightheaded, with tears behind my eyes. I had to breathe deeply to fight them back. "I'm not as strong as you," I said. "Nor as wise."

"You are young and not as alone as I was at sixteen." Dad looked down at his hands and I waited, wondering what was coming and if this was really why he'd sent Lili away. "I need to know, son," he said, "why did you come back? You didn't have to."

"I know," I said, relieved that the question was so easy. "It was my choice. I wanted to come home."

"But you jumped not knowing if it would return you to your time or end your life."

"With the English bearing down on me, Dad, my life was over. Ieuan's life was over. It wasn't just a risk I *had* to take, I didn't even view it as a risk at the time. All my choices had narrowed to two: die on an English sword, or jump."

Dad squeezed my hand. "I have stood on that cliff many times, son. Thank you for coming home. Thank you for saving my life again."

"Everything happens for a reason, Dad. Even if I'd died there, it would have been for a reason. You pray, you try to make the right choice, the moral choice, and then you let it go, and it's amazing sometimes how things turn out."

Dad laughed lightly, containing it so as to not hurt his wound. "I would have to agree, Dafydd. Since you and your sister arrived in Wales, *amazing* is a word of which I've grown very fond."

# 23

*Bronwen*

"**M**mmm," I set the plate of doughnuts on the table in front of Ieuan and sat down.

"What are those?" he asked, gingerly picking one out with his thumb and forefinger. "They look like lumps of dough that have been fried in lard."

"Exactly," I said, grinning. "Except that the dough is sweetened with more honey than usual, and we let it rise once instead of twice."

Ieuan took a bite and his face took on a quizzical expression. "Good," he said. "What do you call them? Dough lumps?"

"Doughnuts, or rather 'doughnut holes' which makes even less sense if you think about it," I said. "Until I came to Wales they were one of my four main food groups, the others being diet cola, onion rings, and coffee."

"I have no idea what you just said," Ieuan said. "Is coffee what you have there?" He pointed to the cup in my hand.

"Yes," I said. "I've had a headache on and off since the day after we got here, and I'm hoping this will help."

Ieuan took the cup from me, sipped it, and grimaced.

"I know. It doesn't taste very good, does it? I put in lots of cream, but no sugar, as there is none. I'm going to have to give it up, I think."

"Prince Dafydd had three sugar packets," Ieuan said, popping two more doughnuts in his mouth and talking around them. "I asked him to bring them here from the hospital. I would give them to you, as part of my betrothal gift, to put in your final cup."

"Ieuan," I said, and kissed him on the cheek. "That's so sweet."

"Isn't it?" he said, looking pleased with himself.

I took a doughnut. They were rather good. One of the things I'd found when I'd traveled the world with my parents was that the memory of certain foods created a longing that was only sated by that particular food. Then, once you had that food again, it not only was no longer a desperate need, but it never tasted as good as you imagined. *I don't think this is the case with doughnuts, though.*

Now onion rings—I was going to try those next. They should be easy.

"You all right, lass?" Ieuan asked.

"I think so," I said. "How long have I been here, in Wales?"

"Six days?" he said, his mouth full again. "Something like that."

"So it's August 14th," I said. "I've known you for ten days."

"A lifetime, really," he said.

I laughed, because he was right, and then sobered. "I've begun my life completely over," I said. I started up from the table at the thought, feeling panic rise in my chest. "Is my professor at Penn State worried about me, or have they already given my office to someone else? Ieuan! What if Elisa didn't find my letters? My friend, Kate, must be frantic!" *What was I thinking? Why do I never think?*

My heart raced as the thoughts tumbled over each other in my head. Ieuan was staring at me, his mouth half-open. "Lass? Bronwen?" he said, a doughnut half-way to his mouth.

"What have I done?" I moaned, sat, and laid my head on the table.

"You've saved the life of the Prince of Wales," Ieuan said.

Suddenly, it was as simple as that. I raised my head. "I did, didn't I?" I said. In the space of a single second, I understood what David had been talking about, back at his aunt's house. What had he said? *This is so much bigger than I am; so much more important that I am. I would be a blind man not to see it.*

"We are, each one of us, here for a purpose, lass," Ieuan said. "You know that."

"I guess I do, at that."

Lili appeared beside Ieuan. "Can we talk?" she asked, without bothering with a greeting.

Ieuan and I glanced at each other. "Let's go where we were before, Ieuan," I said. Privacy was remarkably hard to come by in a castle. There were too many people in too small a space, but Ieuan and I had found a private spot in the kitchen garden where we'd sat late last night before going to bed. There was a bench, screened by a lattice. It had been quiet there.

We left the hall and passed quickly through the kitchen. The workers looked up as we went by, but Ieuan waved them away and they went back to their work. The kitchen garden was a walled enclosure, protected from the wind by a high wall all around it. Many of the vegetables were harvested already, or would be ready soon, but there was nobody inside when we walked in.

"This way," Ieuan said, and led us down a side path to the bench. Lili and I sat and he leaned against the wall, still behind the lattice, but to the left of us.

Lili began, sounding ill at ease, which contrasted sharply to the confidence I'd seen in her so many times before. "I need . . . can I ask you? . . ." She stopped and tried again. "A moment ago, I overheard Prince Dafydd speaking to Lord Tudur of the land from which he came." She spoke faster as the words started to come more easily. "You told me, Ieuan, that he was from the land of Madoc, but he said he was from the future. Prince Llywelyn confirmed it." She stopped.

I kept my voice gentle. "Did you speak to Dafydd about this?"

"Just now, but I . . . I couldn't ask him. That's why I'm asking you, because you're from that land as well and you're a woman so . . ."

I looked up at Ieuan who was regarding his sister. "Prince Dafydd knows that you know?" he asked.

"Yes," Lili said.

"Then I don't see any harm in talking about it," Ieuan said. He sat beside Lili so we flanked her. "He took me there, Lili. The English were upon us and would have killed us both, but the Prince lifted me in his arms and jumped off the edge of a cliff and brought me into his world—Bronwen's world."

Lili clasped her hands tightly in her lap. "And you forsook your world to come here, to marry Ieuan?"

I met Ieuan's eyes. They twinkled at me, obviously amused. "Yes," I said. "I did."

"Prince Dafydd chose to leave, and then chose to come back. You too, Ieuan. Why? That world must be wonderful beyond imagining."

"But it doesn't have you in it," Ieuan said.

Lili had recovered enough to sneer at him. "You're not serious. That's no reason."

"It's reason enough," Ieuan said.

"Could you take me there?" Lili turned to me.

"I don't think so," I said, nonplussed, "and even if I could, I wouldn't. It isn't like a door that just open and closes—one minute you're there and the other not. It's dangerous to go—and I think you have to be in great danger to go there."

"Why, Lili?" Ieuan asked. "Why do you want to go, other than to see the wonders there."

"Because I want to be like Bronwen," Lili said.

262

I was confused. "Why would you want to be like me?" I asked.

"Have you noticed, Ieuan, how she walks differently from any other woman you know?" Lili said. "She holds her head up, like a queen, or I imagine a queen would, and strides like men do. When she healed Prince Llywelyn, she ordered you about. She talks to you as if she believes herself equal to you—as if she is equal to you. She doesn't care what anyone thinks about her. I can't tell if she even knows what effect she has on those around her. If she does, she doesn't appear to care."

"Now I really don't understand," I said.

"She acts like a lord, yet she's a girl," Lili said. "I want that for myself."

"But you do act as I do," I said. "You wear breeches, and shoot a bow. When we first met you were about to take Prince Dafydd's head off with your knife."

"Defiance is not confidence," Lili said. "Bravado is not courage."

"At fifteen, most girls in my country are not confident in themselves either," I said. "You are still very young."

"But girls must see other women like you all the time? You're not unique in your country?"

"I suppose I'm not at that," I said. "I'm no different than a hundred other women I know, yet I understand what you're asking. Girls in my country learn from the cradle to walk and talk and be as I am. I can't help it. Our confidence comes from believing, down to our very core, that we are worthwhile people—smart, capable, educated, confident."

"Can you teach me that?"

"Maturity is a matter of learning to live up to your own expectations," I said, "whether you're a man or a woman. I wouldn't want you to become something other than the beautiful person you are, but we can certainly talk about it, and I think I know some other women who can help too."

"Princess Marged," Lili said. "Princess Anna."

"I imagine that what you want for yourself is exactly what they want for all the women of Wales," I said. "I wouldn't be surprised if they have some ideas as to how to achieve it."

Lili looked from her brother to me. "You accept it in your future wife, Ieuan," she said. "Can you allow it in your sister?"

"That's something you need to relearn, right there," Ieuan said. "You don't need to ask that. Tell me: 'I need this, Ieuan.' Don't ask me what's right for you. Know it. Know yourself well enough to reach out and grab what you need to be a complete person."

Lili nodded. "I need this Ieuan," she said. "I need it more than I can tell you."

\* \* \* \* \*

The talk of the day was the return of Tudur, with the castellan of Aberedw's head in a sack. Ieuan and Goronwy had inspected it, once Tudur finished his audience with David, and then sent two men-at-arms to bury it outside the castle walls. In doing so, they denied him consecrated ground, underscoring for anyone who hadn't been paying attention, the seriousness of his offense.

David spent the rest of the day with his father and didn't descend into the hall until it was time for the evening meal. Ieuan and I sat at a table that ran perpendicular to David's. He sat in his father's chair with the more powerful lords on either side. We'd only just begun to eat, however, when a rider from Hereford demanded entry.

"I have a message for the Prince of Wales," he said. He was of average height, with black hair, beard and mustache, and a pristine tunic. He must have changed before he entered the hall.

"He is unwell," David said, "but recovering. What is the message?"

"Who are you?" the man asked. His chest puffed out a little with his own importance.

Tudur pushed back his chair and stood, his back to the great stone fireplace. "He is Dafydd ap Llywelyn, heir to the Principality of Wales. You were expecting someone else?"

"Er," the man hesitated, looking from Carew, to Tudur, to Goronwy, and then back to David. They all gazed back at him, stone-faced.

"You didn't expect to find me here, did you?" David asked.

"No, my lord," the man said. "I had heard, er . . ." he stopped.

"You had heard that I was dead," David said.

"Er, yes," the man said. He bowed, taking refuge in the enforced formality of David's position.

"What is your message?" David asked.

"I was told to give the message only to Prince Llywelyn," the man said.

"Fine," David said, inspecting the fingernails on his left hand. "Return to your master. It's all one to me."

Ieuan had risen to his feet when the man entered the hall and now stood, his feet spread, with cold eyes and his fists clenched at his sides.

The messenger waffled, and then capitulated. He straightened and called out in a loud voice, in Welsh: "Hear the words of Sir Humphrey de Bohun, third Earl of Hereford, second Earl of Essex, Lord High Constable of England and co-regent for King Edward II."

He paused to breathe and David asked, "Who are the other regents?"

"Er," the man said, confused at being interrupted. "John Kirby, the Lord High Treasurer and Robert de Vere, the Lord Great Chamberlain and Earl of Oxford."

David nodded, though I didn't know if those names meant any more to him than they did to me. "Continue," he said.

"The Lord High Constable has exhibited great patience through the trials of the last years. In his office of co-regent, he orders you to cease and desist in your depredations against his holdings and those of the other English lords whom you and your men have inconvenienced, nay besieged, with behavior unbefitting a vassal to the throne of England. In particular, he claims the castles of Bronllys, Buellt, Dolforwyn, Dryslwyn, Carreg Cennan, Dinefwr, Llandovery, and Pembroke. You are ordered to vacate those castles and quit their vicinity forthwith."

David leaned toward Carew, who sat a few paces from me on David's right side. "We've taken Pembroke?"

Carew raised his eyebrows. "Apparently. I think we'll keep it. What say you, my lord?"

"I'd say so too," David said, rising to his feet. He walked around the table, still rather stiffly, and approached the messenger, who'd backed up a step at his approach.

"How long does Hereford give me to reply?"

"He did not say, my lord."

"Well, you tell Bohun that he can have my answer now," David said. He poked the man in the chest with his index finger. With each poke, the messenger took one step backwards and David stepped forward, such that the words that followed was punctuated by 'poke, step'; 'poke, step.'

"First, Hereford has no authority over me, or any lands, in Wales. Second, in future, we expect any messages from the throne of England to the throne of Wales to be sent in the proper fashion, with the pomp and glory that befits our station, not carried and shouted in the hall by a little weasel such as you; and third, inform your master that from this moment, the throne of Wales is confiscating all holdings in Wales not held by a baron loyal to my father. He and his friends have thirty days to either vacate their former estates and castles, or submit a petition indicating their new loyalty to my father."

"My lord!" the messenger said. David and the messenger had reached the door to the great hall. David towered over him, still poking him in the chest.

"Furthermore, in case your master is confused as to what constitutes the boundary of Wales, there is a wall, we speak of it as the Dyke, built long ago to keep the Welsh penned inside their mountains. We claim all territory to the west of that line and from this moment forward, will defend it to the last man, woman, and child. One of my lords took two castles for me just this week." He tipped his head towards Tudur. "That must be some kind of record, eh, Tudur?"

"As you say, my lord," he said, laughter behind his words.

"If one, just one, of your master's men whom he has sentried on the border between our countries sets foot into our territory, we will not be responsible for the consequences. Do you understand your charge?"

"Yes, yes, my lord," the man said, groping for the door handle.

David spun on one heel and stalked back up the hall. "That man," he pointed back at the messenger, "needs an escort across our border. Ieuan, will you—" David stopped in front of Ieuan. "What? What is it?"

"That man," Ieuan said, his eyes fixed on the man by the door, "is my father."

"Your father?" David said. He swung around to look at the messenger, and then back to Ieuan. "Anything you want, Ieuan. Anything I can do for you or you need. Just tell me. It's yours if it is possible to command it."

Ieuan transferred his gaze to David. At nearly the same height and a foot apart, their conversation was only for each other. "Leave it to me, my lord," Ieuan said. "I will see that he reaches England."

# 24

## *Ieuan*

**M**y skin crawled as I escorted my father across the bailey. "You may rest in the barracks and refresh yourself for a few hours until you return to England," I said.

"I was sorry to find you here," my father said. "You are unchanged."

"*I* am unchanged?" I said, losing control so quickly a red film crossed my eyes. *Hang on! Hang on!* "Hereford? Father, how could you? How could you swear allegiance to such a man?"

"He is not Llywelyn."

"No, he's not! He's Hereford! You taught me to hate him from my first breath!"

"I taught you to hate Llywelyn too, and look where that got me. Times change, son," he said.

"Yes, they do! And for the better!" I couldn't help the rising of my voice, but other men were looking at us and I tried to modulate my tone. "Father, Hereford seeks the end of Wales."

"He does not. He merely wants the lands that belong to him, as I want mine returned to me."

"And this, Hereford has promised," I said, disheartened yet again by my father's attitude. "You've traded your honor for your purse."

"My *honor*." He turned on me. "What do you know of honor? You bow and scrape to *that* man. Llywelyn is a fool and his son an idiot to think he can defy Humphrey de Bohun."

I grasped my father's cloak, no longer trying to contain my anger. "You dare to speak ill of Prince Dafydd? He is the best of men. Even you can have nothing against him."

"He is Llywelyn's son. That is enough."

I released him. "What has Llywelyn ever done to you?" I swallowed. I'd wanted to ask that question for ten years and never had the chance or the courage.

"Nothing! That's the point." We'd reached the barracks and my father turned in the doorway.

"I don't understand," I said.

"I offered him my services. I asked Llywelyn for the honor of leading his men at the first defeat of his brother Dafydd at Bryn Derwin, thirty years ago. He chose Goronwy instead." My father stopped. The silence that followed was painful, for he'd finally spoken the truth.

"So you went to his brother, Dafydd," I said, "and he made you his right hand man. Through all those years, you aided and abetted him, plotting against Llywelyn because he'd hurt your pride."

"I don't expect you to understand," my father said. "I did what I had to do." He turned on his heel and the barracks door closed behind him.

"I'm sure you did," I said.

I felt someone watching me, and turned to look. Bronwen stood on the bottom step, her eyes steady on mine. "Prince Dafydd would see you in his father's rooms as soon as you are able," she said.

I nodded. "I'm ready now," I said. I took her arm and we returned to the keep.

* * * * *

"To what exactly have you committed us, my lord?" Goronwy asked. Everyone had gathered around Prince Llywelyn's bed while Dafydd had related to him the substance of Hereford's message—and Dafydd's response.

Dafydd and his father studied each other, both clear-eyed.

"I've called him out," Dafydd said, with an insouciant grin. He bounced up and down on the balls of his feet.

The other lords didn't look so pleased. "Please explain," Carew said. "I feel I haven't quite caught your intent."

"Don't you see?" Dafydd asked. "Hereford thought I was dead! He thought father was going to die! This is going to blow him out of the water!"

"Why don't you start at the beginning, son. Some of us are slow to catch you up, especially when you speak in that fashion," Llywelyn said.

"Okay," Dafydd said, calming his enthusiasm and starting to pace. "We know that Hereford must have arrived in Lancaster on the heels of our departure. He found King Edward dead, but as neither he nor any of his men had ever met me, assumed the body that Moses had decorated with the discarded dragon surcoat was mine."

"We understand that, my lord," said Carew.

"Immediately, Hereford did two things: one, he sent word to his wife and allies to prepare for action against Wales. With my death and father's injury, which we still don't know enough about, he was counting on our inability to counter him. Two, he took the Archbishop of Canterbury and raced to London, to Edward's son. The sooner Hereford was on the spot, the more likely it was that he would be named regent."

"He was named regent," Goronwy said.

"Yes! That's true. But only co-regent. Vere and Kirby share his power, and do you know what that means?"

"That he can do nothing without their approval." Tudur nodded. "Of course. He had thought that becoming regent would give him near total authority in England and Wales. Instead, he finds himself sharing that authority with two other men who don't support his ambitions and certainly wouldn't support a full-scale—and very expensive—assault on Wales."

"Exactly," Dafydd said.

"No," I said. "I'm still not understanding why you're so pleased."

"Ieuan," Dafydd said, "do you remember when we were in prison in Carlisle, when we concluded that Hereford would try to take advantage of the power vacuum in England?"

"Yes," I said. "And he has done so."

"He hoped he could," I said. "Now, however, he has neither the power, nor the money, to invade Wales, not on the scale he intended, and not when he is facing a Prince Llywelyn who is very much alive."

"Hereford expected his messenger to find us in disarray," Carew said. "He knew that he couldn't invade us, but was hoping we wouldn't know it. His intent was that he wouldn't have to, that we would fold up our tents."

"You exposed his deception," Llywelyn said.

"What will he do now?" Goronwy asked.

"The question is what *we* will do now," Dafydd said. "I may have called his bluff, but I wasn't bluffing. I suggest we continue where Tudur left off the other day."

"Which is where?" Gruffydd said. Until now, he'd followed the conversation without contributing to it.

"How many castles and English holdings lie in the lands bordered by the Severn, the Wye, and the Dyke?" Dafydd asked.

"A dozen, the largest being Montgomery, four miles northwest of Dolforwyn, and Painscastle, to the south and east of Buellt," Tudur said. "The war has taken its toll and there are fewer castles than a few years ago. Knighton, for example, Prince Llywelyn destroyed in 1262 and it has not been rebuilt."

Prince Llywelyn pushed himself straighter in his bed. "So, we do exactly as Dafydd has said, starting with this corner of Wales. We send riders to every Englishman, informing him of the line we've drawn and demanding their departure or their allegiance. It's as simple as that."

"They will resist," said Goronwy.

"Of course they will, and then we'll take them down, one by one, starting with the smaller holdings which are more difficult to defend," the Prince said.

"Hereford won't stand by and let us do this," Gruffydd said. "He can't."

"He will marshal his men and those of his immediate allies," Llywelyn said, "but so many of the Marcher lords are dead with Edward, that he hasn't the ability to gather enough on such short notice, not with the heirs themselves unconfirmed in their holdings."

"When the cat's away, the mice will play," Dafydd said, with satisfaction, "except the mice are not Hereford and his allies, but *us*." He swung around to face his father. "You remember the Rising of 1256? You swept east through Gwynedd, south through Powys, and all the way to Deheubarth in one summer."

Llywelyn's eyes were bright as he gazed at his son. "I have not forgotten," he said.

"Brecon must take precedence," said Goronwy, getting back to business. "It is Hereford's seat."

"That and Painscastle," Tudur added. "It guards the main road into central Wales."

Carew nodded. "I will ride south with my men and reconnect with Rhys ap Maredudd and the other Debeuharth princes who seem to have won Pembroke for us. We will turn east, then, and sweep the English before us."

"I'm for Montgomery," Gruffydd said. "Now that that the Mortimers are dead, I can take it."

"Give the castellan a chance to switch sides," Dafydd said. "My father has good memories of that place. We don't want it destroyed if it doesn't have to be."

Gruffydd snorted. "Yes, my lord."

"And you, son?" Llywelyn asked. "What will you do?"

"I have a couple of errands to run," Dafydd said, looking at me, "and after that, I hope to win the war before it truly starts."

# 25

## *Bronwen*

**D**avid and Lili settled themselves across the table from Ieuan and me the next morning at breakfast. Lili was looking polished, her male clothes forsaken for a green dress and wimple.

"The Prince says we're going on a little trip to get your vehicle," Lili said.

"I for one, would be delighted to stretch my legs," David said.

"With broken ribs?" I asked, and then glanced at Ieuan. He was moving well, but wasn't completely better either.

"What kind of prince would I be if I couldn't ride a horse with a couple of broken bones?" David said. "Besides, it's Taranis I'll be riding. I missed him while I was in England."

"Don't give me that stoic knight crap," I said. "You've not healed yet."

David laughed. "I'm much better; and besides, Lili thinks the ribs are just cracked, not broken."

"Why do you want the car?" Ieuan asked. "You're not thinking of driving it, are you?"

I rolled my eyes. "Oh, yes he is!" I said.

"Not me, you," David said. "The van too, if Mom is willing once she gets here. Can you imagine what it will look like to the English if they see it coming toward them in the middle of the night, headlights in the front, shooting fire arrows at anything that moves?"

"He's gone mad, Bronwen," Ieuan moaned. "Wales is doomed."

"No, no, Ieuan," David said. "It could really work, and it would save Welsh lives in the process."

"You mean to cross the border into England before Bohun sends his forces against us here?" Lili asked.

"Absolutely," David nodded.

"I don't know how Prince Llywelyn will feel about your mother putting herself in danger," Ieuan said. "I don't want Bronwen in danger."

"I can—"

Ieuan interrupted me. "Yes, I know. You and Lili can take care of yourselves. Well, *I* don't care if that is true. The battlefield is no place for women. *My* women."

"That's all well and good for you," I said, my temper rising. "I don't want to have to sit safe inside the castle, worrying about *you!*"

278

"You tell him, Bronwen," Lili said. She popped a doughnut into her mouth. The cook had scattered several trays of them among the tables. Overnight it had become a popular breakfast food.

"We're going to lose this argument, Ieuan," David said, "if we don't come up with some new ammunition soon."

Ieuan picked up his fork and ate a bite of egg. "More immediately, my lord," he said, "how do you mean, *get the car*? It's in England."

"I know," David said. "That's a problem. However, this time we're going to bring fifty armed men with us. We were, what, thirty feet from a track where we hid it? Less than a mile from the Dyke? We're going to go get it and bring it to the Welsh side of the border. I need you girls back in your breeches, though, if that's okay," David said. It seemed like he should have been asking me, but he was looking at Ieuan.

"Don't look at me," Ieuan said. "I'm going to pick my battles very carefully. Bronwen may wear breeches if she likes. My sister embarrasses me in such manner on a daily basis, why not my wife?"

"Your soon-to-be wife," I said, smacking him in the belly with the back of my hand. "Don't jump the gun on me."

"What's this word, 'gun'?" asked Lili. I'd used the word *gwn*, obviously a modern construction, borrowed from English.

I pursed my lips. "Um . . . a weapon that fires a ball a great distance."

"You mean like a trebuchet?" asked Lili.

"Smaller," I said. "You can hold it in your hand."

"That would be very useful," said Lili.

A thoughtful look crossed David's face.

"Oh no," I said. "You can't be serious."

"Not guns," said David, "but black powder certainly. I printed directions on how to make it off the internet while I was at Aunt Elisa's house. All we need is saltpeter, sulfur, and charcoal."

"Better yet, we could make Greek fire," I said.

"Nobody knows the real ingredients of Greek fire," David said. "There's a lot of speculation, but—"

"I do," I said.

"What do you mean, *you do*?" he asked. "How come you do and nobody else does?"

"Well, a lot of people do, really. Anyone who studies ancient Rome like I have plays around with the idea of what it could be made of." I stopped. David raised his eyebrows.

"Okay, truth," I said. "Last spring, the administration at Penn State was all gung-ho about interdepartmental cooperation. They promoted the idea of each department sponsoring interdepartmental potlucks, talks, and little seminars that a bunch of diverse people might be interested in. So, taking the idea to its appropriate extreme, the medieval studies department had this idea that they would sponsor a contest to see who could re-invent Greek Fire using technology from the Middle Ages, circa 1000 AD. Each team had to be interdepartmental, so the teams included chemists, historians, archaeologists, and medievalists."

"Oh, wow! My mom would have loved that," David said. "Did someone make it?"

"Oh yes," I said. "The administration even approved the contest, since the application for the event only mentioned a 'medieval weapons demonstration'. They thought it was going to be jousting and some harmless sword fighting."

"Harmless sword fighting?" Ieuan asked, offended.

"When you grow up with guns, swords look tame," David explained. "Go on, Bronwen. Tell us."

"It was pretty spectacular. In all there were two solutions that worked best. As you mentioned, charcoal, sulfur, and saltpeter. It's best to use the crystallized remains of bat guano from caves as saltpeter to provide the potassium nitrate."

"Saltpeter's a little more complicated than that . . ." David's voice trailed off as I glared at him.

"Am I telling the story, or are you?"

"Sorry, sorry," he said, putting up his hands. "Just trying to be accurate."

"I bet your sister would say you were one of those annoying little brothers who contradicted her all the time, wouldn't she?"

Ieuan cleared his throat. David smiled. "Go on," he said.

"As I said, these three ingredients are the basis of black powder, which you must then grind really fine, like talcum. Once you have the right consistency, you can mix that with oil—making a sort of pitch. It catches fire easily, and when you throw water on it, it spreads."

"We could do that," Ieuan said.

"Well the best recipe belonged to the team that combined lime, bones, and charcoal in the proper combination to make calcium phosphide. They designed a pot with a division down the middle and a stopper in the top. You pour the concoction into one half, water into the other, and throw it. When the pot breaks, the ingredients combine. When combined with water, calcium phosphide releases phosphine which spontaneously combusts on contact with the air."

"My God," David said. "You sound like you did it."

"Well, my team won. That's *how* we won, before the fire department came and shut us down."

"Oh, wow," David said again. "Okay, okay, black powder and Greek fire are going to really make this all work better than I thought."

"Better?" I asked. "There's nothing better than Greek Fire in this day."

"Bronwen," David said, the annoying sound of patience in his voice, "we have at least forty gallons of gasoline within a twenty mile radius of us right now. That's partly why I want to get your car."

"Gasoline! You can't be serious? What are you planning to make? Molotov cocktails?"

"Something like that," he said.

"They're trickier than you might think," I said. "You have to use the right amount of gasoline, the right kind of bottle, the right stopper." I stared at him, horrified. "Think of the people you could kill, David. You can't—"

David leaned forward and grabbed my arm. "Can't I? You know what the English will do to Wales if they defeat us? It's called genocide. You may have heard of it? They'll destroy us if they can, and they'd do it today if my father and I didn't stand between them and our people. Don't tell me what I can't do, Bronwen, because I can do it. We need to win this war; right here, right now, and I have the means to do it."

I pulled away from him and turned my head, but not before tears pricked my eyes. It was Lili who spoke next, leaning in as David had, but her touch and voice were gentle. "Don't believe him, Bronwen. He never kills except when he has to. Do you, my lord?" she asked David. "You're offended that she thinks you would."

I lifted my head. He sat, his arms folded across his chest, his chin out.

"My lord," Lili implored.

"We're going to kill some people, Bronwen," he admitted. "There's no denying that, but mostly," he paused and then grinned, stretching his arms above his head, fists clenched, "we are going to scare the bejesus out of the English!"

"Your plan is to scare them?" I asked, now completely confused.

"So they'll sue for peace," Ieuan said. "That's what you want, really—that they come begging for peace on your terms. The population of Wales is too small to defeat England. What you want to do is make it too costly for them to continue the fight."

"Got it in one," David said. "How did the Americans defeat the English in the American Revolution? By force of arms? Hardly. They won just enough battles to make the English count the cost and figure it too high." He pushed up from the table. "We're going to get my pack from wherever Lili hid it and then we're going to go get the car."

\* \* \* \* \*

David, in his arrogance, had already alerted his men what he was planning before he asked us, so midday found us mounted and riding through the countryside. Thirty of the men-at-arms and knights really were *his* men. He had fifty with whom he trained, but twenty of them were still in the north, hopefully coming this way with his mother.

I rode pillion with my arms wrapped around Ieuan, who was in full armor. He'd complained when he appeared in it that it was someone else's and didn't fit right. Sitting in front of me, every so often his shoulders twitched as he tried to adjust it.

Lili rode behind David. She'd explained that she was going to ride in the car with me, so they didn't want to have an extra horse on the way back, which made *sense*, but I knew the truth, for I'd been present for the argument about it beforehand.

"You are *not* a soldier," Ieuan had hissed.

"I can shoot as well or better than half your men," Lili had replied, her voice rising. "I am not as big as you, but—"

"You're not as big as I am," Ieuan had answered, "nor any man here. Bronwen tells me that in her world, some women become soldiers, but in *this* one, they don't, nor ever will, and especially *not* my sister!"

David had interrupted then. "*I* would really appreciate it, Lili if you would accompany Bronwen in the car."

Lili had hesitated and then capitulated. For a girl who'd claimed just five days ago that she had no interest in men, she was spending an awful lot of time in David's company—and listening to what he had to say, though this time, I thought he was right.

"You have to understand, Lili," David had explained, after Ieuan had stomped out of the room, having got what he wanted but not his way, "that Ieuan's objections have nothing to do with *you* or the fact that you're a woman, despite what he says. It has everything to do with *him*. *He* doesn't want to have to worry about you fighting, but that isn't something he wants to put into words."

"Why do you say that?" Lili had asked.

"Because I feel the same way," David said.

*Oh now, isn't that sweet?*

Not that I was one to talk. I was more than a little annoyed with myself for falling for Ieuan so easily. It was just so *pat*, so *typical*. Already it was *Ieuan and Bronwen* this and *Ieuan and Bronwen* that. *Do I really love him or am I so lost in this crazy place that this is the only thing that makes sense?*

We'd recovered the backpack without difficulty. I'd asked David, as he helped me mount behind Ieuan, if he was worried about accusations of witchcraft.

"History is written by the victors, Bronwen," he'd said. "Either we're going to lose, and Hereford will have my head, in which case I will no longer care—or we're going to win. I don't intend to flaunt my peculiarities in front of my men. However, they already know about Aunt Elisa's van, and we're about to pick up another vehicle, which *you* are going to drive. The more they know of it, see it, touch it, the less dangerous the knowledge becomes to us, and the less we have to live in secret."

We'd taken the road to Aberedw in order to find the pack, and now cut cross-country on a track, skirting the castle of Painscastle to the north. In all, we had only fifteen miles to travel—fifteen minutes in my car—but it was nearing suppertime when we spied the Dyke in the distance. The countryside on both sides of the wall was farmland, nearly as flat as land ever got in Wales, punctuated by stands of trees. The day had started clear, but clouds had rolled in from the west, and as we dismounted in a small wood about a half a mile from the Dyke, it started to rain.

"Perfect," Ieuan said, helping me down. I tugged the hood of my cloak over my head.

"Why perfect?" I asked.

David pulled out a water skin and took a drink before offering it to Lili. "When it rains, men are miserable. It's much worse in the winter, of course, but we want the English miserable, huddling inside their fortifications instead of patrolling the border."

"How long do we wait?" Ieuan asked.

David stepped out from under the tree and checked the sky. The rain plinked off his helmet. "Not long. Let the men rest and eat for a few minutes and then we'll go."

"I'm not sure I understand," I said. "Where's the road I'm supposed to drive the car on?"

"To the south," Ieuan answered. "We left the car due east of here."

"You have the keys, Bronwen?" David asked suddenly, turning to me. "Please say you have the keys."

I laughed. "I have them," I said. "What would you have done then? Hotwired it?"

"Broken a window and dragged it behind us," he said. "It wouldn't exactly have been what I hoped for, though."

The rain came more heavily as we left the trees. I pushed the sodden, stray hairs out of my face so I could see. Once across the Dyke, it took another ten minutes to reach the car. The horsemen milled around it while the four of us dismounted. David and Ieuan lifted off the brush.

I almost cried at the sight of it, but instead got out the keys and unlocked the doors. David opened the passenger door for Lili. "Come, sit here," he said. She obeyed, and he latched her seat belt. After removing my cloak so as not to get the seat wet, I got in beside her. It was nice to be dry.

"Go ahead," I said, with a knowing glance at her. "Touch anything you want. I'll tell you if I need you to stop."

Through the window, I could hear David talking to his men about the car. "This vehicle runs on burning naphtha," he said, "which we in turn are going to use to defeat the English." He gestured to me. "Why don't you start the car, Bronwen."

I twisted the key and the car rumbled comfortingly to life. The wheels caught on the grass and we rolled out from under the trees. David moved to the front of the car. "Pop the hood, okay?" he asked.

He waved his men to him and all fifty crowded around the engine for David's mini-lecture on the internal combustion engine. "Give way, man! I can't see!" "Gruffydd, down in front!" "Rhys! You're the tallest—to the back!"

I tuned them out and turned to Lili. "Tell me what's going on between you and Prince Dafydd?" I whispered. "I thought you weren't interested in men or marriage?"

"Prince Dafydd would never marry me," Lili said, matter-of-factly. "His marriage will be arranged to create a beneficial alliance for Wales. Just as well." Lili raised her chin. "He's too good at giving orders, just like Ieuan."

"Okay," I said. *I'd like to see someone tell that to David.* I'd not known him long, it was true, but it looked to me like he was coming into his own, getting used to giving orders, as Lili said, and the chances that someone else was going to arrange a marriage for him to some woman he didn't know were slim to none. I glanced at Ieuan who leaned against the car with his arms crossed, rain dripping off his mustache, listening to David talk. *I've got my hands full with a certain Welshman as it is.*

The lecture ended, seemingly before everyone's eyes had glazed over, and David closed the hood. It was nearing dusk, now, before what might well be a *very* dark night.

"Here's what we're going to do," David announced. "Bronwen is going to drive the car onto the track. It will be slow going for the first mile because the road is rough. Once she turns south onto the high road from Kington, the drive will become easier, and we can ride faster. The Dyke breaks where the road turns west to Painscastle. Very likely, the English will have guards posted at the crossing and more along the road toward the castle."

David leaned down to speak to me. "Turn on the lights, so they can see them, and then turn them off again." I did as he asked and he straightened.

"Don't be alarmed by the lights. We'll stay together, behind and beside the car."

Beside me, Lili sat stiffly, watching the windshield wipers scrape back and forth. She'd taken out her knife and was holding it in her lap. David leaned in again and looked across me at her. "I'm glad you have that, Lili," he said, "but you won't need it."

"I know," she said, "but I fear that you will." She reached across me to hand David the knife. David took it. They shared a long look before David slipped it into the belt at his waist.

"Thank you," he said and moved away.

I looked over at Lili. She was gazing at her hands, which were face up and open in her lap.

"Do you think something bad is going to happen?" I asked. "Have you felt it?"

"Yes," she said, simply.

I didn't know what to say. Grimly, I started the car and shifted into gear. *Here we go.*

# 26

## *Ieuan*

"What do you think, Ieuan?" Prince Dafydd asked across the roof of the car.

Lili's words had shaken him and he wasn't as confident as he'd been. I didn't know what to say, because she'd been right far too many times for me to doubt her now.

"We can only go forward, my lord," I said. Despite Lili's warning, we'd reached the main road unhindered; we had only a few more miles to safety.

Lili's window descended into the door. When we'd ridden to Bryn Mawr in Bronwen's world, I'd raised and lowered the window upwards of twenty times before Bronwen had informed me that if I did it again, she'd cut off my fingers. Lili had more restraint. "It's nearly too dark to see," she said. "Bronwen wants to know when she can turn on the lights."

"Not until we turn west and are within hailing distance of the guards that bar the road into Wales. Then I want her to hit the lights and the gas at the same time and drive like hell."

"Yes, sir," I heard Bronwen say. She took one hand off the steering wheel to salute him.

"Will you keep up?" asked Lili.

"We'll try," he said. "If we get separated, follow the road past Painscastle until it ends at the Wye. Twyn y Garth is just there."

Just as Dafydd finished speaking, hoof beats rang in the distance. I peered ahead at the soldiers riding toward us out of the murk. Without needing to be told, our men moved into ready formation.

"Damn," David said.

He and I exchanged a look. "No time," I said.

The company of Englishmen came on faster, having apparently decided to strike rather than run.

"Go, go, go!" Dafydd shouted.

Bronwen turned on her lights and sped forward. Our company raced behind her. Dafydd had his sword out and I lifted mine above my head. Ahead, the English company bent away from Bronwen and she sped by them. She turned right, following the road to Wales. That was as we'd hoped, but as her brake lights disappeared, the English recovered and renewed their attack.

Dafydd and I slowed to allow those with pikes to take the lead and ten seconds later, the two sides crashed into each other. The men in the front of the charge were unseated upon impact and went down under the hooves of the men who rode behind. A cavalry charge under these circumstances involved little strategy. It was a matter of who had more men and the room to maneuver them.

When the English had ridden onto the road, I'd had trouble determining their numbers. As I checked Llwyd, however, having come out the other side of the field without even bloodying my sword, I counted the colors showing on the men still seated—our red to the English blue and white. At least twenty men were down, more blue than red, and only three blue remained upright. We'd accelerated more quickly than they had, and our momentum and numbers had carried the day. They should never have taken us on at all.

All three of the English came to themselves at the same instant, dug in their heels, and spurred their horses off the road and into the field to the east. "Follow!" I shouted and ten of our men broke from the battle to give chase.

I turned back, searching for the Prince. He had his back against a tree beside the road. Three of our men guarded him, swords out, as a fourth and fifth dispatched the last attacker. With nobody left to fight, I rode up to him and dismounted.

Dafydd saw me and pushed his helmet to the back of his head. "We got all of them but those three?" he asked.

"I believe so, my lord."

Dafydd shouldered through his guard. He stooped to wipe his sword on a discarded surcoat, sheathed it, and surveyed the dead and wounded on the road. The fighting hadn't even touched twenty of our soldiers. Half of them formed a perimeter around the battlefield while the rest of us picked our way among those on the ground, looking for survivors.

"We'll need torches before it's full dark," Brychan called from across the road.

I pointed at several of the men who knew without further orders what to do. We dragged the dead English off the road, gathered up our men, and prepared to return to Wales. Then, I found Prince Dafydd, who'd taken part in none of this, standing at the crossroads, his hands on his hips, staring up at the starless sky.

"What is the cost?" he asked.

"Always too high," I said. "We have three dead, six wounded and unable to ride unassisted, and six more with minor wounds."

He nodded. "I've lost Taranis," he said.

"I know." I put a hand on his shoulder.

"I slit his throat with Lili's knife, rather than see him suffer."

"You loved him," I said.

Dafydd nodded again. "What bothers me most is that, in my heart, I mourn the loss of my horse more than the loss of the men."

"He was your friend."

Dafydd let out a breath. "We need to get going and we've horses to spare. Find me one that's suitable for the ride home."

"Yes, my lord," I said.

\* \* \* \* \*

At last, we trotted down the road from the Dyke, riding in the open to Painscastle, torches lit. With the road rising steadily ahead of us, patrols on the castle's ramparts could have seen us for the full three miles from the Dyke. Prince Dafydd's face told me that he didn't care and that he didn't believe Tosny, who held the castle, would send men against him.

In truth, there was no reason for Tosny to suspect anything was afoot. The drawbridge and main entrance to the castle actually faced west, as that was the direction from which attacks usually came. The notion that a company of Welshman, with a prince of Wales at its center, would arrive from the east was so unlikely as to be dismissed as soon as it was conceived. As it was, we had no intention of besieging anyone and followed the road as it forked to the north of the castle and continued around it.

An hour later we reached Twyn y Garth. Bronwen had pulled onto the grass to the left of the road, within the shadow of the curtain wall. I gazed up at it. *Home.* It had been a long time, made all the longer by the distance traveled.

We clattered across the drawbridge that spanned the ditch, and through the gatehouse which protected it. We dismounted at the base of the motte. Bronwen and Lili came out of the keep to find us.

"We have wounded," I said.

"I feared that," Lili replied. "We're ready. Rather than bring them up the stairs to the keep, we've prepared the barracks to house them. How many?"

"Six serious, with another six in need of some care."

Lili nodded and began to direct the soldiers carrying the wounded. Bronwen had been standing on the second to last step, and I went to her. She held out her arms; I caught her and buried my face in her hair.

"I was so scared for you. It was the worst feeling in the world to drive away and leave you to face those horseman."

"You did the right thing," I said.

"I understand that now," she said. "Maybe before I didn't; maybe I thought you were just being stubborn and male."

"We lost three men," I said, "and Taranis."

"Oh, poor Dafydd," she said. She pulled away. "I need to help Lili. Bathe and eat. We've food prepared in the keep."

I nodded. "I'll see to the men, first," I said, and we walked together to the barracks.

* * * * *

It was a chastened company that rode into Buellt the next morning. We'd left Lili at Twyn y Garth, as she insisted was her duty, though her eyes had tracked to Dafydd for approval rather than to me. Bronwen drove the car once again, carrying three of the wounded men the last miles home. Prince Llywelyn met us at the entrance to the keep.

"You shouldn't be out of bed," Dafydd said to his father, by way of greeting.

"Leave be, son," the Prince replied. He was pale and thin, though smiling as he grasped Dafydd's shoulder. "It's good to be on my feet. I am well enough. And you?"

"Perhaps not so well," Dafydd said.

"You retrieved it," the Prince said, indicating the backpack which Dafydd wore on his shoulder.

"Yes," Dafydd said. "But as usual, not without a price. I've some things to show you, and whatever you say, you shouldn't be standing." They retreated into the keep.

I stopped Bronwen from following, tugging her away from the steps and towards the battlements. We mounted the stairs to the top. We'd had no rain today and we could see for miles along the river. "I'm sorry," I said.

"What are you sorry for?" Bronwen asked. She allowed me to pull her into my arms, even though anyone could see us.

"For what you've been through these last days; for bringing you here in the middle of a war; for wanting to tie you to me if that's not what you really want."

Bronwen rested her head on my chest. "David was right to think I was unprepared for your world. Nothing I learned in all those years of studying gave me any real understanding of what it might be like to live here . . . or love a knight."

I breathed deeply.

"It's going to take a while to clear my head from everything that's happened," she said.

"I don't know what to say except to repeat that I am sorry," I said. "I can't make it better for you."

"It's better already," Bronwen said.

We stayed together for the rest of the day, and were the first to warn of the riders coming from the north. We heard them before we saw them, galloping their horses across the bridge over the Wye to the north of Buellt. Then Prince Dafydd's banner came into view, streaming from a pole Cadwallon held.

Dafydd must have run all the way from the upper rooms in the keep when he heard the news. "Twenty men have outsped the others," he said.

"That will be Bevyn," I said.

"He's going to kill me," Dafydd said, shaking his head. "This is the second time I've done this to him." He trotted down the stairs and ordered the guards to raise the portcullis. He went through alone, on foot, to wait for his men to come to him.

The last time he was separated from his men, when he'd survived the kidnapping and freed himself, they'd encircled him with cheers and jubilation. This time his men rode forward silently, slowing their horses to a stop ten paces away.

Bevyn dismounted, removed his helmet, and settled it on his hip. "My lord," he said.

"It is I, this time, who must ask your forgiveness," Dafydd said, taking a step towards him.

"Why?" Bevyn asked as he too moved closer. "Did you do wrong? You've paid some kind of price already, I see. Did Ieuan set your nose? He clearly bungled the job."

"Because I didn't tell you the truth, long ago," Dafydd said, ignoring the banter.

"We saw you jump," Bevyn said, and he gestured behind him to the men with him. "All of us."

"And disappear," Dafydd said.

"Yes," Bevyn said. Their eyes met. Bevyn was waiting for something, needing something from Dafydd before he could let it go.

"I took Ieuan to the land of Madoc, to save his life," Dafydd said, "and brought him home again. My mistake was not in leaving, but in not warning you that I might need to."

"Magic?" Bevyn asked.

*He's testing Dafydd. From this moment, Bevyn's loyalty and that of all his men depends on the answer to this question.*

"I only seek to do God's bidding," Dafydd said. "I can't help who I am. I can only help what I do. In leaving you, I saved Ieuan's life; in returning, I saved my father's. We can spend our lives fighting what happens to us, or learn to accept what is given."

"Did you die?" That was Trahearn, from the back of the group. "Did God send you back to us?"

"I went to another place, for a time, one I can't begin to describe to you. Ieuan was with me," Dafydd turned to look at me. I raised a hand. "Perhaps the words will come more easily to him."

It was enough. Bevyn and Dafydd embraced. A cheer went up and the men circled their prince, pummeling his back.

"Careful, careful." Dafydd held out his hands to keep them at bay. "I'm not entirely well. My torso matches my face, perhaps worse."

"Your mother will not be pleased," Bevyn said, with perhaps a bit too much relish.

"And here she is," Dafydd said. More horses thundered across the bridge and made their way up the hill to where Dafydd and his men stood. Aaron, Math, and Anna, tiny Cadell slung across her chest, and finally Marged. The sea of men parted so that Dafydd could reach his mother and help her off her horse.

"Hi, Mom," he said as he set her on her feet. She looked up at him and it was like he broke in two. He folded her in his arms, put his head down on her shoulder, and cried. Her cloak muffled his sobs, but there was no mistaking them. Marged wrapped an arm around his neck and another around his waist and held him to her, absorbing his anguish, with her hand on the back of his head.

Bevyn jerked his head toward the castle and everyone silently filed around the two of them until they stood alone. I met Bevyn and Math at the gate and we hovered there, not wanting to leave them unattended, but not wanting to intrude.

"A man can only take so much," Math said.

"I have much to tell you," I said. "Most of which you won't even believe."

# 27

## *David*

"So what did you do?" I asked. I felt drained, but at the same time happier than I'd been in weeks. For the first time in a long time, what I thought of as my family was all together: Mom and Dad; Math and Anna with Cadell cradled in her arms, nursing; Bronwen and Ieuan; Aaron; Bevyn, who was the only one standing, his shoulder braced against the wall by the door; and Gwenllian, who sat at my feet, whispering to her rag doll.

"At first, we were, uh, *concerned* my lord, that our eyes deceived us," Bevyn said. "I was unsure if you'd fallen onto a ledge and hidden in a cave in the cliff face, or if you'd fallen so fast that I missed where you lay."

"But then an English soldier dismounted at the edge of the cliff and peered over it. He couldn't see anything," Aaron said. "We watched him shake his head and shrug at his companion. They must have thought you'd fallen into the water, though it's not directly underneath the cliff in that location."

"The soldiers were turning away, not even bothering to capture the horses, when we shot them," Bevyn said. "After that, we hunted all over the cliff for you, my lord. We wouldn't have left you if you were to be found."

"It's all right, Bevyn," I said. "We weren't to be found."

"I knew it," Aaron said. "The moment you disappeared I knew what I'd seen. It just took some time for my heart to understand what my brain was telling me."

"How did you explain it to the men?" I asked.

"Aaron told the tale," Bevyn said. "He'll find himself work as a bard if he's not careful. He spoke about the land of Madoc, for those who'd not ridden in the van, and implied that it was a place of safety, from which you would come again when you were ready."

"Like Avalon; like Arthur," Math said. He sat with Anna beside him, while she studied me, her face solemn. We'd have a lot to talk about later, when we could be alone.

"Your men understood the danger you were in, Dafydd," Mom said. "I heard some of them discussing it in the days after they arrived at Dinas Bran, and it has grown since the messenger brought word that you were at Buellt. They called it a miracle—God holding Wales in the palm of his hand."

"It was a miracle," Dad said. "I won't hear anything to the contrary." He sat beside Mom, one hand resting gently on his belly, the other holding her hand.

"Why didn't you tell me that the dragon banner would be seen as Arthur's flag?" I asked. "I'd never have flown it had I known."

"That's why we didn't tell you," Dad said. "You chose it in innocence, and we decided to honor your choice."

"I'm no Arthur," I said. "They can't think it."

"Can't they?" Bevyn said, his voice flat. "You can't stop them."

"Especially considering what he's been up to lately," Ieuan said.

Father eased back in his chair, stretching out his legs in front of him and crossing his ankles. "Our young prince has a plan to expel the English from Wales," he said, satisfaction in his voice. "It's only a matter of time."

\* \* \* \* \*

Eventually everyone left, even Math with Cadell, now asleep, understanding that I needed some time alone with Anna.

"You came back," she said, asking the same question Dad had, though with a slightly different intent. "We had three days between when Aaron and Bevyn arrived and when your message came, in which we feared for you—more than usual, that is." She walked slowly around the room as she talked. She picked up a paperweight and set it down, fiddled with father's pen, and set it down. I perched on the desk beside where she stood.

"Did you think I wouldn't come back?"

"It was more a matter of whether you *could* come back. I assumed you would if it were possible, but didn't know how difficult you might find it to return. I confess, I also felt concern that the longer you were in the twenty-first century, the more natural it might feel, and the easier to stay."

"Aunt Elisa offered to have me to live with her," I said.

"You didn't even consider it, did you?" Anna said.

I shrugged. "I went to the drug store with Aunt Elisa."

Anna's eyes lit.

"Yes, I have things for you!" I said. I pulled her presents out of my backpack.

"A toothbrush!" Anna said. I handed her the rest: pain reliever for Cadell, a couple of the antibiotic tubes, a jar of lotion.

"Anyway," I continued, "it was hard to decide what we should buy—or rather, what I would ask Aunt Elisa to buy—not because so much of it was vital to survival, but because so much of it wasn't."

"You've lived without all of it for three years, so now you can't remember why you needed it in the first place," Anna said.

"Exactly," I said.

"You've got some antibiotics here," she said. She held up two plastic containers, each with a dozen pills.

"Those would be a major exception to what I'm saying. Aunt Elisa emptied her medicine cabinet for me. What they're for is written on the label."

"That's what we really need to make a difference," Anna said. "Medicine like this."

"That's why I brought these," I said, pulling the sheaf of papers from the pack, which was now nearly empty. Anna took the stack and began leafing through the pages.

"Lots of weaponry, here, David," she said. "What's up with that?"

"We need to keep the English at bay, Anna," I said. "Until we achieve peace, we won't be able to make any of the changes in Wales that I'm hoping for."

She looked over at me. "You have big plans, don't you?"

"Yup."

"But you can't do it all, can you?" she said. She shuffled the pages and took out a chunk. "Give the information about medicine to me. I may not be able to fight with you, or want to fight with you for that matter, but this I can do."

"You mean it?" I asked.

"From all the books you've read," she said, "what is the one field of knowledge open to women in this age? What is the only thing I am allowed to master?"

I got it. "Herb lore," I said.

"Well, that's me," Anna said. "I'm good with plants and I know how to learn—and how to read and write. What is penicillin but moldy bread? This is something I can do; something I want to do."

"Okay," I said. "It's all yours."

Anna hugged the papers to her chest. "Thank you," she said. "Thank you for the gifts and for thinking of me."

"I think of you a lot," I said. "I was watching you when we were talking with the others. You know what it meant for me to go back and what it means for me to come home."

"It's funny that the least of your concerns was that the King of England attempted to murder you."

"When it was happening, same as when I'm in the midst of a battle, there's no time for thinking. It's only when it's over that I realize how close I came to dying."

"I don't think I could do what you've done," Anna said.

"You've had a baby in medieval Wales," I pointed out. "I think we're even."

Anna shrugged and changed the subject. "Give the stuff on education to Mom. She's bored. Between her and Aaron, they'll figure out how to get things started."

"You mean, like, delegate?" I asked. "Let other people in on my vision for Wales?" I laughed. "I've had this picture of the future, Anna, that I've been too embarrassed to share. If we are very, very lucky, Wales could become the center of the medieval world. I want that. I want to try to make that happen, but I was afraid to say anything because it sounds . . . well . . . innocent and naïve . . . and unrealistic."

"You aren't the only one to have plans, David," Anna replied. "I'm not exactly thrilled about how society works here either."

"I know that—"

"What I'm saying is that you don't have to go it alone," Anna said. "Everyone may think you're the return of Arthur, but that doesn't mean you have to buy into the myth yourself."

"I don't!" I said. "I'd never think that. You know I didn't ask to be the Prince of Wales."

"But you've chosen it now and you must act the part in public, as long as you realize you have a better, smarter round table surrounding you than Arthur did."

"I do realize that," I said. "I would've realized it sooner if I'd thought about it."

"Good," Anna said. "Now, can we fight?"

"What?" I asked.

"It's been a month since Cadell was born and I'm out of shape. He's taking a nap so I have time *right now*. Can we fight?"

"Sure, I said, "as long as we take it easy and you don't actually touch my belly."

Anna laughed. "Nor mine!"

I sat in a chair and pulled off my boots while Anna slipped out of her shoes. "Eight basic attacks?"

"Right," she said.

"Don't you want to change out of your dress first?" I asked.

"Into what?" Anna said. "I'm a lady, David."

"Why do I always end up apologizing to you for having to live here?" I said. "I'm sorry life is this way, Anna."

"It is this way," she said. "I can cope. Besides, if I'm going to actually *use* karate, it will be while I'm in a dress. I rode here in it; I can fight in it."

We met in the middle of the floor. I was a foot taller and outweighed her by a good eighty pounds, but sometimes being smaller had its advantages, particularly in making her quicker and more agile. I was careful not to hurt her as we went through the motions, because she was out of shape and I was bruised.

"Take him down a peg, love," Math called from the doorway.

I grunted as Anna did exactly that—for a third time.

"So that's how it's done," Bronwen said.

"Don't go trying that," Ieuan muttered.

Math laughed. "There may be drawbacks to having a wife from another land, Ieuan, but the ability to stand up for herself is not one of them."

"Come over here, Bronwen," Anna said, having dropped me on the floor again. "I'll show you a thing or two, something simple you can use in self-defense if you have to."

Bronwen and I traded places. "It's a new world, Ieuan," I said, leaning against the wall beside him. "Best get used to it."

# 28

*Bronwen*

"That was quite a display you put on with your sister the other day," I said, picking up speed and shifting into second gear. "She taught me three simple things to do, and I suddenly feel much more confident."

"Just don't get cocky," David said. "You don't want to have just enough information to be dangerous to yourself, rather than an attacker."

"I know," I said.

"Most of the techniques are relatively simple. You just have to be prepared to use them, and not hesitate, because hesitation will cost you whatever advantage you might have had. Believe me, I know. If your opponent has a knife, every second you delay increases your chance of getting cut."

"That's why you moved in on that guy back at Penn State," I said, beginning to understand. "It wasn't because you were being macho or brave, but because you had chosen to act."

"Better to act than react," David said. "Especially since you're a woman, and like Anna, not a big person. If you have a chance to act, you do it, and you make it count." We rolled over the Irfon Bridge before David spoke again. "Things are going to start happening pretty quickly now."

"As if things have been slow up until this point?" I asked.

David laughed. "I've got Ieuan in pursuit of bat guano—apparently we've more than ten different kinds of bats native to Wales—a lucky happenstance—and Math is overseeing the quest for sulfur and charcoal. Before another week passes, we're going to launch a full scale assault on Painscastle and Brecon. Our black powder is going to bring down the walls and usher in the medieval equivalent of an arms race. The technology exists out there; it's just not widely used or understood. Don't think Hereford is going to take our pre-eminence sitting down."

David's list of weaponry was daunting. He wanted exploding missiles to fire from trebuchets, whether comprised of my Greek fire compound or black powder, fire arrows, black powder kegs for mining under castle walls, and gasoline bombs. I was in charge of the gasoline and the Greek fire.

Another hundred yards and I turned onto a track to the right. It brought us to the bottom of a slope that led to a meadow. Above that was a tree-covered hill.

"Stop here," David said, and got out of the car. He spoke to his men who'd followed behind us as we drove, and had them set up a perimeter around the meadow and the trees by which I parked. David leaned into the car. "We're going through those bushes, just to your left. Follow me."

He disappeared between two thickets and I got out of the car to follow him, trying not to catch my hair in the brambles. I came out the other side into a small clearing. A thick screen of trees surrounded it on all sides. Aunt Elisa's minivan sat in the middle of it. *Wow.* Even after all that had happened, there were times when I felt normal, that thirteenth century Wales didn't seem so different. And then the distance to the twenty-first century would stop me in my tracks.

"So what do you want from me, exactly?"

"Creative uses for gasoline," David said. He opened the trunk and surveyed the contents with satisfaction.

I stepped to look with him. "Oh," I said.

Aunt Elisa was a pack rat. I understood now why David had been so nonchalant about siphoning gas out of the vehicles and the containers in which we would put it. Not only did we have the 6 root beer bottles in my car that Aunt Elisa had given Ieuan, but another two dozen lay jumbled in the back of her car, along with a staggering array of twenty-first century garbage.

"You wouldn't know it by how her house looks," David said. "Maybe it's just her cars." He pulled a six foot length of plastic tubing from the pile of items and held it up for inspection. "I saw this when we drove the van the last time. Poor Aeddan had to contend with all this junk when I stuffed him in the trunk so I could drive the van out of here. I didn't think anything of the hose at the time, but I remembered it later, during the siege of Bronllys

311

in July, and wished I had more time to come up with a way to use it."

I joined him and began gathering the glass bottles into a grocery bag. David lifted up the floor of the trunk and took out a two gallon plastic gasoline container.

"Okay," I said. "We need to start the siphon, and then it's a piece of cake."

"This is the part that I was most worried about," David said. "Is it as easy as it looks on television?"

"I can do it," I said. "My youth was apparently more misspent than yours."

Bevyn strode into the clearing. "My lord!" he said. "Tudur and Goronwy have reached the castle and your father requests your presence, as soon as possible."

"Thanks, Bevyn," David said. He turned to me. "Can you handle this? Just fill the container and bring all the bottles back to the castle. You can prepare the bottles there."

"Go," I said. "I'm fine."

David nodded at Bevyn, who held the branches open for him to pass.

"My lady," Bevyn said before he followed David, "I will send Cadwallon to you, and leave you a further ten men for your protection."

"Thank you, sir," I said.

I returned to the task at hand. The key with siphoning gasoline was not to get any in one's mouth, which I'd watched my father do once when his car was out of gas and our neighbor's wasn't. Clear tubing, such as Aunt Elisa had bought, helped. I shoved the tube into the minivan's tank, stepped into the trunk so I stood higher than the top of the van, and sucked. The gasoline rose up the tube until it was about a foot from my mouth. I stopped it with my tongue, and then my finger, before climbing down and lowering the end of the hose into the plastic carrying container. *Done!*

Cadwallon appeared just as it finished filling. He approached me and the vehicle with obvious trepidation.

"Did you ride in it before?" I asked.

"Yes, my lady," he said. "It was an experience of a lifetime."

"But you wouldn't like to ride in it again?"

He shook his head vehemently. "I would prefer to leave the Prince's miracles for him and him alone."

His words could have been full of fear, but instead he spoke with reverence. I straightened and Cadwallon looked at me, his face shining. "You are a lady of Avalon too," he said. "I'm honored to assist you."

*Uh oh.*

"Then carry this for me," I said, and pointed to the gas canister.

He hefted it easily. I shut the trunk, we walked back through the bushes to my car, and Cadwallon put the container inside. I tried to figure out what to say to him. I didn't want to diminish David's authority, but surely such worship wasn't healthy.

I'd wondered initially how a high school kid could so easily—not that it was 'easy,' granted—make the transition to being a prince of Wales. But really, many Americans behaved routinely just like the sons of the British aristocracy had two hundred years ago: they played lots of games; they cared about fashion; they attended college in great part to go to parties and have a good time; they wore their entitlement like a cloak. They walked the streets as if they owned them—*which in the United States they did!*

"You realize, Cadwallon," I finally said, "Dafydd doesn't claim to be Arthur."

"But he wouldn't, would he?" Cadwallon said. "He already serves Wales in the same fashion as Arthur did. It's up to us to remind him who he really is. He's everything Arthur was. You can't deny it."

I gazed at Cadwallon. He *believed* it.

\* \* \* \* \*

The sun was bright for once. On a whim, I climbed to the top of the castle wall and walked all around the top of it, the breeze on my face, and contemplating the green countryside around me. Lili's parting words passed through my head: *Prince Dafydd has lost control of this. He can't stop it now. Tell him he shouldn't try.*

I turned to the south, thinking of Lili's prescience and wishing I shared it. I found the road that would return Ieuan to

Buellt, but no dust stirred it. With a sigh, I stepped inside one of the rounded battlements. Anna sat cross-legged on the stones nursing Cadell, her back against the eastern wall. I hesitated, one foot forward.

"Come in," she said. "You won't disturb us. Every castle has at least one spot for me to hide, and this is it for Buellt."

"I thought it was only me who looked for places like that," I said. "I didn't know you were shy, too." I looked west, my back to Anna. The sun shone in my eyes and the breeze pulled at my hair. Someone had told me that this signaled a change in the weather. *Rain then.*

"Math has gone off on a quest for David, and Ieuan too, I hear," Anna said. "Looking for the ingredients for weapons."

"Bevyn told me when I entered the bailey that David, Prince Llywelyn, and your mother are closeted with Tudur and Goronwy. Apparently three of the English lords chose to side with us."

"Really?" Anna asked. "That's unexpected."

"Maybe they like Wales too," I said. "Or maybe they realize that the crown of England is weak and think this is the better option."

Anna sighed. "Why can't the English just leave us alone? Wales is beautiful, but there isn't much else here, is there?"

I smiled. Below us, the river Irfon wended around the village. The hills rose just beyond, becoming mountains in the distance. It wasn't even sufficient to say the air was clear.

Twenty-first century people have no idea how clean their air used to be—could be again one day, given effort.

"Can I ask you a question?" I said, turning back to look at her.

"Yes."

"You married Math. What made you decide that you could make a life here?"

"You're thinking about you and Ieuan?" Anna said.

"Yes," I said. "But also about you. You're younger than I am, and younger still when you came to Wales."

"I chose to grow up," Anna said.

I hesitated over my next question. "And Math?" I asked. "Can it really work for Ieuan and me?"

Anna laughed. "Love helps a lot," she said, "but it isn't enough. You have to look at the kind of person they are; figure out whether you can live with their character for the rest of your life. That's even more important here, where divorce is so rare, though it happens. I didn't want to follow my heart with Math at first. I tried to persuade him that he wasn't interested in me. David is the one who encouraged me to look at him more closely, because he and Math had become such good friends. Finally, Papa, David, and I sat him down and told him where we were from, and explained what that might mean for him and me."

She stopped.

"And then what?"

"It was such a relief for Math to realize that it wasn't *him* that I was afraid of, but committing to *this* life. After that, I couldn't lie to myself anymore. We married soon after."

"And since then?"

"I'm so thankful I didn't choose differently; that I have Cadell and Math and a complete life here."

"Your feelings haven't changed even with the knowledge that you might be able to return to the twenty-first century?" I asked. "Like David did?"

"Life is the people you live it with, not the time you're in," Anna said. "That life is so far removed from what and who I am now. I can't imagine trying to fit in as a teenager in Oregon having lived as I have. I'd have to pretend that none of this had happened; that it was all a dream, like my mother had to when she went back before David was born. I have a child now, as she did. How could I choose to go back? Mom wouldn't have either, had she been given the choice." Anna stroked Cadell's head with her free hand.

I stared into the distance.

"Don't jump," Anna said.

"Excuse me?"

"In the first weeks I was in Wales, I used to stand at the top of the wall at Castell y Bere, before the English burned it to the ground, and think about jumping. I thought maybe I wouldn't hit the ground, but be transported home, and perhaps I was right."

I looked over the battlements. It would be so easy to step off the edge and fall. Could I return that easily, or would it kill

317

me? Either way, the thirteenth century and Ieuan would be lost to me.

"What stopped you?" I said.

"I didn't want to be a coward, and I didn't want to abandon David."

"I don't want to go back." *I don't want to go back!* The realization flooded through me and I felt like someone had lifted off the top of my head and filled me up with emotion. I swung around to face Anna. "It may sound crazy, but despite everything that has happened to me since I came to Wales, I love it here."

"Do you really?" she asked. "When David told me he'd brought you back with him; that you were going to marry Ieuan, I was, quite frankly, shocked. I asked myself, *why would anyone* choose *to come to the thirteenth century?* Even for an historian, the fascination can pale pretty quickly, once the absence of anything resembling a hot shower sinks in."

"But . . ." I said, and gestured to the land around us. "Wales is beautiful, and I hardly miss those things. Most are more of a burden than a help anyway. Admittedly, I grew up without much in the way of material possessions, what with the yurts and the shacks my parents called home."

"I see your point, even if most of the time my inner child doesn't agree," Anna said. She lifted Cadell, put him on her shoulder, and kissed his little cheek as she patted his back. "There's a thirteenth century equivalent for most things that we *need* that are manufactured in the twenty-first century, but that didn't stop me from crying over the baby fingernail clippers David brought me, or Mom over her cotton socks. I *like* luxury." She reached out a hand and I helped pull her to her feet.

"Those first hours and days in Wales, totally overwhelmed me."

"And now?" Anna asked.

"Now I wouldn't even consider jumping," I said, and meant it.

# 29

## *Ieuan*

I rode towards the western side of Painscastle with my lord Dafydd and Goronwy. It was near the end of the day and the setting sun lit the castle, earlier now that September was only two days away.

"Your men must have worked like demons!" Dafydd said, dismounting from Aneirin, his new stallion, named for the great bard. The tunnel that Goronwy's men had dug began at a low point, a hundred yards from the southern castle wall. The troops had set up wooden barricades to shield them from watchers' eyes. The majority of Goronwy's men camped at the edge of the trees, two hundred yards away and out of bow range. Dafydd walked into the entrance and gazed down the long tunnel. Timbers supported the roof, which stretched into the darkness.

"As you can see, my lord, we've begun the undermining process," Goronwy said. "The men are near the castle walls now. Conveniently for us at this stage, the rampart is in front of the ditch. The wall's foundation is deep, however, and it won't be easy to bring it down."

"The black powder should take care of that," Dafydd said.

"We captured the messengers Tosny dispatched to England," Goronwy added. "No others have left the castle since."

"Good," Dafydd said. "Edward has been dead nearly a month, and this is the last thing any of the English lords want or need. We take this castle, and Brecon after that, and they'll come begging for peace."

"Hereford won't," I said.

"Hereford won't have a choice," Dafydd said. "He's more than a Marcher lord now. As regent, his responsibility is to the whole of England—a new concept for him, I admit, but one that the other regents will force him to see. I want to take the castle before Tosny's reinforcements arrive, if they arrive."

"Tonight?" Goronwy said.

Dafydd canted his head toward the wagons behind us. "We should be able to bring down the castle wall with the powder we've made. If it works, that is. This could be very dangerous, so I need your most experienced miners to set it up."

"I will see to it," Goronwy said.

"Just let me know when you're ready."

"Yes, my lord."

Dafydd nodded and he and I returned to our horses. Bevyn had brought Llywd home for me. He'd weathered the trip with no difficulties. It still rankled Dafydd that circumstances had required him to leave Taranis in a ditch beside the road in England. I assured him that dying in battle was a noble ending for a warhorse, but he wasn't comforted. He viewed Taranis' loss as careless and—*stupid*, was the word he used.

Back in the trees again, we rode north along a path that was just out of bowshot of the walls, and reached the line of archers that hovered on the edge of the woods, occasionally firing off a shot in the direction of the ramparts. It was exactly as it had been at Bronllys, except the terrain here was less hilly.

Dafydd dismounted again. "My lord?" I asked, wondering why he'd stopped, and then saw who'd caught his attention: *Lili*. As we watched, she pressed and loosed an arrow. Despite my misgivings at her presence, I congratulated myself on teaching her such good form. In truth, she was wasted in this company. A mass of arrows, fired in unison at the enemy and which came down like a rain of hail would win the day, not accuracy.

Once darkness descended, the archers and siege engines could move closer without being seen from the castle. The archers would shoot our new fire arrows, the trebuchets would throw caskets filled with black powder and metal fragments we'd laced with gasoline, and the powder would explode the castle walls.

"I feel your disapproval like a black cloud over my head, my lord," Lili said. She looked at Dafydd over her shoulder.

He spread his hands wide, conveying his innocence. "Did I say anything?" he asked. "I don't recall saying anything."

"But you thought something," she said.

"More along the lines of 'what's *she* doing here?' I admit," he said.

"Your sister and mother are to the rear, aiding the wounded," Lili said. She glanced at me. "Bronwen is there too."

"We'll see them now, before it gets dark and the world goes crazy," Dafydd said.

"Aren't you going to order me away from the line?" Lili asked.

"No," said Dafydd. He stepped away and remounted Aneirin. "You've sworn you can take care of yourself. I expect you to do just that."

Lili's face was a pale circle in the darkness under the trees. "Yes, my lord," she said. We left, me with my mouth shut and my tongue between my teeth.

Marged greeted us as we entered the pavilion for the wounded. Dafydd stopped short—given pause by the number of men who already lay on the ground around him. "What's this?" he asked his mother.

"Accidents, mostly," she said. "One poor man over there almost chopped off his foot with an axe."

I whispered in his left ear. "Malingering, my lord?"

Marged overheard me. "Don't say that," she said. "That's the last thing we need, though I don't see it as a concern at all. Overall, my impression is that morale is very high."

Dafydd looked past her to Anna. "What are you doing here?" he asked.

Anna's brows furrowed. "What are you talking about? Why shouldn't I be here?"

"What about Cadell?"

"He's sleeping in the car with his nanny. Like every other baby ever born, he fell asleep within minutes of starting the car. Wena promised to come get me when he wakes and Bronwen will drive me back to Aberedw."

"Right," Bronwen said, from her post at a man's side. She was winding a strip of cloth around a cut on his wrist while he sat on a stool in front of her. I walked over to her and patted the man on his shoulder.

"You're in good hands," I said to him.

"I know it," the man said. "And not just because of your beautiful lady. This is just a scratch. It could have been an arrow's wound. I was walking up the hill and slipped in the mud just as an arrow shot over my head. I'll be back in the line by sunset."

"They're all like this, Ieuan," Bronwen said. "Not one of them will hear of staying behind."

I kissed the top of her head and turned to leave, but Bronwen grabbed my hand and followed me out of the tent. "I heard that you're going to lead the assault through the breach in the wall, if the black powder brings it down as David hopes," she said.

"Bronwen—"

"I heard you volunteered to do it."

I wanted to touch her, but she'd folded her arms across her chest. "This is who I am, Bronwen," I said. Goronwy had offered to lead the footmen in their attack on the castle, but Prince Llywelyn had dissuaded him of it. That job belonged to a younger man. *Me.*

"Why?" she said, anguish in her voice. "When we rode with Dafydd to get the car, I had no idea what we were getting into. Now, I do." Her shoulders sagged and she softened her stance. Recognizing that her need matched mine, I tugged her into my arms.

"Because it's my job," I said, "and I'm good at it."

"What if you don't come back?" Bronwen said, looking up at me. "What is there for me here without you?"

"There are two answers to that question, Bronwen," I said, "and you already know them both. The first is that I don't believe I'm going to die tonight. I don't feel it, but I can't promise you that I won't."

"Then don't go," she said, her voice muffled in my chest.

"I could die tomorrow, next month, next year. Your happiness can't depend on me, as much as part of me wants it to. If I die, other people here will still love you."

"And that's the second answer," Bronwen said.

I pulled her closer and bent my head to kiss her. She tightened her arms around my neck. "Come back," she said. "I need you to come back."

"You're not the only one who needs it," I said, my voice soft in her ear. "I will come back for you."

\* \* \* \* \*

The battle started as soon as it got dark. We had only two trebuchets because they are expensive to build and complicated to work. Dafydd let me hold his binoculars so I could watch the flaming casks hit. The first one fell short, as the men who manned it tried to find the range. Meanwhile, a stone from the other trebuchet slammed into the side of the curtain wall, ripping off the top crenellations. I glanced at the Prince. He wanted more. He didn't just want to destroy Painscastle, he wanted to demoralize the English.

With the next shot, the men manning the first trebuchet got going in earnest. Each cask arced through the air in a magnificent trajectory of light, then disappeared over the curtain wall into the bailey. The screams of the defenders were audible from where we stood. In an hour, we managed twelve shots.

"Have they put up a flag?" Dafydd asked. "I don't see one."

"No, my lord," I said.

"Tell Goronwy before you join your men that he can bring down the wall whenever he's ready and Madog to move the archers forward," he said. "Make sure they're properly shielded."

"Yes, my lord."

Madog was the captain of the archers, whom I'd not met personally before. I'd made it my business to become acquainted with him, however, once it became clear that Lili was determined to fight amongst his men. "If anything happens to her, I will personally rip your head off," I'd told him.

"She'll be well protected, my lord, but safer yet would to have her at home, weaving among your women."

I growled at him. "Did you tell her that?" I'd asked.

He'd grinned at my ferocity. "Me?" he'd said. He held up his hands, palms outward. "Worth more than my life to tell her anything, I think. That's *your* job, my lord."

Now, the foot soldiers and I crowded behind and to one side of the archers. They'd provide cover for us for the two hundred yards separating the tree line from the castle walls. In the momentary lull, I pulled my sword from its sheath, stabbed it into the ground in front of me, and knelt. *Dear God, keep me safe. Let me return well and whole.* I kissed the point of the cross and with each heartbeat that passed, locked my emotions more tightly into a box in my mind and put it away, on a high shelf. Some men fought angry and it gave them power. I strove to feel nothing—no anger, hatred, love—that would distract me from the task at hand. *I've no love for Bronwen; no fear for Lili; no regret for a life half-lived. There is only the sword in my hand and my men beside me, with death a widening abyss beneath my feet.*

A commotion came from the tunnel entrance. A man ran out, shouting, "It's lit! It's lit!"

*Whump!*

I felt the power of the blast, more than heard it. Less than a second later, the ground shook and Painscastle's curtain wall exploded into the sky. Fragments of stone and dirt shot fifty feet into the air. They came down like rain, thudding into the ground on both sides of the rampart.

Then the archers started firing their arrows over our heads and we ran across the grass towards the castle, screaming our battle cry until our throats went hoarse. I shouted at the top of my lungs, my sword raised high, but even I couldn't make sense of what I was saying. The trebuchet fired a cask; it exploded on the keep and shot metal fragments (shrapnel, Dafydd said) in every direction.

It took us thirty seconds to reach the wall—fast considering the rough terrain, but the men had spent the day preparing themselves for battle and were fully charged with courage. We stormed through the breach in the wall, the men stumbling over the stones that descended out of the opening on both sides and filled the ditch behind the wall. The men behind were pushing hard, and some of those in front went down. I grasped one man's collar and hauled him to his feet as I passed him.

Painscastle was lost the moment we passed the wall and surged into the defenders, who'd been slow to fill the gap. If they'd been able to meet us at the top, we would have fought, pressed against each other so closely a man could hardly wield his sword. Instead, I got three paces down the other side of the pile of stones before anyone countered my advance, and my men spilled into the bailey behind me.

All the buildings had caught fire and metal littered the ground. I hoped Tosny had pulled his non-combatants into the keep, because any left out here would be dead within the half hour. We outnumbered the English, and no matter the ferocity of their defense, now that their wall was breached, they would lose.

I faced an Englishman, his helmet askew and wearing a scorched surcoat. Our swords met, but we were pressed so close together, I only managed one swing before I gave up and bashed his face with my shield. He staggered back, tripped on the stones behind him, and fell. I lost track of him instantly as I had to meet the sword of the man behind him. This one was much larger, but like his fellows, shocked by the barrage and the explosions. I caught his downward slash with my shield, and slid my sword under his guard and into his belly. He fell, and I moved on to the next man. And then the next.

Finally, I reached the barbican—the fortified gateway that protected the motte on which the keep sat. I swung around. We'd charged the wall with nearly two hundred men and encountered less than a third of that number. Most of Tosny's men had fallen, but it was not my job to finish the rest. I grabbed the arm of one of my men, one of the youngest.

"Run to Lord Goronwy. I need archers atop these battlements," I said, gesturing to the walls that surrounded the bailey—those that were still standing, that is. "Tell him we've penned Tosny in his tower. We need to keep him there until he sues for peace."

"Yes, my lord," the boy said. He flitted through the wall and was gone.

The intensity of *being* that always filled me during battle began to fade and my vision cleared. Soon, my men had finished their work in the bailey and archers began struggling through the gap in the wall. Lili was among them, but before I could berate her, she grasped my arm.

"I'm a messenger, only," she said. "Your man, Brychan is here, and knows what to do. Prince Dafydd asks that you return with me. He would have your counsel as to what comes next."

\* \* \* \* \*

We met in the early hours of the morning. Bronwen had taken Anna to Aberedw Castle, and returned with Prince Llywelyn. He stood with Dafydd and his other lords, including Goronwy and Math, who'd ridden in from Brecon an hour before.

"Tosny refuses to surrender?" Math asked. "Why?"

"Perhaps he fears we will put him to the sword," I said.

"Edward would have," Goronwy said. "Edward did, in fact, most recently at Castell y Bere. For all the years he's lived in Wales, Tosny knows little of its Prince."

"The only thing standing between him and us is a barbican," Math said. "Two barrels of powder at its base and it's gone. He must know by now we have the means to take his keep. Painscastle can be ours if we're willing to raze it to the ground, along with everyone in it."

Prince Llywelyn shook his head. "Give him a few days to think about it. His choice is to surrender or die and he knows it. He'll see reason eventually, and if he doesn't, we can still take the castle."

Dafydd turned to me. "How is the men's morale? Are they still willing to fight?"

I laughed. "You couldn't stop them, I don't think. They're drunk with the power of being Welsh."

"Drunk with victory, and soon to be drunk with mead," Bevyn said. "We'll need to keep an eye on them if we hope to have any fighting men left to watch the keep."

"Two cups each," Goronwy said. "That's what I ordered. If a commander allows differently, he knows that he'll regret it."

"Good," Prince Llywelyn said. "We need the men alert and awake. I don't want to just defend the border, I want to control it. I need every man who can walk or ride divided into companies within the hour. From this moment, no Englishman may set foot in Wales without my leave." He fisted his right hand and slapped into the palm of his left as he spoke.

"This is our hour," Goronwy agreed. "We must make the most of it."

"See to it," Llywelyn said. "Hereford has three days to admit the error of his ways. After that, we will move again, and any Englishman who stands against us will pay a stiff price."

# 30

## Bronwen

Ieuan was in a hurry. I could feel him urging the car faster as we left Painscastle behind us, heading east to England. His face and shoulders reflected his intensity. We were going fifteen miles an hour, which admittedly in a car feels like a slow crawl, but it was far faster than we would have been going on horseback. The dashboard glowed blue and red, but otherwise we were riding without lights.

Molotov cocktails and the pots of unmixed Greek fire filled the backseat and trunk. The pots exploded on impact, no matter if we threw them on the ground or at buildings. The glass bottles which contained the cocktails, on the other hand, were proving a more sturdy container than we'd anticipated, having been invented in a land of pavement and concrete, of which there was none in the Middle Ages.

"Why didn't you tell me it was so soon?" I asked.

"Prince Llywelyn's orders," Ieuan said.

"It's only been two days, not the three that Prince Llywelyn gave Hereford," I said, trying not to feel betrayed.

"Events encouraged us to pick up the pace," Ieuan said. "Pull over here, to the right."

I parked fifty feet from the Dyke beneath two beech trees that had become intertwined in a mass of branches and brambles that marked the edge of a farmer's field. The Dyke lay just ahead, lit by an unexpectedly bright moon after a long day of rain. We didn't want to alert any nearby English to our presence by driving the car any closer. In the twenty-first century, the sound of a vehicle was like nothing—so common you hardly ever noticed it. Here, where the only sounds were natural, it stood out.

Ieuan eased the door open. "Stay here."

"Where are you going?"

Ieuan stopped by the trunk, listening. I waited, and then heard what had caught his attention: hoof beats. Ieuan shrank into the shadow of the trees. The pounding rang out as rider passed us a few feet from the car. Even I recognized the horse, the armor the man wore, and the set of the man's shoulders. *Tudur.*

"There he goes," Ieuan said.

"You expected him?" I asked.

"I did," Ieuan said. "And now we'll see if the bastard is true to his word."

Keeping to the grass beside the road, Ieuan cat-walked to where the Dyke rose above him, a bulk in the dark. He climbed down into the ditch and up again, to the top of the wall, and then scurried over it. I waited. Nothing.

*This is unacceptable.*

I got out of the car and ran in a crouch to the point Ieuan had gone over the Dyke. I knew he wouldn't like it, but as long as I stayed on the Welsh side of the wall, I thought I'd be all right. I climbed to the top of the earthen wall, my feet losing their traction repeatedly in the mud, and crawled on my stomach across the flat top to the far edge. Fortunately, I managed to bury my gasp in my sleeve.

Below me, a dozen yards away, a campfire blazed next to a small hut. A disarmed Ieuan, with his hands out, stood back to back with Tudur, who'd lost his helmet. A sword length away, a thickset, bearded man glared at them. On the edge of the camp, just within range of the firelight, a company of English soldiers in full battle armor waited.

I spent ten seconds trying to find my breath, my head down on my arms, and then pushed backwards off the Dyke and dropped to the Welsh side. I turned to run back to the car and froze. *Worse and worse.* Ten men on horseback surrounded my car. They must have heard the thud on the grass as I fell, or sensed my movement, because they turned as one to look at me.

"Bronwen!"

I ran towards Prince Llywelyn, who dismounted to greet me. I spoke through choppy breaths. "Ieuan . . . Tudur . . . English soldiers . . . the other side of the Dyke . . . must save him!"

"How many men?"

"Forty?" I guessed.

"Ach," the Prince said. "They outnumber us four to one."

"Not the way I see it," I said.

I popped the trunk and everyone gazed down at my Greek Fire canisters. They resembled small urns, with a narrow top and base and a septum down the center that separated the water from the powdered mixture. When the pot broke, the ingredients spontaneously combusted. I was quite proud of them and would have been prouder if we weren't going to use them to kill people— or at the very least injure them.

I handed one to each of Prince Llywelyn's men and put the remaining five carefully on the front passenger seat. I moved the box of Molotov Cocktails to the floor, under the glove box. Meanwhile, Llywelyn tied his horse to a tree.

"What are you doing?" I asked, then kicked myself for leaving off the 'my lord.' He didn't appear to notice.

"Coming with you. Someone has to throw those weapons, and it can't be you if you're driving."

I was too concerned about Ieuan to argue. Ten minutes had passed since I'd seen him. *Please be alive! Please still be alive!* "The men are to the left of the road," I said. "If you stand in the doorway, you can hang on with one hand and throw the devices over the top of the car with your right arm."

I started the car, Llywelyn grasped the interior handle, and put one foot on the seat and the other on the rim of the car. He pulled the door more closed so he was sandwiched between the door and the roof.

"I'm going in hot," I said.

SARAH WOODBURY

I gunned the engine, we skidded, and then picked up speed as I pulled onto the road. I flipped on the headlights and rocketed along at nearly forty miles an hour, with Prince Llywelyn's men thundering along behind me; we drove through the cut in the Dyke and into England.

"Ieuan, down!" I shouted, at the same time the Prince barked, "Tudur!"

Llywelyn lobbed the first pot of Greek Fire. Ieuan threw himself towards the Dyke, his hands over his head. The canister hit the back of an English soldier's metal helmet. It exploded with a sharp crack, engulfing the man's head in flame.

*Crack! Crack! Crack!* Llywelyn's men threw their pots. One settled in the grass without igniting, but the rest blew, throwing fire everywhere. The men who survived ran for their horses. I lobbed a Molotov Cocktail out the window in the direction of the camp fire. It bounced once and rolled into the flames.

*Oh my God! What have I done?* I ducked below the level of the window in anticipation. The bottle exploded.

Glass shot in every direction and the fire burst upward. Men screamed. It was as if a high wind had come up and blown the English to the east. Within two minutes, the only men remaining lay on the ground.

I brought the car to a halt and ran to Ieuan. The first pot had sprayed him with fragments and fire, but he'd rolled in the dirt to extinguish the flames. He sat up and I threw myself at him, nearly knocking him over.

"It's all right, *cariad*," he said, wrapping his arms around me. "I'm only singed."

"Do we pursue, my lord?" called one of Llywelyn's men, still seated on his horse.

"No," Llywelyn said. "Not yet." He surveyed the camp, and then strode to the smoldering body of a man who lay face down in the dirt. He crouched beside him and his face fell. "Tudur," he said.

Tudur moaned. I crawled over to him and helped the Prince roll him over. I pressed my ear to his chest. "His heart is strong," I said.

The Prince blew out a sharp breath of relief.

"And Hereford?" Ieuan asked. "Where is he?"

"He, I would pursue," Llywelyn said, "but we should regroup and prepare to support Dafydd and his men when they come. It's bad enough we used all their spare ammunition."

Llywelyn's words washed over me. I knelt in the grass beside Tudur, my breeches muddy, my hair undone, my heart still pounding from the tension of the scrimmage. For the thousandth time since I'd come to Wales, I felt like I was in the middle of a rising river, flooding over a waterfall in a rush, headlong towards an impossible future. More than fear or uncertainty, I felt incredulity. *How is it that I'm here? How could any of this be real?* But the wounded man before me was real, the Prince who loomed over us, his hands on his hips, jaw set, was real, and so was his son, who'd soon come pounding up the road with a hundred men, all set on rewriting history books that had not yet been written.

\* \* \* \* \*

"I'm a firm believer in overwhelming force," David said an hour later. David, Ieuan, and I stood on a high spot on the Dyke, watching the Welsh archers fire one flight of arrows after another at the English encampment near Huntington Castle, not far from where I'd first driven into England from Pennsylvania.

Goronwy and Math had ridden with their companies along the road to the north of Painscastle before crossing into England and riding south. David had met Carew at Hay and fanned out across the English countryside, burning as they went. It was total war. We weren't looking to defeat the English *army*, we were looking to defeat the *English*.

It wasn't that the English hadn't posted sentries or were unaware that we were dangerous, but they weren't prepared for the speed and ferocity of our night attack, and for the new weapons we used. Although the Greek Fire was spectacular, and now that we knew that the Molotov Cocktails exploded nicely in a campfire they were useful, it was the fire arrows and the gunpowder that truly won the night.

The bowmen shot, and shot, and shot again. Even though we had only a hundred archers, each one could shoot at least six arrows a minute. *Anyone can do the math and reach an inescapable conclusion . . . we're going to win, this round*

338

*anyway.* Our archers shot arrowheads laced with a sticky mixture comprised of black powder and oil, with the consistency of pitch and set on fire just before the archer shot it. They landed in the English camp and were impossible to extinguish, especially as the grass was wet from a downpour that had just ended. The moon was again behind us, but otherwise, the only lights was from the arcing arrows, flying one after another.

Another flight of arrows left the bows and descended to the field two hundred yards away. Lili had determinedly kept with the company of archers. I moved closer to Ieuan.

"Did you speak with her?" I asked.

"Yes." He handed the binoculars to David, who put them to his eyes.

"Lili is very reasonable in her unreasonableness," Ieuan said. "She insisted on joining the men, and swore, once again, that she wouldn't deliberately expose herself to danger."

David put down the glasses. "She still wanted to fight, then? I was hoping it would lose its allure."

"I don't think she wanted to," Ieuan said. "I think she felt it was her duty."

"Huh," David said, and despite the mayhem going on around us, I had to smile at the totally American expression that said everything and nothing in one simple syllable.

"We've won," Ieuan said as another hundred arrows hit and exploded. Every English tent was alight and the archers had started to aim their arrows over the castle walls at the defenders on the battlements. "We don't even need the castle."

"Don't you?" a voice said in English. An arm snaked around my waist, jerking me backwards until I was three steps away from David and Ieuan. The man held a knife at my throat. "We will turn defeat into victory, I think."

The men had turned at the voice, but now stood frozen, staring at the man behind me, their swords not even a quarter out of their sheaths. Then four English soldiers materialized behind Ieuan and David. They'd been lying prone all this time, right at our feet.

"You're not the only ones who can orchestrate an ambush," the man said. "Don't look for your men. They're dead."

*Cadwallon; Gruffydd; Madoc.* I choked back a sob.

"Bohun," Ieuan said. "Trust you to use a woman as a shield."

"You," Hereford either didn't understand his words, or ignored them. He gestured with the knife, "Royal whelp. Stand apart."

"Nothing ever quite works out the way you plan it, does it?" David said. He spoke under his breath to Ieuan, and in unison, they each took a step, Ieuan to the right, and David to the left. At that, three soldiers surrounded Ieuan, swords out. He had his hands to his sides, palms out.

One of the soldiers shoved at his shoulder, turning him north in the direction of Huntington. I'd been looking at David, who had only one man on him, the soldier's sword held in the small of his back and I realized from the distribution of the soldiers that Hereford thought Ieuan, not David, was the Prince of Wales.

"Wait my lord!" The man who guarded David spoke. "You have it wrong. This one is the Prince of Wales!" It was Ieuan's father, Cynan.

Hereford snorted in my ear. "You're mistaken, old man. The other man is the one from the campfire."

"But—" Cynan began.

"Move!" Hereford said. He urged me forward. I obeyed. Ieuan walked stiff-legged ahead of me.

Hereford still had his arm around me, and it was awkward to be held so closely while trying to walk. We struggled along the Dyke. Twice in the first fifty feet, I stumbled on the uneven ground and each time Hereford clenched me more tightly around the waist and pulled me upright.

Cynan tried again. "My lord, this man here is the Prince of Wales. He and I spoke at Buellt when I delivered your message. The other one is an imposter."

Hereford appeared to be listening now. "Who is the other one then?" he asked.

My throat constricted in fear for Ieuan, but Cynan didn't answer. Perhaps he didn't respect his son, but didn't want to see him die on Hereford's sword either. David must have been thinking similar, desperate thoughts, because he interrupted the Englishmen, speaking in Welsh into the silence Cynan had left hanging. "Bronwen, remember your work with Anna?"

Cynan had to lower his sword to do it, but he cuffed David in the side of the head. "Quiet!"

"Yes," I said.

"Now!"

I bent my knees, tucked my chin, and drove the back of my head into Hereford's nose. He staggered backwards, releasing me as he tried to recover his balance. I dropped to a crouch, underneath whatever line of fire might come my way.

David, meanwhile, took a quick step forward, spun to the right, and knocked Cynan's blade away with his right forearm. Then he grabbed the hilt of Cynan's sword with his left hand and drove his gauntleted fist into Cynan's belly. The chain mail the man wore wasn't stiff enough to protect against such a punch, especially since it had the force of David's entire body behind it. Cynan went down and at the same time David relieved him of his sword.

Leaping over Cynan's body, David strode toward Hereford, who was on one knee, holding his nose with his left hand. David kicked the inside of Hereford's right wrist with his foot. As at Penn State, the knife skittered away.

"Halt!" David said. The three soldiers with Ieuan had turned back at the noise and now stared at us in disbelief.

David stood to one side of Hereford, his sword aligned with the back of Hereford's neck, as if he was about to chop off his head. I scurried after the knife and came to my feet on the other side of Hereford, holding the knife as David had taught me, at my side, the blade pointed behind me.

"Let him go," the soldier said, "or we will kill your Prince."

"Cynan was right. He's not the Prince," David said. "I am."

Hereford grunted and spoke, his voice altered by his clogged nose. "I should never have listened to Tudur."

David barked a laugh. "He's spent a lifetime in service to the Prince of Wales. That means more to him than whatever you could promise. Now, drop your weapons."

The soldiers didn't move and David gently rubbed the back of Hereford's neck with the edge of his sword, drawing blood.

"Do it!" Hereford said. The soldiers dropped their swords. Ieuan moved three steps behind the soldiers and pulled out his own sword. Cynan moaned on the ground.

"Do we have something to tie their hands with?" David asked in Welsh. "That was their mistake and I don't want to repeat it."

I stowed the knife at my waist and pulled at my hair for the ties that bound the top and bottom of my braids. "Tie them," David said, and though my hands shook, I managed to secure each of the soldiers, plus Hereford, at the wrists, their arms behind their backs. Ieuan helped his father to his feet and tied his hands with the leather thong that held his own hair out of his eyes.

"Let's go," David said, when we'd finished. He grasped Hereford underneath his left arm and pulled him to his feet. Ieuan prodded the other soldiers forward and we made an awkward group as we walked back the way we'd come.

After twenty minutes, we reached the spot where we'd left the car, just off the road that led to Huntington, and picked our

343

way down from the Dyke to the English side. David didn't stop at the car, however, but kept going until he reached the command center that Prince Llywelyn had established.

"My lord!" Bevyn said, hurrying over. "What is this?"

"Hereford, and four of his men," David said. "See that they are well contained in the dungeon at Buellt, will you? I need to speak to my father."

"He is near."

"Good," David said. He turned away, and then hesitated. Bevyn was watching him and when their eyes met, Bevyn bit his lip.

"Your guard, my lord. What has become of them?"

"They're dead, Bevyn, along with so many others."

Bevyn placed a hand on David's shoulder. "Every victory has a cost, my lord," Bevyn said.

"Witless sap," Cynan muttered under his breath. He spoke in Welsh, and that could only be because he wanted to ensure that we all understood him. In response, Ieuan spun on his heel. His hand flew up, but David caught it before he could backhand his own father across the face.

"Lord Ieuan!" he said, and then more softly. "Ieuan, no."

Hereford spoke over the tension that had encompassed our little group. "Release me and I'll see that you live, Prince Dafydd. Edward once offered your father lands in England. I could be equally generous."

David laughed, and it even sounded genuine. "You think you're arguing from a position of strength, do you? I'll take my chances, Bohun," he said. David took a step closer to him. "Did you not notice my surcoat, Hereford? It shows the red dragon of Wales. As long as I live, this is where I'll be, standing between you and my people."

Within the hour, Bevyn and a troop of men rode away with Hereford and Ieuan's father under guard, in chains in the back of a cart.

Ieuan shook his head. "I wouldn't have believed it," he said. "Not in all these years of meeting in discord and resentment did I ever think I would see him thus."

"Do you want me to release him, Ieuan?" David said. "You have only to ask."

"No," Ieuan said. "I can't ask that, and he wouldn't want it. It gives him one more thing to hold over my head. I'll not deprive him of the pleasure."

"Can you explain to me about Tudur?" I asked. "I'm still not clear what happened with him."

"He made his choice, Bronwen," Ieuan said, but then hugged me to take the sharpness out of his words. "And this time it was the right one."

"That he's injured near to death is my fault," David said. "I finally convinced him to tell me the truth about his involvement with Hereford. Once he admitted it, he swore his oath to my father again and agreed to play double agent."

"Double what?" Ieuan asked.

"To spy for us, while making Hereford think he spied for him."

"I can't believe you didn't tell me," I said, hurt.

"Again, that is my doing," David said. "Only Father, Goronwy, and I knew at first, and then I told Ieuan so he could keep an eye on Tudur tonight. Any more and we'd have found the charade difficult to maintain. A simple gesture at the wrong moment could have given the game away."

Ieuan shook his head with regret. "I popped my head over the top of the Dyke right into the arms of a sentry," Ieuan said. "He hauled me into the camp. Tudur and Hereford were surprised to see me, but of course, only Tudur knew who I was. Hereford was prepared to run me through, right there and then, but Tudur stayed his hand."

"By telling him you were the Prince of Wales," I said.

"Yes," Ieuan said.

David stared off into the distance. "I doubted him," David said. "I won't again."

# EPILOGUE

## *David*

**M**y father and I sat together on our horses, our lines of men stretching for two hundred yards in either direction along the top of the great Dyke.  Below us, in a field not far from where Bronwen, Ieuan, and I had appeared two months before, lay the English camp.  We wouldn't have a repeat of what happened in Lancaster.  This time, the English had come to us.

It was a clear day for October, with only a threat of rain in the air.  Hopefully, we'd be long gone before the skies opened.  But it didn't matter if they did.  We'd won.  *Wales* had won, and the world was never going to be the same.

"I see the Archbishop," my father said.  We walked our horses forward, followed by a company of a hundred knights.  Carew was with us, along with Math, the princes of Debeuharth, and Gruffydd ap Gwenwynwyn, whose eyes were alight with glee and only a little malice.  Gruffydd had never liked Hereford either.  Tudur was still recovering from his wounds, but would live.

"I don't want any surprises," I said.

"Hereford will have something up his sleeve," my father said. "John Peckham is honorable in his own way, but he's a tool of the English crown, thinks little of Welsh law, and will bend to the regents if required."

My father and the Archbishop had spent the last weeks in constant communication. Our final raid into England had done what the taking of Painscastle, Montgomery, and Brecon had not: convinced the regents they must sue for peace, else they squander the resources of England on a war they weren't winning, and which only Hereford and a few remaining Marcher lords cared about winning. Defeating Wales had been a matter of pride to King Edward, not practicality. As far as the vast majority of English landholders were concerned, we were a poor province that drained the exchequer and brought them little in return. Hereford had been forced to give way.

Hereford, unsurprisingly, was not a happy man. He rode to my right, under guard. We were exchanging him, as a matter of our good will, for the entirety of Morganwg and Gwent in southern Wales. It was a huge concession, but we'd refused to settle for anything less, and the English hadn't the stomach for a full scale assault on Wales. Not now. Not without Edward. Whether Hereford would have any clout left, given the high cost of ransoming him, remained to be seen. *And isn't my problem.*

We reached the pavilion, our men positioned behind us in a 'v'-shape, forming a safety zone between us and the road to Wales.

"Noble lords," Peckham said. He'd been sitting in an elaborate chair, cushioned and carved, but now rose to his feet. "Let me make you welcome."

My father and I dismounted, followed by Math and the others. Hereford was allowed to join his co-regents behind Peckham. My father and I stepped into the pavilion, but didn't accept the chairs that Peckham offered. As a result, all of us stood, the Welsh on one side, and Hereford, Vere, and Kirby on the other, forming two half circles, with Peckham in the middle. Behind the regents, other great lords of England gathered, including Roger Bigod, whom we were forcing to give up Chepstow Castle, and William de Braose, who was losing castles along the southern coast of Wales. At the same time, these lords *were* still alive. They'd benefited profoundly from their decision *not* to obey King Edward's orders to travel to Lancaster.

"We are here to bring peace," Peckham said. "The lords of England agree to quit Wales, forgoing their holdings to the west of the great Dyke and the River Dee, which the Welsh have so bravely defended. In turn, the nobility of Wales agree to forfeit whatever claims they might have to land in England in perpetuity, and to return Lord Humphrey de Bohun, Earl of Hereford and co-regent of England, to his countrymen. At this time, I am also revoking the edict of excommunication against the throne of Wales and welcome your lordships into the Christian fold once again."

I managed not to laugh. We'd done just fine without his blessing and this whole peace charade was a direct product of that fact. It was important to my father, however, so I controlled myself.

My father and the three regents stepped forward to the document table, taking their turns to sign and seal the treaties. When they were finished, Peckham signed the documents as well, before speaking again. "The final agreement, without which this treaty is incomplete, is the formal engagement of Edward II, King of England, with Gwenllian, daughter of King Llywelyn I of Wales."

The silence in the tent was so loud my ears rang with it. My father froze in the act of handing his seal to Goronwy. His knuckles went white with the tension in his grip, and the two men studied each other, speaking without words. I could almost hear their thoughts in the stillness: *Do I ruin all by refusing?*

My father turned to Peckham. "Although you insult our person by not inquiring in advance whether or not such an agreement is acceptable to us, we choose not to be offended. We accept in principle your proposal because I desire peace between our nations from this moment. But know this, no claim may be laid to the throne of Wales through her. That assumption will lay the foundation of any charter between us."

"Of course, King Llywelyn," Kirby said. He and Vere bowed. "We meant no disrespect and were unaware of your ignorance of this provision." Vere turned his head very slightly, but it was enough for me to realize whose idea it had been. *Hereford.* Even languishing in our dungeon, he still had power.

Another paper produced, another treaty signed, and it was done. We mounted our horses and rode back the way we'd come. If Hereford had his way, my father and I would never set foot inside England again. *Fine by me.*

# About the Author

With two historian parents, Sarah couldn't help but develop an interest in the past. She went on to get more than enough education herself (in anthropology) and began writing fiction when the stories in her head overflowed and demanded she let them out. Her interest in Wales stems from her own ancestry and the year she lived in England when she fell in love with the country, language, and people. She even convinced her husband to give all four of their children Welsh names.

She makes her home in Oregon.

**www.sarahwoodbury.com**

Made in the USA
Lexington, KY
19 November 2012